CHRIS BUDD lives in Somerset with, at the time of writing, his wife, two children, and Luna the westie.

His writing covers both fiction and non-fiction, and is rooted in a belief that the world would be a happier place with a little more compassion and a little less competition.

Aside from writing, his obsessions include music and cricket. He has built a business, a youth cricket section, and an institute, and loves to share and hear ideas.

He is happy to be on the stage, but prefers to be at the back.

I0610043

Also by Chris Budd

Fiction

A Bridge of Straw
Manners From Heaven

Non-Fiction

The Financial Wellbeing Book
The Eternal Business

THE VANISHING POINT

CHRIS BUDD

SilverWood

Published in 2021 by SilverWood Books

SilverWood Books Ltd
14 Small Street, Bristol, BS1 1DE, United Kingdom
www.silverwoodbooks.co.uk

ISBN 978-1-80042-047-2 (paperback)
ISBN 978-1-80042-048-9 (ebook)

British Library Cataloguing in Publication Data
A CIP catalogue record for this book is available from the British Library

Page design and typesetting by SilverWood Books

For Susie, Ella and George

Phase 1

The Message

Chapter 1

The Future Has Already Happened

When asked by a journalist, decades later, about her role in ensuring the continuation of humanity, Hannah Siggers would mischievously reply that fate had simply knocked on her front door at random.

Hannah's response revealed a perspective on destiny forged from having been given the chance to discover her own. It is fair to say, however, that the Hannah Siggers digging out a tree in the warmth of a midsummer evening did not have the same degree of poise and perception that her older self would be given the chance to demonstrate.

No story is ever finished. Even though the human race might be been propelling itself towards its own extinction, life on the planet would still continue in some form.

A similar thing can be said for the moment *before* a story begins. Clearly, the story of the Earth long predates that of humanity. And the story of Hannah Siggers did not start with her aged forty-five, in the back garden of her cottage in the middle of the Mendip Hills in Somerset, England, wielding a spade and shouting at a tree root. But that is where we now find her.

Propelled with greater force than was strictly necessary, the blade sliced across the root. It failed to inflict a clean cut, slamming instead into the mud and wrenching the handle from Hannah's grasp. Her leg, the primary source of the propulsion, continued its momentum, and Hannah stumbled forwards, twisting at the last moment to land heavily on her backside. She cursed the root in terms that would leave it in no doubt of her feelings. If the root had been able to protest its innocence, to point out that it was merely a passive participant in the incident, its words would have fallen on deaf ears. That Hannah's anger at the root was not the fault of anything the root had done would not have improved the prospects for what remained of the stag's horn sumach tree.

The tree had been earmarked for extraction some time ago, but the events of the day had finally given Hannah the impetus required to take action. This was more like therapy than gardening. Even the cows in the field adjacent to the cottage, who had initially come to watch the excitement, had now moved away, as if respectful of Hannah's considerable desire to be alone while exorcising her angry thoughts. Agnes, her ageing West Highland White terrier, lay on the grass admiring Hannah's every move, oblivious to the tension.

Sometimes it takes an ordinary person to do something extraordinary. Hannah Siggers did not consider herself to be either ordinary or extraordinary. She had never held any great desire to be thought of at all, at least not by the public at large. Leadership was not a skill she felt that she possessed, nor admired in others. Opinionated, helpful, intrusive, argumentative – yes, all those things – but never desirous of leadership, never *ambitious*. One teacher had written in Hannah's school report that she was a solution in constant search of a problem. Her grandmother had not disagreed.

Breathing hard, she took a moment to survey the puzzle in the soil below. Reluctantly she admitted that this was time for a planned attack, not just brute force. Pushing on the remaining length of trunk to further expose the roots, she spotted the source of the resistance. Placing the blade of the spade at the troublesome spot, she stamped hard. The spade sliced into the root. She withdrew, preparing for the final cut.

The cottage was situated on top of the Mendip Hills at the end of a long lane, a situation that was even bleaker than Hannah's current job prospects. It was as if the further she moved away from social contact, the further the world shrank back away from her. The view from every window was farmland, fields defined by hedgerows and sheep confined by fields. Up until today, groceries had been purchased on her way home from the office in Bristol.

After today things would be very different, as she had just left the digital marketing company that she had helped to found ten years ago. 'Stormed out of' would be a more accurate representation of her exit from the business. Either way, she would not now or for the foreseeable future be dropping by anywhere. Instead she would be planning specific visits to the supermarket in Wells, a twenty-minute drive away. This meant lists, and possibly weekly meal planning. She struggled to decide whether this excited or wearied her.

There were friends, such as the book group, who met once a month. She might cycle to the pub in the nearby village once or twice a week. Occasional romantic entanglements lay peppered across her more recent past like weathered trig points, directing her memory back to more socially active times, should she wish to take that journey. She did not. Hers was now a social life lived entirely on her own terms. It seemed that her career was about to follow the same path.

An entire decade of being the only woman of four directors. One person for each side of the boardroom table. Equal in theory only, as the day's events had proven. It had already started to feel like another time, even if it was too soon to focus on the future rather than the past. Further rumination was required; built-up resentment needed exorcising.

She lined the spade against the cut and forced it through. This time it went all the way – and made a hollow sound as it slid into the mud.

Dropping the spade, Hannah knelt next to the hole she had created. Pushing her fingers into the cold, damp soil, she was surprised to touch what felt like a wooden box. She retrieved the trowel from the home-made cotton holster attached to her belt, and carefully dug out more of the soil. When two sides were visible, she pulled the box from out of the ground. Embossed on the top and side were the words *King Edward Invincible*, although the label had rotted away. She stood, placed the trowel back into the holster, and took the cigar box over to a bench, situated under the shade of a tall eucalyptus tree on the edge of the garden, facing across the moor down towards Cheddar Gorge.

After four failed attempts, Agnes succeeded in jumping onto the bench beside her. Hannah took a moment to close her eyes and acknowledge the fading warmth of the evening sun as it began to descend behind Gibbet's Brow. Strange, she thought, to think that in a few months' time it will already have been dark for several hours by now.

A pigeon in the tree above her cooed, as if imitating Morse code. Long long, short short. Cooo cooo, coo coo. Repeat. Then another pigeon joined in, slightly out of sync with the first, as if an echo. The two continued for a few rounds, then abruptly stopped at exactly the same time, mid-coo, as if suddenly embarrassed to realise that Hannah was listening to them.

She placed the box onto her knee and opened the lid.

It was a time capsule. That much could be guessed from the top item, a 1971 annual from the children's television show *Blue Peter*. She placed the book on the bench next to her and rummaged through the rest of the contents: pre-decimal coins; a lock of white hair in a bag, with the word 'Snowy' written in spidery handwriting; a copy of *The Times*, with a lead story revealing the collapse of Rolls-Royce; and photographs of the children who, presumably, had lived in the house at the time and had prepared the time capsule.

A message from the past in the form of a snapshot in time. What had the future looked like forty-seven years ago, two years before she had even been born? The optimism of the sixties was over, the violence in Northern Ireland was at its peak. Would the parents of these children have been excited about their future, or would they have been just as fearful as she felt concerning her grandson Atticus? She herself would have been only a possibility in 1971, an idea at best. Her existence would have been the subject of excited, possibly fevered, debate. Her parents would have been in love and thinking of the future together, of exciting opportunities and building a nest of security, before the cancer took her mother and the booze grabbed hold of her father.

She picked out a picture of a small girl, probably aged seven or eight, standing near the very spot where Hannah was currently sitting. The girl was wearing a dark Brownies uniform and white socks, and was holding a white rabbit close to her face as if it were her special blankie. What did the future hold for that little girl? The future as the past, written but not revealed. The idea gave Hannah a perverse comfort, pouring a soothing balm on her anger. If she had known that the last ten years would end here, would she still have joined her three erstwhile colleagues in setting up the business? Probably. If she had known that having a son would end in him moving to Switzerland with his family, would she still have had the child? Of course. There is no such thing as an ending; there are only points in time.

Hannah replaced the items, closed the lid, and placed the box carefully on the bench. She returned to the spade, launching a final and successful assault on the roots of the stag's horn sumach.

She put the tools back into the shed before taking the box to the back door. Leaning against the wall, she removed her Hunter boots and went inside, holding the back door open for Agnes to hop in as she did so. She went through the utility room and into the kitchen and placed the cigar box on the counter. She filled the kettle, poured a little too much pasta into a saucepan, and lit the gas under the remainder of yesterday's bolognese sauce.

As she waited for things to boil, she stared at the box. She should probably bury it again. Perhaps add something of her own. But what? She struggled to find inspiration. The very notion of her sending a message to the future felt arrogant, presumptuous, as if anything she might do or say could affect the actions of people in the future.

It was too soon. She needed time to process the fact that her own imagined future had been so abruptly altered; to mull and mope; to roll her disappointments around and around until they became mute. This exhausting process of endless reflection happened without form or sense of destiny. It did not seek her permission; it soaked up the processing power of her brain until her anger was beaten into submission and all the feelings were safely squared away where they could no longer reach her.

A mile away, Hannah's future was in fact walking towards her front door. There are stories that are told about people which seem to contain too much coincidence, in which the main character just happens to be in a certain place at a certain time. This is not one of those stories. This story is not about Hannah Siggers. It's just that Hannah Siggers is the person the story happens to. You do not choose your destiny, it chooses you – although you do have to be at home when it comes to visit. The future is not your playground. You do not decide that you will be great; it is a judgement conferred upon you by others. Hannah Siggers did not one day decide to change the course of history, because the history of the future had already been written. The knock on her door that would occur in sixty minutes' time would lead to the revelation of a future that was considerably different even from the one that Hannah was trying to prepare for.

Chapter 2

The Conclusion of Evolution

It arrived in the darkness of the night sky without a whoosh. There was no distant sighting followed by rising confusion and mayhem amongst the general populace as it drew ever nearer; no moment of realisation when the fuzzy distant outline solidified into an actual spaceship; no sighting of a mysterious cigar-shaped object in the sky; no headlines blazing across the newspapers of the world. It was simply a case that there was a space in the air where it wasn't, followed moments later by an absence of space in the air where it was.

Considering that it was the first spaceship ever to appear on the planet Earth; that it was hovering silently some fifty metres above the surface of the Earth; and taking into account the myriad of dramatised predictions of the moment when aliens first make contact with the planet Earth – bearing in mind all these factors, it could even have been argued that the first (known) arrival of aliens on planet Earth was somewhat anticlimactic.

Ever since the first realisation that some of the twinkly things in the sky were other planets, humans have wondered about the possibility of alien life. The moment of their coming has been predicted in a multitude of ways. Invariably the starting point has been the assumption that we are actually a planet worth conquering – a sign of the self-importance of a species that considers itself to be the epitome of life on the planet, the conclusion of evolution. Humanity has long viewed itself as the end result of millions of years of incremental change, rather than just one of many variations on a theme. If popular culture is to be believed, aliens have been waiting on the periphery of the universe, waiting patiently for the time when we have evolved sufficiently to warrant being attacked. The actual moment of the appearance has been the subject of particularly florid speculation, whether it be one giant spaceship attempting to make friendly contact or huge numbers of killer machines landing all over the world. The first contact with humans is invariably shown as a moment of historical importance commensurate with the gravitas we attach to our existence as a species. The idea that aliens might, for example, choose to make their first contact with a rabbit rather than a human has not, so far, occurred to writers of science fiction. Had those writers seen the actual moment of arrival of the very first spaceship, therefore, they *might* have been rather disappointed that the reality did not match their lurid expectations.

That *might* have been the case, had it not been for one detail: the ship itself.

The spaceship that appeared was a cube, each side one hundred metres long. It seemed to be made entirely of black glass, and yet no reflection came from its surface. In the dark, the only way that one might determine the outline of the spaceship was by what it prevented one from being able to see, rather than any features on the spaceship itself. There was no obvious form of propulsion, no protruding jet nozzles or docking stations. It simply hung in the air, occupying space.

For a full five minutes, nothing further happened after the initial burst of coming into being. The spaceship simply hovered, providing menace merely by the fact that it should not have been there at all. It hung in the air, heavy with expectation yet exuding an impossible lightness, if only due to the fact that it was, indeed, hanging in the air. Then, with as little warning as the ship had given when it arrived, a light appeared in the cube as a door slowly drew back. It was situated in the very middle and lowest part of one of the four vertical sides of the cube. The light that came from the ship oozed out of it almost reluctantly, as if it had been on a long journey and needed to stretch. It was not a blinding light but a glow, suggesting an interior design of the spaceship that was based around an intensive course in uplighting.

A figure appeared in the doorway. It was human in form, female and dressed in a tight-fitting light blue one-piece suit, with a grey belt which seemed to be for hanging things from rather than holding up trousers. She stood, arms on hips, legs slightly apart, adopting a stance that had clearly been rehearsed for such a moment. It was a stance that made a statement. She — it? — stood just inside the ship, surveying the scene below. She narrowed her eyes, blinked, and peered into the darkness. Then, taking a step forward, she held onto a handle just inside the door, leaned out, and looked down. Alien or human, this was clearly not an entity that suffered from a fear of heights.

The figure in the doorway stepped back and turned to look back into the spaceship. Apparently addressing another, she shrugged, gesticulated, then threw her hands up in exasperation. An argument continued for a minute or so before she turned back to the open doorway. She stepped to the threshold, bent forwards and, cupping her hands to her mouth, yelled at the top of her voice.

"Hello!" she shouted towards the ground in a voice that was plainly not from around those parts. Indeed, had anyone heard it, they would have harboured strong suspicions that it was a voice that was not from any other parts either. "Is there anyone there?"

Fifty metres below, a flock of sheep looked at each other. Unable to look up, they wondered as to the source of the voice they had just heard. In the next field, twelve cows continued to sleep.

Chapter 3

A Dark Matter

At precisely the same time as the spaceship was converting fresh air into occupied air, a young man in the town of Humlebæk, Denmark, was having the living daylights completely and utterly scared out of him. For several years he had been applying theories of astrophysics that he did not fully understand to building a machine, and he had just switched it on successfully for the first time.

There is a philosophical theory which holds that if you put an infinite number of monkeys in front of an infinite number of typewriters, one day one of them will write the complete works of Shakespeare. Torben Christiansen was like that monkey.

Torben was a graduate whose hobbies included astrophysics, string theory, and avoiding social contact. A complete lack of friends was made easier by two important facts. One was the inability to project any form of memorable personality; the other was the absence of concern at not having friends. Torben had discovered over the course of his twenty-five years that, in the main, other human beings irritated him, and that the feeling was entirely mutual. Possession of an intellect higher than his peers but not by so much as to make him special, combined with an impatience not justified by that disparity, meant that school breaks spent in the physics lab had been to the benefit of everyone.

Whether this was a state of mind that had been caused by his social inadequacy or one that had *caused* his social inadequacy was a moot point.

Throughout school, during university, and now into an unavoidable adult life, Torben had dedicated himself exclusively to the pursuit of astrophysics. His parents had relocated to New Zealand following an opportunity to run a turtle rehabilitation centre. Torben had been given the choice of joining them or not in this exciting new phase of their lives, and had preferred the option that required the least change to his own life. Although he loved his parents – and assumed they loved him – the fact that he would have the family home entirely to himself had proved to be a greater attraction than the security of the familial bosom. His parents had provided him with an income commensurate with the guilt they felt at leaving their only son behind.

Humlebæk sits on the long coastal region north of Copenhagen known as the Whisky Belt, so named for the many expensive houses that look out across the Nivå Bugt bay to Sweden. Torben's family home stood as one of a long line of houses that were desirable partly for the ease of the commute to Copenhagen and partly for the panoramic views across the flat bay to the equally flat landscape beyond. Cormorants and gulls would catch the eye of even the casual observer, who might have been relaxing in the early evening with an Akvavit and beer chaser, sitting on the terrace or walking down to the water's edge. Oystercatcher, dunlin and sandpiper; grebe, goose and goldeneye; all provided detail and colour for those who took the time to notice. No house along the Whisky Belt was complete without a book on native birds and a strong pair of binoculars perched on the windowsill, waiting to be grabbed in case of a suspected sighting of a migrating flock of lapwing. Torben's father had spent his weekends indulging the hobby of whittling, and the house was dotted with life-sized wooden replicas of the fowl that surrounded it.

For the most part, properties on the Whisky Belt are expensive for a third reason: their size. Torben's lifelong home differed in this regard. The house in which Torben now spent some ninety-five per cent of his time was a smaller three-bedroom affair, sandwiched in between the grander properties. He had long suspected that it had been built on a plot of land carved out of one of the neighbours' gardens. A sliver of land snaked down to a tiny section of beach, which featured the obligatory boat tied optimistically to a short jetty.

With no need – or desire – to rent out a room, and no expectation of anyone wanting to visit him, Torben had converted his parents' bedroom at the rear of the house into a study. He would sit at his desk in front of the French windows, looking out towards the island of Hven, which lies in the middle of the bay. Days would be spent reading and researching, the weekends coming and going unnoticed, as he slowly began to apply the theories into building the white box that now sat on the table in front of him.

Machines are built for a purpose. They are built by human beings in order to serve a function that humans will find useful, usually by performing a task that the humans would rather not have to perform themselves. All of the great innovations throughout time have occurred through one of two motivations – laziness or to fulfil a purpose.

There had been no specific purpose in building this machine, which is why it was able to do something nobody had managed to make a collection of inanimate parts do before. Torben had had no outcome in mind when he began its construction; he had simply wanted to apply what he had learned. Occasionally a great invention or discovery is made through unspecified curiosity, and Torben harboured a deep appetite for putting things together just to see what might happen. His old college professor at Copenhagen University, Professor Flensberg, had inspired in him a love of the unknown, and it was to this territory that Torben regularly found himself drawn. He came from a long but thin line of scientists who put tab A into slot B purely for the thrill of seeing what might happen. In this way he less resembled a scientist and more a philosopher or a small child. Which, in many ways, are the same thing.

A large portrait of Danish physicist Niels Bohr hung on the wall to the right of his desk. Bohr's work on quantum theory had changed the world, and he had altered the future of many people by helping them escape the Nazis. It was the thought of creating something that might emulate such achievements that inspired Torben to work late into every night.

Having graduated with his dissertation on Bohr's theories of modulated neutron initiators, Torben had retreated to his family home (if no longer having to attend university could be counted as 'retreating'). He had spent the next few years turning some of the theories that he had learned into practical use. He had begun to build something – even though he did not know what. He had ventured out of the house only to get groceries, chosen on a calculation based on ease of preparation and nutrition. Fresh food had generally been ruled out, except for apples, of which he would eat half a dozen each day. His computer would beep an alarm each day at ten, two and nine o'clock to remind him to break for food, which would constitute a frozen meal, a pizza or a bowl of porridge, depending on the time of day. A second alarm would remind him to take the meal out of the oven and consume it.

He had researched theories of astro- and quantum physics, studied computer coding, and hadn't totally understood any of it. He had maintained a sufficient grasp of the concepts that he had studied to take the theories and build a...*something* machine. When he had first switched it on, nothing had happened. Actually, he did not know whether something had happened; he just knew it had not happened in his vicinity. He had been playing with theories of time and space and, for all he knew, switching the machine on might have caused a black hole to open three million light years away. He might have created two wormholes that opened on opposite sides of the galaxy. He hadn't really known what he was doing, and he had loved every absorbing moment of it.

That morning, after getting dressed in his standard attire of chinos, blue shirt and blue tie, he had made some changes to the programme running inside the white box, based on a research paper on string theory by a professor at Princeton University. There had also been a tricky decision to make about the frequency at which his machine would produce its output. He had had to flip a coin in the end to help him make the decision. Furthermore, unbeknownst to Torben, a spider had crawled inside the white box as he had obeyed the alarm and run down to the kitchen to make his porridge. Upon his return he had screwed the side panel of the white metallic white box into place, trapping the spider inside and thereby changing the entire course of history of the human race.

The white box in front of him now was the twenty-third version of the mystery machine that he had constructed. He called the machine 'Niels'. Consequently, written on the side in large black letters were the words 'Niels mark 23', right next to the orange button that turned the machine on. Spooning porridge into his mouth, Torben sat down at his desk and pushed the button, idly speculating at the possible waves he might be about to send across the universe.

Instead of the usual nothing, however, the white box gave off an initial pulse so deep and intense that it knocked Torben off his chair, spilling porridge across the floor. It was as if a wave had formed out of the substance of the space around the box and had thrown itself outwards.

As Torben looked up from his sprawled position on the floor at the machine sitting on his workbench, he now saw a bubble of colour extending outwards, with the machine at its core. The bubble continued to spread itself in every direction, including towards Torben, who scrambled to his feet and backed away. The edge of the sphere stopped just in front of him and seemed to quiver and shake, as if trying to hold itself together. Across its translucent surface, brightly coloured shapes merged and coagulated with each other, creating patterns that were ever moving. They seemed to come together, almost forming something recognisable, then drifting apart again. Swirling, they teased with possibility before dispersing back into a random series of images. In one section, Torben thought he saw a face – a woman's face – looking back at him, distorted as it was stretched across the surface of the bubble.

Slowly, driven on by the curiosity that had led to the creation of the machine in the first place, Torben reached out his hand towards the face. Slowly, closer and closer, until the final moment of decision. He pushed his fingers one millimetre further and touched the bubble where the image of the face peered back at him.

Suddenly he was no longer in his room. He was no longer... anywhere. And yet he was everywhere. He felt like a superbeing, in all places and times at once, unable to choose which came into focus. He felt as if everything in the universe was happening to him at the same time. The images and lights and colours were too overwhelming to comprehend. Sounds he could not identify, sounds that seemed to be within him, that he experienced rather than heard.

Whirling around and around, it was as if the machine were searching for something, seeking a signal from the cosmos. Torben was an interloper, a voyeur; he had no right to be there. It was the machine, sending out its signal, waiting to connect. So many lights, so many images, too much to process.

And yet…there was one light that seemed to remain constant, one shimmering blue something that remained stationary as everything else formed the maelstrom which was threatening to send Torben into unconsciousness. And in the light was the morphing face, stretching into new shapes, peering, not seeing him, but still searching for something. And then Torben saw – no, *felt* – the machine reach out to the blue light, as if making a connection. The two got closer and closer, the noise in Torben's head got louder and louder, until they connected, and then…

Nothing. Torben was standing in his study, with porridge on the floor in front of him. The white machine was still on the workbench. Nothing had changed. And yet, Torben knew, everything was different. He just didn't know how. Or where.

Chapter 4

Poohsticks

Having rinsed away the soap suds under the cold tap, Hannah placed the bowl on the draining board next to the spoon, the fork, the pasta strainer and the two saucepans. Then she refilled the wine glass with a French Chenin Blanc that had been given to her several years previously by a client, put the half-empty bottle back into the half-empty fridge, and transferred herself into the front room.

She straightened the throw and rearranged the cushions before flumping into the sofa, grabbing a local newspaper from the low table on her way down. Agnes registered the interloper on her sofa by looking up briefly. Hannah stared at the newspaper without taking anything in, then, in an admission of distraction, threw it onto the sofa next to her.

The tinkle of Westminster chimes came from the grand-mother clock which dominated the small stone-walled living room. Hannah absorbed the information that the time was now fifteen minutes past ten o'clock in the same instinctive manner that she knew that the stream that ran through the garden was still carrying water to the pond at the other side of the fields.

The clock brought a gravitas to the room that soft fur-nishings could never manage. An inheritance from her own grandmother, Nana Siggers, the clock had been one of the few constants in Hannah's life. An only child, she had lived with Nana between the ages of twelve and eighteen, after her mother had been taken from the family by a tiny lump that had not been spotted soon enough.

*

Her father might possibly have succeeded in coping with the twin challenges of bringing up his daughter at the same time as recovering from the blow of losing his wife. However, the third yoke of a crippling dependency on cheap gin and German wine proved to be a burden too many. Of those three challenges, Hannah was deemed to be the easiest to solve.

Hannah was sent to spend the weekend at Nana's, during one of which her father fell down the stairs at three in the morning. He woke four hours later unable to move anything but his left arm, which – through happy chance or bitter fate, depending on your viewpoint – was within reach of the telephone. He needed three months in hospital to regain the ability to walk, during which time he also received counselling and support for the ongoing grief and the debilitating drinking habit, which (the counsellors informed him) were so closely linked. He then demonstrated a wilful determination to prove them wrong by recommencing his drinking upon his return home.

The grandmother clock occupied pride of place in Nana's tiny front room. It would later fulfil the same role in Hannah's cottage, thereby providing Hannah with a link to a very happy period of her life. There was no judgement while she lived with Nana. What is it about a generation skipped that begets patience; forbearance, even? Lessons already learned, perhaps? Did Nana approach the parenting of Hannah differently to Hannah's father because she had already been through the process? Perhaps we are not destined to repeat every mistake of the past after all, as long as the angle of attack is different.

Nana made no assumptions about her granddaughter, and received no judgement in return. Hannah appreciated the space that this gave far more than Nana was aware. At school, the other children would judge her constantly: that she was too feisty and not worth the bother; that she was in shock and needed support; that she was an easy target. Hannah learned to keep her head down. She chose her GCSE subjects by what was recommended to her, and A-levels by the same nonchalant criteria. She was happy to go where life was taking her, to be a stick floating down a river. That other sticks were floating quicker than she had never been a concern.

Nana just…was. She grieved the loss of both a daughter-in-law and, at least until he managed to reverse his descent, a son. She had her own crosses to bear, as the black and white photographs of a long-deceased husband adorning the mantelpiece testified. Slowly but surely Hannah and Nana helped each other convalesce, if only by providing each other with something to worry about other than themselves. Bustle and noise in the house, a person to cook for, the occasional purging argument. Looking back, Hannah suspected that outsiders were uncertain of who was actually caring for whom.

Nana's stolid demeanour was even maintained when, at the age of seventeen, Hannah provided them both with a third person to worry about.

The identity of the father of the baby to be christened Gareth Siggers was never clarified. It didn't seem a priority. Hannah did inform three of the four possible candidates in a frenzy of telephone calls. Two instantly proposed marriage, while the third instructed her to get an abortion. They each received a similar response. The fourth of the suspects could not be contacted, as he was stepping onto the stage of a small club in a provincial market town some two hundred miles away. Each was ignorant of the other; the bass player had also been ignorant of her age. More accurately, he had not asked.

Predictions by others for what her future would look like if she chose to have the child were universally bleak. Advice came unbidden from all quarters, many of them women who had been friends of her mother and felt they had a role to play in Hannah's life. The one exception was Nana, who offered only support for Hannah's decision, whatever it might be.

Being pressured to terminate the pregnancy settled Hannah's decision to have the child. With Nana's help she passed her A-levels: art, English literature and sociology, two Bs and a C, enough for a good university – an option that was not even considered. Instead, she entered the world of work, only to discover that twelve years of schooling had done nothing to prepare her for adult life. Employers of the 1990s had yet to wake up to the potential of the single mother, and Hannah's job options were driven by the need to contribute to the household bills.

When Gareth began attending school, Hannah found the school gates an even harder place second time around. The distance that the other mothers placed between themselves and Hannah could be measured in years as well as metres. The few who did speak to her began from the assumption that the twenty-two-year-old was hired help, not the mother of the child that came running into her arms three afternoons each week.

She floated through a variety of jobs which required her to produce unimaginative graphic design for even more unimaginative clients. She settled for inanity because it allowed her to drop off and pick up Gareth, then stayed when he became old enough to ban her from the school gates.

Her world collapsed for the second time at the age of thirty-five when Gareth left home for university. One cannot prepare for what one cannot imagine, and even though the empty nest had been looming, she had declined all opportunities to address the issue. In a series of life changes that she later realised were not unconnected with the exit of Gareth from her daily life, she moved into an isolated cottage in the Mendip Hills, and accepted an invitation from three colleagues to join them in starting their own business.

Now, twenty-eight years after Hannah had become a teenage mother, Nana had been taken by cancer and Hannah had left the company she had helped to found. Gareth was living in Switzerland with a French wife, Monique, and a son of their own. The chime of the grandmother clock prodded a reminder of her own inactive role in relation to her grandson. It dawned on her now that the only grandmother in the house that could realistically be considered to be serving any useful purpose in life was that clock, standing so obediently against the wall. She was not aware of any specific event that had caused a rift with her son and his wife, although she did suspect that her reaction to them naming her grandson 'Atticus' may not have helped.

All those years of something, and now, after walking away from her company, her job, there was nothing. A very real nothing: real time, her time, not anyone else's. A nervous nothing, but exciting too. Maybe this expanse of time stretching away in front of her would allow ideas to come again. Perhaps she could write. The other three directors had agreed to buy her shares from her, which meant there was no financial pressure to get another job. Whenever she took time off work, her brain would slowly begin to work differently. It took a week or so, but eventually the lack of decisions requiring her attention allowed new thoughts to come. They were old thoughts, ideas that humans had contemplated since Siddhartha himself. It was as if there were a world of contemplation that was held back by the daily grind, like a shadowy delicatessen full of scrumptious cheeses and pickles that was never open. After a couple of weeks of not being at work, she would feel its presence, even get to snack on an idea or two. But then she would return to a mass of work emails and the door would slam shut and the shop again fade away.

Maybe now that there was real time ahead, a delicious nothingness, the thoughts and ideas might come again.

She reached across Agnes to the side table and picked up a postcard and pen that she had begun writing earlier that evening. It was addressed to Gareth, informing him of the day's events. The picture on the front was of Cheddar Gorge. She liked the idea of Atticus seeing something arrive through the letterbox. The chance that a little piece of her might be pinned to the door of the fridge was another, if slightly more guilty, motivation. A Trojan postcard.

She read the postcard again and, satisfied, placed it on the sofa, on top of the magazine. Then, with a start, she quickly picked it up again and added a postscript.

PS All my love to Monique.

As she returned the postcard and pen to the table, the sound of the ticking grandmother clock was suddenly joined by the considerably louder noise of the iron knocker being banged on the front door. Agnes barked once in reflex then settled back down, clearly of the opinion that she had performed her guard-dog duties. Hannah put a hand on the nearest arm of the sofa and eased herself up, a loud clicking emanating from both knees simultaneously.

She walked thoughtfully and barefoot across the floorboards into the hallway. There were three reasons why a visitor was a cause for concern. The first two were to do with the remoteness of her location and the lateness of the hour. The third related to the lack of people who might feasibly want to visit her at all. She placed the chain on the door, pulled it open, and looked out through the gap.

Standing on her threshold was the tallest woman that Hannah had ever seen. She was smiling in a way that was so friendly that Hannah was immediately wary of her motives. Aside from the grin and the way she held her hands together in front of her with each finger touching the tip of its opposite number, Hannah was also drawn to what the woman was wearing. A light blue one-piece trouser suit was split at the middle by a grey belt. A pouch was attached to one side of the belt. It was a strange enough outfit if seen in a fashionable district of London, or even a marginally less fashionable district of Bristol. Appearing on her threshold late on a Monday evening in late spring brought an incongruity which caused Hannah to grip the door considerably tighter.

"Hello!" said the woman brightly. "Please don't be afraid!"

Hannah quickly shut the door.

Chapter 5

The Agent of Change

From this particular study, David Armitage enjoyed a view across Lake Iseo of which he thought he could never tire. The room was on the third floor of the villa, which was perched on the top of a small island, which sat in the middle of the lake. The former site of a monastery, the island had changed ownership just three times in the last two hundred years. The Armitage Foundation had secured ownership, partly due to being the highest bidder but also due to owning certain photographs which had resulted in it being the only bidder.

As he stood at the giant windows which dominated the southern wall of the room, David Armitage rolled the Dalmore 1926 whisky around in the glass. With the time in Italy nearing midnight, the view consisted mainly of lights. There were the lights on the much larger island of Monte Isola, blinking at him from across the water with the threat of civilisation. His main focus, however, was on the lights on the rear of the boat that was speeding away from the island. It was returning to the mainland, carrying: a glamour model who wished to become an actress; an actor who wanted to become a politician; a politician who wished to further his business interests; a businesswoman whose daughter wanted to be a singer; and a singer who wanted to be a glamour model. Each was returning with their hopes of achieving their ambitions increased, but also with far greater understanding of the tithe that would need to be paid. The sound of the retreating boat died slowly away, leaving David Armitage with his precious peace and quiet.

The studies in his other thirty-five houses, spread almost equidistant across the globe, were furnished exactly the same as this one. Naturally the view altered, but, from the Regency mahogany writing desk to the Poul Henningsen standing lamps, the interior design was identical. Even the books in the Eichholtz bookcases were the same – autobiographies of Churchill and Thatcher alongside the collected poems of the likes of T. S. Eliot and Robert Frost. Books to inspire, not to be read.

There was no meeting area in the studies – this was a room for David Armitage alone. It was where he plotted and planned and made things happen. His toolbox consisted of 'other people'; something he used to achieve those plans, and something he tried to avoid spending time with unless in that capacity. Friends were not something he found necessary.

Things were quiet – or at least as quiet as they were ever likely to be in the world of David Armitage. The new POTUS was still in his honeymoon period with the American people following his recent election. The data harvesting exercise had proven extraordinarily effective and was being put to use at that very moment in other countries. No such measures were necessary in large parts of South America and Italy, where any of the politicians who came to power were only too happy to mainline into the Armitage Foundation. Indeed, the suspicion of golden rewards that lay waiting beyond the election victory is what drove many into politics in the first place. Some palms were much easier to grease than others, but David Armitage had learned over many years of living behind the scenes that everyone in a position of influence was corruptible.

There had been a suggestion in some of the more inquisitive newspapers that the politicisation of social media in order to inf-luence voting patterns might itself become a media story. One telephone call to each of the three old white men who controlled the majority of the Western world's media had soon ensured that the story died at birth through a lack of oxygen.

In the 1970s, when Armitage had been growing up in a dull suburban English town, the son of dull suburban English parents who led dull suburban English lives, the family would sit down together on a Saturday night to watch the 'light entertainment' shows offered by the BBC. The gurning presenters, performers and contestants on end-of-the-pier programmes and family gameshows had seemed to the pre-pubescent child to be the epitome of the limitations of the people that surrounded him, both at home and at school. These formative years would instil in the young child a lifelong derision for the common man, seeing no nobility in the struggle for survival. Where Springsteen would find heroism in the sweat and toil of the blue-collar worker, Armitage could find only failure and weakness. He preferred to get other people to sweat and toil for him.

The one type of performer that left a lasting impression on him from those evenings spent wilting in front of the television was the plate spinner. A dozen poles rose from a long piece of wood in front of him (it always seemed to be a 'him'; the only roles for women in the seventies were those of acrobat or glamorous assistant). The performer would place a plate on top of a pole which he would then twizzle, sending the plate rotating. Quickly, he would set up a second plate on a second pole, then a third, and so on until all twelve plates were happily spinning away. The performer would then run to whichever plate began wobbling and give it a swift twizzle, moving from pole to pole. The plates did the work, they were the ones expending the energy. But it would be the performer's fault if they fell. David Armitage revelled in the accountability of others.

He had spent over thirty years setting up his own plates, slowly gaining the confidence and building the influence of ever more powerful people. Now he just needed to give those sticks the occasional twizzle. Provide a prostitute for a Russian diplomat here, bury the news of a murder by a US governor's son out of his head on booze and pills there. He was in charge of nothing and influencer of everything, the power behind the Wizard of Oz. He did not seek adulation. Over many years he had engineered himself into a position of anonymous indispensability. The idea of the glory to be found in a certain type of success was one that he found fascinating. Some people chose their definition of success to be 'money'; others preferred 'fame'; and for a third, it was 'power'. The definitions changed marginally, be they yachts or islands, votes or readership, but the true motivations of those who aspired to be rich and powerful were tediously similar.

This did, however, make his job much easier. One simply had to work out which of the three motivations drove the individual who required manipulating, and either promise to provide it or threaten to take it away.

The only kind of person that David Armitage was truly afraid of was the person without hope. They could not be controlled. It therefore became his mission in life to ensure that everyone had something – or someone – that they wanted to live for.

Of course, the name 'David Armitage' never appeared in the published lists of wealthiest people. Only people selected by David Armitage appeared in such lists. It did, however, mean that he could buy the level of influence that had once enabled him to persuade a Canadian politician-of-the-people to reverse their decision not to allow an oil pipeline across Ontario by providing their children with life-changing sums of money.

And so it went. Round and round. Until even this view across one of the most beautiful stretches of water in Europe failed to lift his heart. For many years now he had been finding purpose in the exquisite delight that came from having control. It had been the ability to make people do things that they did not want to do that gave him an almost orgasmic pleasure. Anyone could bribe a politician, or pay a pop star enough money so that they would play at the wedding of the son of a Middle Eastern tyrant. No, the real satisfaction had come when he could get what he wanted without having to spend any money at all. He had spent a lifetime amassing his 'levers', a huge dossier of weaknesses of the influential that allowed him to control the people who controlled the world.

And yet, as beautiful as Lake Iseo might be, as comforting as it was to know that he could buy any view in the world at any point in time, that he could change the course of the election of the biggest economy in the world, he was starting to feel that there was something missing. He understood motivation as well as anyone in the world – he had, after all, spent a lifetime recognising and exploiting it in others. But now, even as he received a text from an operative in Laos reporting that the illegitimate daughter of the prince who was next in line to the throne of an oil-rich Arab state had been located, he felt something was missing. Ten years ago he would have been excited by having another future world leader under his control. But now he could not shake the feeling that there was something missing. He had built the machine to do his work for him and then had begun to miss the days when he got his hands dirty. Each morning was starting to feel like it was the beginning of just another day at the office.

David Armitage had lived his life in the shadows, albeit shadows that he had carefully created himself. And yet he wondered if his true calling was yet to come, if the future was to be more of the same or was yet to be written. He had reached the top and seen the view. It was a spectacular view, but he had seen it now. The trouble with getting to number one is that the only challenge left is to stay there. He recognised the gestation in himself of what he took advantage of in other highly successful people: the desire for something different, something longer-lasting.

A legacy.

A plan in formation is infinitely more interesting than a plan that has been completed. He envied the young if only for the fact that they got to experience life for the first time. He felt, at the age of forty-nine, that he had seen and done everything that he had wanted to see and do. It was time he found something new. Something that would provide meaning to his life's work.

There was a word that he had been avoiding for some time now. He knew that 'legacy' was an insufficient word, a word used by the sort of people he controlled. The word he had in mind was up another level again. He had been suppressing the emotions it represented; he realised that now. But it could not be ignored any more. With a smile he felt it arrive. His lips formed the word and spoke it aloud through the window, over the lake and out into the world.

"Immortality."

It felt good to finally discover a new challenge – to uncover his true purpose.

But how could he succeed where so many others had failed? Who were the true immortals of humanity? Who had been remembered longer than any other person? Jesus? Plato? Zoroaster?

Julius Caesar? An Egyptian king? How could David Armitage ensure that he would be remembered in a thousand years' time?

Such opportunities did not just fall out of the sky. David Armitage held the destinies of individuals and the fate of nations in his hands. If anyone could solve the unsolvable puzzle, surely it was he.

David Armitage turned from the window, sat at his desk and began scanning through the online reports that constantly arrived in his inbox from his operatives around the world.

Chapter 6

One in Seven Point Five Three Billion

"Hello," said the woman through the closed door in a sing-song voice. "We very much need your help. Please may you open the door?"

Hannah could not place the accent. There was a definite American lilt, and yet there were tinges Russian in there too in the phraseology. It was an accent that suggested a person who had either been schooled on three different continents or at one extremely expensive international school.

She reopened the door on the chain and peered from her one metre seventy upwards at the woman, who she now estimated must be at least two metres ten tall. Her shoulder-length blonde hair was worn tucked behind both ears and somehow managed to stay there. She put Hannah in mind of an oversized mouse. Her age could have been anything between twenty-six and forty. There was something androgynous and ageless about her. Her expression was so beatific that Hannah feared for a moment that a religious cult might have set up a commune nearby.

"Please," said the woman again, cheerfully. "May I come in? I need to talk to you. My name is Rachel. I need your help with something. It's...quite a big thing. But I need to be explaining it thoroughly." The woman smiled again in a way that reminded Hannah of a naturalist mimicking the actions of an animal in order to gain its trust.

"Why not just tell me here?" said Hannah. "I'm sorry, I don't get many visitors at the best of times. What are you doing up here at this time of night?"

"Up here?" repeated Rachel. "What do you mean, 'up here'?"

"Up here on the hills. Surely you noticed you were going upwards when you drove up here?"

"Ah," said Rachel, as if laughing at a private joke. "We are on a remote hill? That explains many things." She stopped smiling abruptly and adopted a serious face. "So! Are you ready for a rather significant surprise? It is something that may well make you the most famous person on the planet! May I take your name?"

Hannah closed the gap a little further. "Are you selling a religion?" she said. "Because you have no idea just how much you are talking to the wrong person."

"Please, come walk with me. What is your name?"

"Hannah. And I'm not walking anywhere with you. You're weird."

"Hannah, please understand that I need to show you something which is very important. Something that will change your life."

"What makes you think I *want* my life changed? Okay, you can fuck off now. Thank you. Goodbye." Hannah went to push the door fully shut, but couldn't. She looked down and saw a strange-looking shoe preventing the door from closing. It was blue, seemed to be made of a material she did not recognise, and was attached to a leg. Opening the door back to the maximum the chain would allow, she looked up the leg, and then up a body which was dressed identically to the woman, arriving at a bearded male face grinning benignly at her through the gap that remained.

"Argh!" she shouted at the face, taking several steps back and letting go of the door in her surprise. A hand appeared, holding what looked like a metallic pencil. The hand drew the pencil down to the chain and sliced through it as if it had not been there.

The door was pushed open and the two strangely-dressed people stepped into her house. They were both smiling as if they had only just learned how. He was a little shorter than her and walked rather bashfully behind her shoulder. It created the very clear impression that she was his superior. They both seemed to exude good cheer and positivity from every pore of their bodies, which only had the effect of making them appear even more creepy. Surely no one with intentions that pure would feel the need to demonstrate it with their eyebrows?

"Please," said Rachel. The two of them continued to advance at an identical pace. "There really is no reason for you to be worried." The man nodded enthusiastically; he was not as tall as his colleague and was therefore partially obscured by her. His beard came into and back out of view behind her shoulder. "We just want to talk to you."

"We come in peace," said the man, on tiptoes. Rachel turned slowly to look at him; her eyes widened in annoyance. "What?" he replied on seeing her glare of irritation. He shrugged his shoulders innocently, then turned to address Hannah. "I've always wanted to say that," he said.

Hannah stepped across to the fireplace and grabbed a poker. "What do you want from me?" she shouted, flailing the poker in front of her. "I've got a panic button, you know. I only have to press it and the police will be here in two minutes."

Rachel had reached the sofa, where she sat down next to Agnes and folded her hands on her lap. She seemed completely unperturbed by the threat of being thwatted about the head with an iron poker. The man remained standing, arms in front of his body, one hand held by the other, grinning like a gibbon. The lack of jeopardy in the room had the effect of making Hannah feel a bit foolish. There was nothing whatsoever about the two of them that exuded danger, other than the fact that they had barged into her house. She felt as though her home had been broken into by two Sunday School teachers looking for unpaid work.

"We are very sorry to have walked in on you like this. However, yours was the first house we came to," said Rachel. "Please allow me to explain. You may wish to sit down, as what I have to tell you may come as a shock." Hannah remained by the fireplace, but the poker was no longer being brandished. Rachel continued, "We come from a distant planet. Our spaceship is parked a short walk from here. We need your help in announcing our arrival to the world. We clearly have landed in a remote area, and fate seems to have brought us to your door. Even though you are not impressed to be meeting us. I think it is fine to say that we have not so far had the impact that perhaps we might have hoped for."

"A spaceship. Distant planet." Hannah stood up straight, placing her hands on her hips, the end of the poker just missing a vase filled with daffodils. She saw Rachel wince, looked at her hand, then leaned the poker against the large flagstones around the fireplace. "Oh, right. Of course. How stupid of me not to realise it immediately. You're an alien. Who dresses in Gucci. Fuck right off."

"What you see is a hologram, using a holo-ferro drive," Rachel replied patiently, sitting upright on the sofa with her hands in her lap. "My real body is on the spaceship. I have sent this hologram in the form of a human so that you will not be scared by our real form. My real body is...squidgy. I don't think you would like it very much. I have been projected and sent to you in order that you will come back to the ship and explain to us how things work on this planet, so that we can best communicate with those with whom we need to communicate with. We have a message that needs to reach as many people on the planet as possible. This mission is very important." She gestured to her colleague. "I am the captain of the ship, and this is my second in command, Clarence." The man bowed almost to horizontal level, then back up to straight. Rachel rolled her eyes a little, then began to stroke Agnes, who lifted her head marginally from her recumbent position then let it flop back onto the sofa. Even the arrival of an alien was not sufficient to rouse Agnes from a nap.

"Right," said Hannah, placing her hands on her hips. "A hologram. Something ferro – didn't understand that bit. Space-ship. Okay. This has got to be the most convoluted burglary I've ever heard of." She ran her hand through her hair, then reached mechanically into her pocket with the other hand, plucked out a band and tied her hair back. She began pacing in front of the unlit fire.

Rachel stopped stroking Agnes, who rolled onto her back in expectation of a tummy rub. Instead, Rachel stood, took a step forward and faced Hannah. At no point since entering the house had Rachel's expression lost its rapturous haze. "Would you hold out your hand for me?" she said to Hannah. "Just stand still for a moment and hold out your hand?"

Hannah stopped pacing at a point where she could stand facing Rachel, or at least Rachel's shoulders. She weighed up this stranger through half-closed eyes. Clarence was still standing in the same place that he had reached when Rachel had sat down, and seemed happy to be a spectator. Hannah took a breath, then thrust out her hand, palm up, like a schoolgirl bracing herself for a ruler slap from a burly male metalwork teacher.

Rachel reached into a breast pocket that Hannah could have sworn had not been there a moment ago, and brought out a flat, diamond-shaped lump of metal. Rachel didn't seem to be actually holding the item; it was more that she was coaxing it to move. She placed the diamond almost onto Hannah's palm, where it hung in the air, point upwards, not touching the skin. Hannah lowered her hand a little, and the shape lowered too, maintaining the same precise distance from her increasingly sweaty palm. Hannah turned her hand sideways and the shape became horizontal. Just after it had turned ninety degrees, now beyond vertical, the shape suddenly dropped away from her hand, bouncing onto the floor.

Hannah bent to pick the diamond shape off the floor, but to her surprise it began unfolding itself. One side of it bent back as if on a hinge, then another side, then another, each revealing further sides underneath. As the unfolding continued, so the shape grew larger and larger until it began to grow arms and legs, and finally the shape of a small child began to emerge. The unravelling gathered apace, until the colour of the metal changed to a shiny, translucent blue. Two black vertical and one horizontal rhombus shapes became the eyes and mouth. The change stopped as quickly as it had started. The lights flickered into a dull glow, and the mouth flashed as it looked up and said: "Hello, Hannah Siggers."

"What in the name of...of...what the hell is that?" said Hannah, who had taken several steps back during the transformation and was now flat against the wall next to the fireplace. "And how did it know my name?"

"It is my proof to you," said Rachel, "in order to attempt a conviction that you will believe me, Hannah. Rupert has the ability to scan the room for information. Rupert, how did you discover Hannah's name?"

"Hi! I discovered Hannah's name because there are plastic cards in that bag over there that have the name 'Ms H Siggers' printed on them, and a letter on the table addressed to Hannah Siggers."

"Rupert?" said Hannah. "You have a robot and you called it Rupert?"

"Yes," said Rachel, looking hurt. "Isn't it not a good name?"

"It's a *great* name – for a *rabbit!*"

"Does this convince you that I am from a more advanced place than Earth? Perhaps you would now follow us to visit our ship?"

Hannah shook her head carefully as if testing a new crash helmet. "It's like I'm in the weirdest children's book ever. I've got to follow Rachel, Rupert and Clarence into the night to visit their spaceship. What the hell. Let's go for it. How much weirder can this get?"

"You might want to bring a camera and a dressing gown, if you have one."

"A dressing gown? Why, are you going to perform some strange experiments on me?"

"No," replied Rachel. "It is cold outside."

Chapter 7

A Pollinating Zeal

Hannah sat with her head tilted sideways at a forty-five-degree angle, her stare reaching well beyond a thousand yards. She was perfectly still. This was due less to dissociation than to the fact that her brain had shut down any extraneous movements in order to direct all processing capacity to the task of assimilating what she had just been shown. Namely, that she was sitting in the control room of a spaceship.

She held a dainty cup and saucer. The cup was filled with a brown liquid that looked and probably tasted like tea but which was now at best mildly warm. Rachel, sitting behind an unfeasibly large desk with her arms resting on the surface in front of her, was regarding Hannah with a level of consternation that was increasing incrementally with every passing minute. Two other chairs sat unoccupied, one either side of her. The ubiquitous Clarence stood behind the captain's shoulder, and he too was observing Hannah with concern. The desk was empty except for two items: (1) a table lamp, which was projecting a spot of light onto (2) a simple control panel in front of Rachel.

The room in which they now sat was devoid of any other furniture of fixtures. Rupert hovered silently somewhere to the side. It was a large room, and yet the desk seemed to impose itself over the whole area. The entire wall behind Rachel and Clarence was a window, looking out into the empty night. The walls, ceiling and floor were cream in colour. The desk rose out of the ground with pleasing curves, as if the whole entity had been carved out of one giant white pebble. Hannah's first impression had been that she was walking into an eggshell. There was no obvious source of light in the room. The ambience both looked and felt like daylight, warm on the skin, and yet they had arrived at ten thirty in the evening.

The walk to the spaceship had taken fifteen minutes, Rupert the robot 'walking' alongside them. Clarence had spent the journey asking a series of questions about everything he saw or touched. Fortunately, the moon was only halfway through its lunar cycle and visibility was therefore impaired. This had not prevented Clarence from asking about the sheep (what was their purpose?), barbed wire (what was its purpose?) and hedges (why is the land enclosed in this way?). Hannah had provided the occasional answer when Clarence paused long enough to allow her to do so.

The person called Rachel claiming to be an alien – Hannah was not nearly ready to consider the possibility that it actually was an alien calling herself Rachel – had taken a direct-line approach to navigating back to the spaceship. The only words that had passed between them had been when Hannah suggested it might be easier and quicker to take a small detour through a gate rather than walk through a patch of stinging nettles.

Hannah's doubts as to the veracity of Rachel's story magnified when they arrived at the site of the spaceship. Rachel stopped in the middle of a field and turned to Hannah.

"We are here," she said.

Hannah looked around her. She saw only the outline of trees and hedges. Then she looked around her again. "I am guessing it has an invisibility force field surrounding the ship?" she said. "To protect it from attack from a herd of particularly aggressive sheep?"

"No," said Rachel, seemingly impervious to sarcasm. "Invisibility is not possible. We realised that two hundred years ago. It is against the laws of nature and therefore simply cannot be done. You may have been referring to cloaking, whereby a camera on the back of the object relays the images onto the front. This can create a form of invisibility, but it is not perfect, and can be detected quite easily when one knows what one is looking for."

"Excellent," said Hannah, one eyebrow extravagantly arched.

"Well. As pleasant as it has been traipsing across the moors in the middle of the night in my dressing gown, I think I might just toddle off home now, if that is all right."

Rachel looked puzzled. "Home? Will you not come onto the spaceship?"

"Ha ha, yes, well, nice idea," replied Hannah, taking a step backwards. "Except that, given there is no actual spaceship, I thought I would just make my excuses and leave."

Rachel shook her head as slowly as an elderly piano teacher grown used to disappointment. "Rupert, would you please help Hannah to comprehend our spaceship."

The lights that constituted Rupert's mouth flashed as he spoke. "Hi! I will help you comprehend our spaceship by politely suggesting that you look upwards." As he finished the sentence, a bright floodlight shone directly upwards from the top of his head.

Hannah followed the beam of light and promptly fell backwards with a tumble of expletives.

"Rupert, note that these are not words we require you to learn," said Rachel. Rupert switched off his light, and the sky was once again darkness. "Clarence, please help Hannah to her feet."

Clarence was already walking over to Hannah. He offered his hand. Hannah took it dumbly.

She found herself being helped to her feet – and onwards. Her feet left the ground as she continued upwards. The four of them rose into the air as if inside an invisible lift. Looking up, Hannah saw a rectangle of light seemingly floating in the air. As they neared, she could make out that it was a doorway into the spaceship that she had just seen outlined in the sky. After fifty metres of slow rising they stopped in front of the door and stepped inside. Hannah was led meekly across the room by Rupert and invited to sit, an invitation she accepted as if in a trance. Rachel and Clarence waited for her to regain composure.

As if waking, Hannah snapped her head upright and focused on what she understood to be the hologram of an alien's interpretation of a human being, sitting across the table from her in the welcome lounge of a spaceship hovering above the fields. A few minutes ago, she had been walking across those fields. In the intervening minutes she had seen enough to convince her that Rachel and Clarence were telling the truth, and whoever else – *whatever* else – was on this ship was, indeed, *not* from planet Earth. As arguments went, theirs was pretty conclusive.

"So," said Rachel, as she settled back into her chair. Clarence lowered himself stiffly into the chair to her left, as if unsure whether this was allowed, and expecting to be told off at any moment. "Tell me about you, Hannah. What are you?"

"What do you mean, *what* am I? What sort of question is that? I am…I am a mother." She sat slightly more upright for a moment. "Is that what you mean? I don't have a profession as such. I mean, I'm not a scientist or anything. I was a director until recently, but I'm not sure that helps you. I am… Yeah, I guess. I'm a mother."

Rachel paused. When she spoke, it was as if she was reading from a script of how to make small talk and build rapport. "Do you have a child?"

"Yes, although he is not a child. He is twenty-eight." She recognised the flash of bafflement that crossed both their faces. "I had him very young. He lives in Switzerland now with his son. And wife. Is this…important?"

Rachel smiled gently, and for a moment Hannah wondered if she had children too. "No," she replied, "it is not important to us. But we do have a message we wish to share to the people of Earth, and we wish to find the person best able to reach as many people as possible. So what we want of you is – well, we do in fact want you to…" Rachel paused to throw a sheepish glance towards Clarence. "Take us to your leader." Clarence grinned, sharing their private joke. "Well," Rachel continued, "to clarify, we do want to meet with your leader, but we really would rather prefer it if they would come here to meet us."

"Which one?" asked Hannah.

"Sorry?"

"Which leader?"

"There is more than one? Oh, you mean there is a council. Well, we will be content to see a representative. We have a message, and we wish to see the Earth leader who will be able to spread our message across the planet."

"Yeah, but, you see, there isn't one leader. There's loads. About a hundred and eighty, probably. That's about how many countries there are. Although some are more important than others. Well, they think they are, anyway."

"You don't have one planet leader?"

"No, we've got lots of leaders spread out across the planet. And they tend to argue with each other a lot."

"How very strange. Mind you, that does explain a lot."

"How so?"

"Oh, never mind. Look, we have a message that needs to be seen by as many people as possible, and we want to do it quickly. How can we get the attention of the world leaders?"

"You're an alien spaceship. I shouldn't think it would be very difficult. Come daylight I'm pretty sure someone will notice you."

"We would like to be a little more…proactive in reaching the leaders. Our message really is very important."

Hannah smiled. "Well, there is one way," she said. Standing, she took her phone out of the pocket of her dressing gown. "Why don't we just get news of your arrival out there and see who turns up, eh? Hey, Rupert. Smile!"

"Hi! I cannot smile as I do not have emotional reflexes. However, I can do an imitation of a human smile, in order to put you at your ease." With that, the robot's mouth-lights flashed.

"That's good. Do that."

Hannah held the phone to her face and began recording. "Hi! My name is Hannah, and I am currently standing inside an alien spaceship!" She turned the camera to pan around the room, alighting on Rupert. "This is an alien robot. He's called Rupert. Hey, Rupert, what's the news?"

Rupert's mouth flashed as he spoke. "Hello, Hannah. The news is that we have just arrived on your planet Earth, and we are very pleased to meet you."

Hannah turned the phone back to herself. "Yep, I am actually on a spaceship that has just landed on Earth in the middle of the Mendip Hills in the south-west of England. Sounds bonkers, huh?

Well, it's true. Aliens have landed. And they're really nice! So listen, authorities, why don't you come and see them? Just go to Bristol and keep going south. You can't miss it."

She stopped the recording, tapped for a few moments then, after just the briefest of pauses, pushed 'send'.

"Well," she said, turning back to Rachel. "To quote my Nana, that should get the sausages pricked."

Chapter 8

Between The Thorns

The British Prime Minister removed his underpants and threw them over his shoulder with a flourish. His discarded clothes were now scattered on the floor around him. His confidence at not being disturbed was total, thanks to the two Secret Service police officers standing outside the door. Indeed, there was armed security dotted all around the hotel. As he had earlier commented to his foreign secretary, "If there is one place you can walk naked around a hotel room with complete faith that you will not be photographed, it is the G7 summit."

He paused to glance at himself in the mirror. He looked like a waxwork model. It was as if someone had heated his face sufficiently for it to go soft, smacked it with a cricket bat, then allowed it to cool. He breathed in deeply, turned sideways, then exhaled quickly, giving up on the pretence.

Walking over to the bed, he bowed his head. Then, holding onto the bedside cabinet for support, he knelt by the bed. Clasping both hands in front of his chest, he closed his eyes, head bowed. He paused before beginning to pray, probing for the connection with his God, to feel the celestial touch upon skin. He breathed in deeply and exhaled slowly, releasing as he did so some of the pressures and irritations of the day.

And it had been *such* a long day, and an even longer night. The debates had been varied but always intense. He was expected to be up to date and knowledgeable on each one. Only one vote remained: that on the policy that his own government had proposed on reducing the freedom of movement of people between countries. It had been a key plank of his party manifesto, and he knew that the rabid element of his party, always waiting for a fresh opportunity to create the havoc in which they so revelled, would be baying for his blood if he did not come back with a positive result. The meetings had finally come to a close at ten o'clock. It was now two in the morning, he had taken a few whiskies, and he so longed for the comforting blanket of sleep.

"Dear Lord," he began, in confident tones. "Please give me the strength to be the person you need me to be. Help me to find the path that your son, our saviour Jesus Christ, showed in his infinite glory." Wait, was it God or Jesus who possessed infinite glory? He slid the palm of his right hand away from his left and rubbed at his eyes for a moment before ploughing on. "Take my hand, dear Lord, and guide me along the path of righteousness. Help me to make the right decisions, help me always to govern in the way that my constituents would desire."

He paused, waiting for his thoughts to catch up with him. He leaned to the right and stretched his left leg. The joint of his knee cracked, and a small fart took the opportunity to escape. His eyes remained closed, and he once again genuflected.

"Dear Lord, please look over my family and my people and ensure they remain safe from harm. Keep them from evil and from other people, from those who would seek to do us harm and take away our freedoms. I remain your loyal servant. Amen."

He placed both hands flat on the bed in front of him and pushed himself to standing position. A loud knock on the door startled him briefly. He grabbed the hotel dressing gown from the bed, the monogram *Hôtel du Palais* emblazoned across the breast, and placed it around him. He shouted at the door in response to a second knock.

"Who is it?"

"I have been sent to get you," came the terse response. He recognised the voice as belonging to the Brigadier.

He tied the cord around his waist and walked to the door. Looking through the spyhole, he opened the door. The Brigadier walked into the middle of the room. The British Prime Minister turned and addressed him with cautious irritation, like a schoolboy trying to banter with a teacher for the first time.

"Good God, man. What is it now? It's been a bloody long day."

"We have a situation," replied the Brigadier in the finest Etonian accent. "Mr Armitage requires your presence in ten minutes' time."

"Jesus, really? Is this absolutely necessary? I am totally knackered and really need to get to sleep. Can it not wait until the morning?"

In reply the Brigadier held up his phone and tapped the screen. The video of Hannah announcing the presence of the aliens to the world played for the British Prime Minister. His jaw slowly dropped and his eyes widened, having the combined effect of lengthening his head by several centimetres. When the clip had finished, he looked at the Brigadier.

"An English accent. Have they landed…?" His eyebrows raised more in hope than expectation.

The Brigadier's expression was impassive as he nodded to confirm to the other man that the arrival of aliens had indeed occurred in the country of which he was currently the head of the government. The British Prime Minister clenched his fists and uttered a quiet "Yesssss!"

By four in the morning (French time), the members of the G7 group of countries had been fully briefed on the situation currently occurring in the area known as the Mendip Hills in the United Kingdom, and had moved on to discussing what action should be taken next.

The Italian Prime Minister had the room; he was being all arms and argument. He finally finished speaking, sat back in his chair and folded his arms; it was the first time they had not been flailing around for a full three minutes. The heads of the remaining G7 countries, all seated around a large oval oak table, stared back at him in astonishment. All except the French President, who was leaning back on his arm and staring thoughtfully out of the window at the statue of the Virgin Mary standing atop the Rocher de la Vierge, and beyond that across the Bay of Biscay.

The German Chancellor was the first to respond to the proposal that had been so eloquently made by the Italian Prime Minister. "Marco," he said slowly. "Please forgive me if I speak plainly. However, I think it is wise that we do so at this time. I think that – judging by the looks on the faces I see before me – I speak for all of us in saying that we have a different assessment of the situation from the one you make. I'm sure everyone would agree with me when I say that there are others around this table who would be better suited than you to representing the planet Earth in its first meeting with the aliens."

"There are people better suited in the kitchens of this hotel than Marco," said the US President to everyone in the room except the Italian Prime Minister. The UK Prime Minister laughed loudly. The Canadian and Japanese Prime Ministers allowed themselves a minor smirk, which they quickly removed.

"And on what do you base that assessment?" the Italian Prime Minister responded, leaning back in his chair so that the front legs came slightly off the ground. He reached up and patted his hair into place on the top and then at the back.

"Aw, shit, Marco," said the US President. He stood abruptly and threw his arms dramatically in the air. "Come on, let's get real here. It is four am here in France, three am in the UK. We had so much on the agenda for this summit as it was. Now we are discussing aliens and you're telling me that I have to explain to you why you, the fifth-longest-serving Italian Prime Minister since the war because you've been in office more than six months, why you aren't the best person to represent the world to the aliens? I don't even know why Italy is even part of this summit. Just because France felt lonely back in the seventies and invited you in. I'd rather have China here. At least then we'd have the same person around the table two summits in a row."

The Italian Prime Minister abruptly leaned forward, thudding the front legs of his chair on the floor, then quickly stood up, sending the chair scooting backwards across the slate floor with the backs of his legs.

"That is a disgraceful remark," he said, pointing a quivering finger at the US President. "I demand that you retract it immediately."

"All right, all right," replied the US President, sitting back down and waving his hands to indicate that his colleague on the council should do the same. The German Chancellor, who was sitting next to the Italian Prime Minister, stroked his arm gently and made cooing noises.

"Keep your wig on," continued the US President. "The point remains, if anyone is going to represent the Earth, it is only logical that it should be the most powerful man on Earth, right? The President of the mighty U S of A. The office I hold represents more people than you lot put together, if you exclude Japan – something I would never want to do, madam Prime Minister." He nodded towards the Japanese Prime Minister, who nodded back. The heads of Canada and Germany rolled their eyes at each other. The US President had been flirting with the Japanese Prime Minister ever since they had arrived at the summit the previous morning.

"I do think that is an excellent idea, Davis," said the British Prime Minister. "However, I would recommend one small amendment – nay, addition. It seems to me eminently sensible that two people should attend. Given the unique position Great Britain holds in world history, I would like to put myself forward."

"Oh, yeah, certainly unique," the Italian Prime Minister muttered to the German Chancellor. "The country that gave us cricket and the pork pie." The German Chancellor continued to stare with a non-committal smile at the British Prime Minister, expending maximum effort in not being seen to respond to the Italian Prime Minister's quip in any way whatsoever.

"Furthermore," the British Prime Minister continued, with a level of disdain that comes only from a very expensive education, "I would remind you that the spaceship has touched down on British soil. Finally, if I may be so bold, given the special relationship between the United Kingdom and our friends in America" —the Italian, French and German premiers all let out a groan— "it is only natural that I should be the one to accompany Davis."

"If I may be permitted to offer a contribution?" said the Japanese Prime Minister.

"Of course, Kyoko. Please," said the US President, sweeping his arm across the table as if the room and all its contents belonged to him.

"It seems to me that we should consider the request from the aliens, rather than arguing over who is the most important person amongst us. They said that they have a message for the population of the Earth, and they have asked to speak to the person who would best be able to spread that message as widely as possible. With our voice in Asia, Japan should surely be represented in this meeting with the aliens."

"Madam Prime Minster," said the French President, still sitting sideways on his chair facing the windows, with one leg tucked under the other. One elbow rested on his knee, with the hand flopped back at right angles. It looked as if he had been holding a cigarette in a holder that had just been snatched from his grasp. "With the greatest respect, I fear that you are missing a very important point." He turned his head and looked around the table at the various heads of state, creating a moment of drama the likes of which had created his reputation. "Let us remember just *why* we are sending someone – or two people – this is a good suggestion from Douglas, I think." He wiggled the hand in the vague direction of the British Prime Minister, who nodded appreciatively in reply to the compliment. "It is to *hear* this message. It is not to simply relay the message. What if the message is one that the population of the Earth are not ready to hear? It could create panic around the world. *Non*, what we need is someone who is able to negotiate with these aliens. And therefore, as the only person around this table with legal training, I think I should be one of the two people who go."

"Aw, come off it, Gabriel," said the US President. "We've all seen your negotiation style here. Remember last year when we were negotiating climate change? Your entire approach was to sit there with your arms folded while I tried to talk sense to you. That's not negotiating, that's sulking."

The French President flung his floppy hand in disgust. "That is because climate change is not something that can be negotiated!" he replied, now leaning lazily across the table and jabbing his finger across the cultural vacuum that lay between the two men. "You think only of your own country, of 'protecting American jobs', while killing all life on the planet. Well, this, how you say, parochial attitude is shown for how stupid it has always been, now that aliens have landed! Eh? How could you represent the planet Earth when you have eyes only for your own re-election? Eh?"

"Guys," said the Canadian Prime Minister, leaning forward onto the table on her elbows, palms facing the rest of the G7 leaders. "Hey guys, come on now, this isn't helping. Each and every person round this table would be great at this. What are we even arguing about? I suggest we draw straws for it. Look, I'll write the words 'Representative' and 'Deputy' on this piece of paper. Then I tear it up and fold each of the pieces. Brigadier, would you be able to rustle up some kind of receptacle I could put these in? You really are very kind. Thank you."

The Brigadier, standing with his back to the door, paused for a moment. Then he turned, opened the door and spoke to someone on the other side before shutting the door again. A few moments later the door reopened and a young woman passed a brass pot to the Brigadier, who brought it over to the table.

The pot was wide around the middle. At the top was a funnel of a size that would accommodate even the largest hand. The British, Japanese, US and Canadian premiers looked at the pot doubtfully.

The Brigadier placed the pot on the table in front of the French President.

"Holy mother of God, what the damnation is that?" said the US President. "We are about to create a moment that will be discussed for centuries to come, and you want us to pull paper out of a chamber pot? Well, I guess people will be able to write in the history books of the future that we did at least have a pot to piss in."

"It is not a chamber pot," said the French President. "It is an antique Indian water pot. It represents the essence of life and the sharing of knowledge and love. I had it kept nearby in case a vote would be needed. I thought it would be ideal for such a historic moment."

The Canadian Prime Minister put the small pile of papers into the top of the pot, then picked up the pot with both hands and swirled the papers around. "Okay," she said. "Who wants to go first?"

"Ladies first," said the British Prime Minister, gesticulating towards his Japanese counterpart sitting next to him, who reached in, pulled out a piece of paper and opened it on the table. Blank.

The British Prime Minister took his turn next. He also placed a folded piece of paper in front of him, then opened it. Another blank. He muttered an obscenity.

The Italian Prime Minister was next. He peered into the pot, then put in his hand, pulled out a piece of paper, leaned back, and opened it like a hand of poker. "*Meravigliosa!*" he shouted, and threw the piece of paper onto the table with a flourish. It showed the word 'Representative'.

"That doesn't count!" shouted the US President. "You cheated! You looked in the pot first! Draw again!" He stood up and walked around the table, grabbing the piece of paper and throwing it back into the pot. "Null and void, draw again. Not fair, you peeked. Go on, draw again. Come on," he continued to shout, as he stood over the Italian Prime Minister.

Throughout this outburst the Italian Prime Minister looked as innocent as a teenage boy on prom night. He spread his arms in a gesture of peace and goodwill, then clasped the palms together again as if he were about to pray. "How could I cheat?" he said. "All the papers were folded. I looked in out of reflex, I could see nothing. Nothing. Please, my friend, sit, let us continue."

"No shitting way, that was bang out of order," said the US President.

The Japanese Prime Minister stood, took POTUS gently by his elbow and led him back to his chair. "Come along," she said tenderly, as if escorting a small child who had wet the bed. "There is always number two still to be drawn out," she said to him in a soothing voice. He was still complaining quietly to anyone who would listen as first the French Prime Minister then the German Chancellor drew a blank.

The US President took his turn, opening the paper close

to his face. Then he shouted "Fucknuts!" towards the ceiling, screwed up the piece of paper, threw it to the ground then stood, kicked away his chair and walked over to the windows, where he folded his arms and kept his back to the room.

"Well," said the Canadian Prime Minister. "I guess that means I'll be your number two then, Marco." She took out the final piece of paper and unfolded it, revealing the expected word 'Deputy'.

"Oh, well, ain't that the big surprise," said the US President, turning around with a flourish. "Managed to get your boyfriend along for the ride, didn't ya, Olivia?"

"Davis! That is an outrageous thing to say!". The Canadian Prime Minister's face had turned a crimson colour similar to the leather desk blotter on the table in front of her. "My relationship with Marco is entirely professional."

"Ha, yeah, I bet it is." He pointed a finger at the Italian Prime Minister. "I don't know how you swung that one, but you're going to pay for it one day, you mark my words." The US President turned back to the window to resume sulking.

"Never mind him," said the German Chancellor. "The important thing now is to get you two ready for the meeting. There are three hours before you need to leave. We need to agree objectives and protocol. The fate of humanity may well be in your hands."

"Huh," said a dull suburban English voice. It came from an armchair in the corner of the room. "God help us all if this is how you lot behave in a real emergency. Now, if you children have finished picking teams, it is time to get on with the game. I will send in the negotiators to prepare you for the meeting. Now, if you will excuse me, I have arrangements to make."

David Armitage got up from his chair and left the room.

"Good Lord," said the British Prime Minister to his peers. "That made me jump. I'd quite forgotten he was here. I do hate it when he does things like that."

Chapter 9

Handwheels And Cranked Handles

Like most people in the world with access to a television or the internet the following morning, Torben Christiansen was staring at news footage of a spaceship hovering in the air in the south-west region of England. Unlike every other person in the world, however, the reports of the contact with alien life did not make him feel tiny and insignificant, but instead terrifyingly important.

Seated at the wooden kitchen table, he took another nervous bite from a slice of rye bread smeared with strawberry jam. On the laptop computer screen in front of him, the twenty-four-hour news channel went into its third loop of the arrival of the alien spaceship since he had logged in, without imparting any additional information. The screen showed the cube-shaped spaceship hovering in the air. This was then replaced by one of the two videos that Hannah had posted onto social media the previous night.

As Rupert the robot came onto the screen yet again, Torben felt a pang of existential dread, in common with billions of other people around the globe.

Hannah now filled the screen again. Her features had been such a part of his morning that he had reached the stage of wondering if maybe they had actually met before. He hit the 'mute' button, not feeling the need to hear the journalists' interpretation of events, yet still eager to see every possible rerun of whatever footage of the spaceship was available. He was quite happy to accept that aliens existed in principle; it just required a period of assimilation.

As a boy, Torben had grasped an early understanding of the principle of acceptance: when to acclimatise and when to adapt. Firstly in order to survive, subsequently to thrive in isolation. While several of his male peers reacted with belligerence to a school system which imposed rules to obey and instructions to follow, Torben found the pleasure to be had from accepting that which was outside his control. There was also the joyful side effect of minimising the number of things he was required to think about. As his love of the mysteries of the universe evolved, so his interest in social conventions and etiquette diminished.

He found himself increasingly on the end of regular beatings from other boys, and sometimes girls. He would patiently wait for the bullies to finish before continuing on his way, limping off to his next lesson without complaint or reaction. As they approached him with their menacing threats and demands, he would place his briefcase gently on the floor, bow his head, hunch his shoulders, bring his arms across his chest and brace himself for the inevitable blows, waiting for the onslaught to end so that he could continue on his way to the lunchtime physics club. Eventually his tormentors turned their attention to other victims who would provide them with greater satisfaction in the form of wailing and crying, and even the occasional visit to the headmaster's office; they seemed to collect such visits like notches on a headboard.

The study of physics provided Torben with an escape route. Unlike English or art, he found that physics did not attempt to unearth skills within him. It was a discipline in understanding, not explaining. He certainly found it to be a wholly more satisfying enterprise than trying to be liked in the playground.

As he developed his understanding of the workings of the universe, through high school and into university, he became increasingly interested not only in the unbreakable laws of the universe but in how those laws meshed and mingled together. His few friends at the University of Copenhagen were from the science fraternity. They would gather in the Studenterhuset bar, huddled over their coffees, earnestly discussing the universe, from things too small to ever be seen to things too big to fully comprehend.

Other groups of students in their own corners discussed that same universe in terms of poetry, or business, or sport, or history. Where the other students focused on the why of the universe, however, Torben and his friends fixated on the what. Each group would occasionally glance at the others in a mildly condescending fashion, wondering why they were bothering to debate such subjects when there were clearly more essential matters at hand.

The poets found the scientists to lack imagination; the scientists thought the business students to be materialistic; the business students considered the jocks to be frivolous; the jocks believed the history students to be an irrelevance; and the history students thought the poets had missed the point. Amid this maelstrom of judgement and pigeonholing, only Torben and a young chemistry major called Tilda sported a genuine and comprehensive lack of interest in the worldview of the members of the other faculties.

Tilda had been the first to invite Torben to join their group. He had only left his dormitory because the chaos theory major in the room next door was hosting a rowdy poker night and Torben could not concentrate due to the noise. He had taken his book, *The Little Book of String Theory*, down to the Studenterhuset, ordered a burger and a coffee, and seated himself on a dark leather sofa, placing his bag next to him to ensure no one could join him. Tilda had approached him once the burger had been eaten as much as it was likely to be. She later told him that she had recognised a kindred spirit more due to the self-imposed isolation than the choice of reading material.

Tilda convinced Torben that chemistry was about putting different elements together and seeing what happened, whereas physics was about understanding things that had already been put together. He developed the idea that the beautiful mathematical rules behind physics could be combined with what he saw as the chaos and recklessness of chemistry. He would take the rules of the universe and combine them in random ways, simply for the joy of seeing what might happen. The intellectual spark that Tilda had lit within him translated itself into his studies and his research and, eventually, into the white box with 'Niels mark 23' written on the side.

The spaceship had arrived at an estimated time of ten o'clock the previous night, the very moment that Torben had switched on his machine. Approximately an hour later, the woman who called herself Hannah had posted her video on the internet. Some twenty minutes after that, five Tornado jets had flown over the stationary craft and confirmed it to be an unidentified flying object – although, as Hannah had pointed out in the second video she released later that night, it was only unidentified to the government and the Army. *She* was perfectly able to identify the inhabitants of the craft.

In that second video, recorded some half an hour after the first, Hannah had stood in a field facing the camera and explained that the aliens were not only peaceful but actually rather sweet, and that they had a message for the people of Earth. They had wanted to speak to the leader of the planet in order to pass along that message, but when Hannah had told them there wasn't such a person, they'd got a bit confused. Anyway, Hannah had said, she was just holding the fort, and was looking forward to someone official taking over. She had also attempted to explain the whole hologram thing, although she admitted that she didn't really understand it. She had reported that, although it felt a little creepy that the real aliens were in another room and she didn't know what they actually looked like, the hologram versions had seemed very friendly. And, in case anyone still didn't believe her, she had said: "Here is the spaceship." At which point Rupert had turned on his floodlights, and the floating spaceship had come dramatically into view behind Hannah.

When Torben awoke at seven am – six am in England – and turned on his phone, the news bulletins immediately made him aware of the breaking story. He fired up his computer and logged into the news channel, to see that a tall and imposing brigadier was talking to a group of reporters. His head seemed to be almost perfectly spherical under the fatigues cap, his baby face smiling as he spoke. There was something in his green eyes, however, that gave Torben the impression that he had a very definite line, and woe betide the person that crossed it.

The reporters were reflecting concerns expressed across social media as to whether sending the British military as the first point of contact was the best thing to do, or if it was in fact creating the worst possible first impression. The Brigadier left them in no doubt not only that it most certainly *was* the most prudent response but also that *he* was the ideal individual to cope with the developing situation.

Finishing his coffee, Torben closed the lid of his laptop, tucked it under his arm and walked up the wooden steps to his study. The fog was hanging over the bay this morning, a single isolated cormorant floating gently on the undulations in the water that lapped soporifically at the shore.

He walked over to Niels. The orange button taunted him, daring him to press it. Would it have the same effect? Would the bubble pulse surge out of the unit a second time? Would another spaceship appear hovering above the surface of the Earth? What *was* this machine that he had created?

His right arm moved slowly and without permission. He had not commanded his hand to thrust itself towards the box, nor had he intended for his finger to extend towards the orange button, and yet here it was, reaching out, ever closer and with purpose. This wasn't just any old extension of his arm, out for a feel or to explore. This was a finger with intent, a digit that meant business. It was as if the button held an utterly irresistible attraction, like that of a West Highland White terrier to fresh fox poo. If there was a button around, the finger seemed to be saying, then it needed to be pressed, and I am just the finger to do the pressing.

Torben regained sufficient control, as contact was made between flesh and the orange plastic, to delay the inevitable for just long enough to take a deep breath and brace himself. Was this wise? If he really had unleashed a spaceship onto the planet, should he not wait until the true nature of the interloper was known before he repeated the exercise? He felt reckless for a moment – and it felt good. He felt rebelliousness. This was not a feeling that he had ever experienced before. The closest he had gotten to being a rebel in his life was handing in homework early. And yet was this really such a silly thing to do? Surely it was in the spirit of scientific adventure to press the button? Did he not have a duty to repeat the experiment, to gather more data, in order to work out what he had actually built?

Injected with a new confidence, Torben took the brakes off. The finger dabbed forwards and pressed the orange button.

And then.

All of a sudden.

Nothing happened.

After waiting a few extra seconds to eliminate the possibility of a delayed reaction, Torben sat back in his chair, momentarily disappointed. Like any good scientist, however, he quickly realised that there is no such thing as a failed experiment; there is only additional information to analyse.

Firstly, the fact that nothing had happened in the room did *not* mean that nothing had happened anywhere. Secondly, this apparent failure did not necessarily mean that the *previous* pressing of the button had *not* been the cause of the spaceship appearing. Thirdly, the fact that he had felt initially disappointed *did* reveal that he had actually wanted to press that button, and for Niels mark 23 to have been the cause of the arrival of the spaceship. He had wanted to be successful. He had wanted to prove the world wrong and show 'them' that he *was* a genius, not just a bespectacled loner. He had wanted to make a difference.

It was this latter revelation that drove his left arm to reach for the telephone. He dialled a Copenhagen number, then stabbed the 'speaker' button and put the phone on the table in front of him. After five rings, a voice answered in Danish.

"Hello?"

"Professor Flensberg?"

"Yes. Who is this?"

"It's Torben Christiansen. I need to talk to you."

There was silence on the table. Torben leaned forward to look at the signal, checking that they were still properly connected. They were. He leaned back again, still staring at the phone.

"Torben Christiansen," he repeated. "From your astrophysics class. Three years ago. We had a discussion once about string theory."

"Yes. Oh, of course, Torben. Yes."

The tone of voice was not convincing. Torben sighed.

"I was the student who stayed behind every lecture with extra questions continuously for a four-month period. You told me it was a record."

"Oh! Torben! Oh. Torben."

"Professor. I need your help. I think I have invented something. But I don't know what it is. I do, however, think it may involve the spaceship in England."

"Torben, how do you have this number?"

"Um…you, um…left your phone behind in class one time."

"You hacked into my phone?"

"No, I just put in your passcode."

"How did you know my passcode, Torben?" Professor Flensberg was starting to sound annoyed.

"I just guessed. It was 1234." From the lack of response, Torben guessed that the passcode of Professor Flensberg's phone was still 1234. "I would like to come and see you, professor. I need your advice."

"Torben, I'm just leaving for the university, I really don't—"

"Great, I'll see you in your tutor room at one o'clock."

Torben pressed the 'end call' button quickly, choosing to ignore the tail end of a protestation that he might or might not have heard. Okay, that he had heard.

From the cellar he retrieved a pink rucksack from underneath a pile of paint-splashed sheets and carefully placed Niels mark 23 inside. He threw a T-shirt on top, tied down the lid of the bag, swung it onto his back, and headed out the door.

Chapter 10

Love as Destiny

The eucalyptus tree provided more than just shade for Hannah and Agnes. It provided a source of happy memories as well as a location for their contemplation.

Situated across the broad stone courtyard, and then on past the strip of grass that the estate agent – with barely a trace of irony – had termed a lawn, the tree stood on the edge of the property, outgrowing all comers. It was at the furthest point from the road and could not be seen by visitors approaching the house. Hannah had purchased the bench when the tree had grown to a sufficient size to offer meaningful shade on a summer's day. She and Agnes would sit gazing over the fields that formed a saddle down past Velvet Bottom and on towards the top of Cheddar Gorge, where ambitious cyclists could often be found trying to recover their breath.

The tree had been planted as the result of a joke between her and Julia. With Gareth having left to start finding himself at university, Hannah had begun the rebuilding process, and had allowed herself the luxury of finding solace in the company of another. She had met Julia while attending a local folk music festival. The two had been sitting on the grass next to each other and had fallen into chatting between bands. Prior to Julia, lovers had been exclusively impermanent and male. Her time with Julia changed many of her preconceptions.

Love as destiny had been such a feature of her childhood books and films. Love, like life itself, seemed predetermined: a path to follow; a future that is mapped out and decided in advance, just waiting to be revealed. Hannah found herself entangled in contradiction. Having a son had made her want to rebel against inevitability. She sought options, even when a decision seemed obvious. The notion that Gareth's life was preordained repelled her, and she became fixated on ensuring that her son would have a different childhood to her own. She oscillated between the concepts of inevitability and destiny, depending on whether she was considering her own life or that of Gareth.

As the boy grew into a young man and began the slow process of breaking her heart into tiny pieces, so Hannah grew more cynical of her own search for meaning. If she had long ago rejected the notion of destiny, if the future was to be a vast wilderness with no paths or signposts, then she came to embrace the joy of small things. Having found nothing but fear and uncertainty in the enormity of the future, the present became a place where happiness could be found. Life happened to her, and she allowed herself to be carried along by it.

Then Julia occurred, and the concept of destiny once again seemed hugely appealing. Like praying to God while waiting to see the headmaster, she found herself using the concept of destiny as something to be brought out as and when required.

They spent increasing amounts of time in each other's company. Returning from a weekend in a small hotel in a fishing village in Cornwall, they visited a garden nursery. Julia had been teasing that Hannah needed something new to nurture now that Gareth had left, and had bought a eucalyptus sapling, arguing that, like parenting, Hannah would not be able to fuck it up.

Back home, Hannah had pretended to forget about the seedling, leaving it in the car. While Hannah was preparing dinner, Julia had sneaked out and planted it. By the time Julia died from the same bastard illness that had taken Hannah's mother, the tree had proven its ability to exist, as if taking over Julia's position on Earth. It had already grown sufficiently for Hannah to sit underneath and mourn her friend.

The tree was out of place – it belonged in the outback of Australia, not a back garden in Somerset. The propagation of a species of plant requires a third party intervention; a bird or animal to eat the fruit and then excrete the seeds. Or a flower such as the dandelion, which needs the wind to carry the seeds that it releases into the air. But here was a tree which had been offered a new way to migrate and continue its species. Julia was the bird, Julia was the wind. Julia was everything to the story of that tree, just as she had been to Hannah. Now the timeline of Hannah's life had taken Julia away from her.

There were moments when Hannah would sit under the shade and rejoice in the short time they had been allowed to spend together. There were other times when she did not want to sit there at all.

Events moved even more swiftly than Hannah had anticipated following the posting of the video. The military were quick off the mark, finally being able to put into practice plans that had been pored over and reviewed countless times since the very first response to the foo fighter sightings during the Second World War. First there was a jet flypast to confirm what satellite navigation had already showed them, and then, just twenty-five minutes later, the arrival of soldiers in trucks, who surrounded the spaceship and started digging holes and putting up tents as if they were setting up an emergency Cub Scout jamboree.

The local teenagers had an even faster response time, however. They had arrived three to a motorbike straight from a lock-in at the local pub, bouncing along the lanes and over the fields, with a few stragglers on pedal bikes joining them shortly after. The first can of cider was hurled towards the ship around eleven thirty. Air rifles arrived soon after as the youths realised the ship was floating just beyond their can-throwing range. One of them pulled out a large spliff; someone else had a packet of mushrooms. Two of them wandered off into a small copse for a fumble, only to come running out again ten minutes later when the first of the Army trucks rumbled noisily into the field.

Through the night, the Army village continued to assemble below the ship. A wire fence quickly appeared, with the teenagers and anyone else not a member of the armed forces or in the direct employment of the Armitage Foundation being swiftly moved to the outside. Tents were erected, equipment was moved in, generators were started, and floodlights were switched on to eradicate the darkness.

Watching all this activity on a bank of screens that rose out from the desk, Rachel expressed alarm to Hannah that those in charge had decided to send an army to greet them. Hannah pointed out that the people in charge were mostly men, and that was how they tended to react to any sort of confrontation. Rachel seemed to understand the point, and even found it funny. Hannah wondered if the aliens had the same gender issues as humans. Indeed, it occurred to her that differences between the sexes may even have been a universal truth, like gravity and fire. Perhaps, throughout the universe and far beyond, there were multiple genders who didn't really understand each other.

At Rachel's suggestion, Hannah then used the invisible lift to float down to the ground and greet the soldiers. Rachel, Clarence and Rupert the robot stayed aboard the ship, keeping themselves at a distance from the gathering might below, at least until Hannah could assure those in charge that the aliens were peaceful.

Descending slowly through the bright, floodlit night sky, Hannah was acutely aware that, to the soldiers gathered below, it would appear that she was floating down through the air. They were all dressed in white anti-contamination suits, their faces covered by masks. They reminded Hannah in the moonlight of the will-o'-the-wisps that she saw when walking back from the pub across the moors at night. As she looked down at the tented village assembling all around the ship, she could see more people approaching her landing spot, staring in wonderment. One person, larger than the others, started to run, clearly under the impression that she was falling, but stopped after a few steps.

As she reached the ground, one large ghostly figure stepped forward and introduced himself as the Brigadier. He asked her to follow him to one of the larger tents, in a tone that made it clear it wasn't a request. His deep baritone voice revealed no trace of surprise that her feet had only just touched the ground as he addressed her.

Inside the tent, a medical team immediately began shining lights in her eyes, taking blood and generally having a thorough prod. She kept trying to explain that she just wanted to talk to someone who was in charge, and that Rachel The Alien was waiting for her to return. One of the will-o'-the-wisps, whose voice revealed her to be a woman and who seemed to be in charge of the examination, explained in a kindly but incontestable tone that Hannah would be placed in quarantine until they could be sure that there would be no risk of contamination. Hannah's reaction to this was terse; however, she quickly realised that the offer of quarantine was not one borne out of concern for *her* wellbeing.

Finally, at four in the morning, she was shown to a new tent, which contained a table, a sofa and a cot bed with a blanket and pillow. She lay on the cot and tried to sleep. The enormity of what was happening began to sink in, and she found it difficult to slow down her racing thoughts. She wondered if Gareth had seen the video, and whether Monique would allow Atticus to see his grandmother on television in the morning. Then she realised that of course they would all see it; everyone in the world would see it.

A rising panic began to envelop her. Everyone in the world. Who *wouldn't* have found a television in the hope of seeing the first ever pictures of aliens? And she had put herself in the middle of it all! What had she been thinking? She wished that she had followed her instincts to turn and run the moment she had seen the spaceship hovering above. Instead she had allowed curiosity to get the better of her, and what good had it done? Oh, if only she had not answered the door to Rachel, if only she had kept her head down and not gotten involved.

Once again she was bouncing around on a tide of events not of her making. Why had Rachel chosen her door to stop at? That was a foolish thought; it had been completely random. The chances of the knock being on her door were some 7.5 billion to one, but someone had to be that one. That wasn't destiny, it was sheer bad bloody luck.

She had long ago begun to wonder if her journey through life might be less a search for the thing she was meant to do and more just a question of hanging on while life happened to her. The search for true purpose meant believing that there was a true purpose to be found, which in turn meant that her future was somehow preordained; yet these two concepts remained incompatible for her. Surely a world so filled with poverty and injustice could not have been inevitable? A world in which a tiny few hold the power and wealth of the world; who seek to profit as humanity sets the path for its own destruction; where the seas rise and entire species of animals and birds die, yet those in power do nothing, because to do so would mean losing some of that power; surely such a future cannot have been the destiny of the past?

Fate – destiny's evil twin – seemed to be waiting around every corner. Rather than fighting the future, rather than attempting to carve out a path of her choosing, Hannah had chosen to be a passenger. She would find meaning in the life which was happening now, and accept that the future was not something that she could control. Whatever it would throw at her, whoever (or whatever) might knock on her door, she would deal with as and when she was required to.

But now she realised that that approach had been based on the assumption that nothing interesting was going to knock on her door. It was a way of accepting that she was not special, of abandoning potential and enjoying the smallness of now. In doing so, had she made herself small? If, in fact, she had known what fate had in store, would she still have taken such a path? Or had fate chosen her precisely because she had not been interested in being chosen?

She eventually fell asleep with none of these doubts chasing around her thoughts. This was not because there was nothing to worry about, but because there were *so many* things to worry about that she could not decide which ones to focus on.

She was awoken by the Brigadier shaking her gently by the shoulder. She woke with a start, sat straight up in the cot, and swung her legs to place her feet on the floor. Having accomplished this, she took stock. She looked up at the Brigadier blearily.

"Good morning, Hannah."

"Timezit?" she mumbled.

"It is nine hundred hours," the Brigadier said.

Nine o'clock. Perhaps five hours sleep. That was okay, she could function on that.

Hannah stretched her shoulders back and felt a few satisfying clicks at the top of her spine. She rolled her tongue around inside her teeth, as if setting her mouth free. "I think I'd like to go home now," she said, rubbing her hair and looking up at him. "No more tests, okay?"

"Yes, ma'am," he replied. "That is our intention. Your safety is paramount to us, and the tests have come back negative. We are therefore able to move you back to your home."

"'Move me?"

"Yes, ma'am." The Brigadier had adopted his natural stance, feet apart, hands behind his back.

"What are you going to do, get a helicopter to airlift me there? I am quite capable of walking to my house."

"Ah, I very much doubt that, ma'am. Your video has caused quite a stir."

Hannah opened her mouth to speak, then decided it was too early for an argument and, besides, her main interest was getting home. Agnes would be worrying about where she was. At least, she would be wanting to be fed. She decided the Brigadier's offer was easier to accept than decline.

An Army truck waited outside the tent. The Brigadier walked with Hannah to the rear, where a soldier pulled back the green canvas and reached down to help her climb up. The Brigadier went round to the passenger seat of the truck's cabin. Hannah saw in the gloom of the truck that three further soldiers, two men and one woman, sat on benches which ran down either side. No one spoke, and Hannah remained uncertain as to whether they were there to protect or restrain her.

As the truck rolled and bounced forward, Hannah stood to look out the back, but as she rose, each of the soldiers immediately stood as well.

"Whoa, easy, fellas," she said. "Just having a look, okay?"

The soldier who had helped her onto the truck smiled. "Of course," he said, then waved his hand at his colleagues to indicate that they should sit back down and perhaps even chill out a little. Hannah steadied herself against the bouncing of the truck by holding on to the frame, and pulled aside the canvas flap.

It was only as she looked out from the elevated vantage point of the truck that she realised the scale of the world's reaction to her videos. She saw the spaceship, hovering impressively and impossibly. She saw a high wire fence which, she guessed from the way it disappeared out of sight to the right and left, surrounded the spaceship. Across several fields she could see cars, trucks, tractors, motorbikes, mountain bikes all approach the fence, bringing people to see the first aliens to make contact with Earth. A crowd of people were already standing, pressed against the fence, their hands grabbing the wire as if holding on for dear life, their mouths open as they stared silently at the spaceship.

The truck slowed to pass through a set of gates into a smaller compound, itself fenced off. The array of vans and trucks with antennae sticking out of their roofs, and from which men holding cameras were at that very moment jumping, suggested that this was a media village. Hannah watched several soldiers quickly shut the gates behind them. Shouting voices suddenly surrounded them, as if they were in the middle of a riot. A soldier pulled her back onto her seat just as a swarm of photographers ran towards the rear of the truck. Suddenly the inside was lit with blinding flashes as cameras were poked through the flap. Hannah thrust her hand over her face. The truck accelerated, and Hannah heard screaming as someone seemed to bounce off the front.

The shouting continued from behind them, but lowered in volume as they pulled away from the chasing paparazzi. Hannah now turned her head to watch through the windscreen as they approached another gate. It opened to allow the truck to speed through without slowing. Hannah dared to peep out the back of the truck again, and saw a variety of vehicles weaving and bouncing across the field in pursuit.

The truck turned out of the field and onto the road, waved on by a soldier. After five minutes, it turned onto the drive towards Hannah's house. The driver ignored more paparazzi jumping from the bushes, clipping one particularly brave camera-man and shattering his camera into tiny pieces. The truck sped across the front lawn and skidded to a halt next to the front door. The four soldiers jumped out the back of the truck. She ignored the outstretched arm of the soldier who offered to help her, and instead jumped down from the truck and strode towards her home. She could hear cameras click behind her, and looked back to see the soldiers walking backwards while keeping back a group of journalists who were shouting questions at her, with more jumping out of cars and trucks and running towards them across the flowerbeds. The Brigadier appeared at her side as she fumbled with her keys then finally, among a blinding barrage of flashes, managed to open the door. She and the Brigadier tumbled inside, slamming the door behind them.

Agnes ran out of the lounge to greet them, barking once then lying on her back. The Brigadier bent down to tickle her tummy.

"Shit!" shouted Hannah, less used to such drama. Just at that moment, someone started banging on one of the windows and shouting her name. She turned towards the noise and saw a soldier roughly grab the man, and then both disappeared from their view. She ran over and closed the curtains, repeating the action at every window.

Entering the kitchen, Hannah put on the kettle, filled Agnes's bowl, then stood with her back to the counter. The Brigadier stood stiffly in the kitchen doorway. "Bloody hell?" she said to him, framing the words as a question. When he did not respond, she continued, "What the hell am I supposed to do now," this coming out as a statement rather than a question. The kettle boiled behind her, and as she turned away she spoke for a third time. "Tea?"

This time the Brigadier did respond. He held up his hand as if stopping a suspicious vehicle going through a checkpoint in Kabul. "Thank you, no," he said. Hannah shrugged as she took out a mug and threw in a tea bag as if was all the tea bag's fault. She poured in the water, ignoring the considerable spillage, then turned back with folded arms to face the unwelcome guest in her home.

"I need to return to the site," continued the Brigadier, as if explaining his declinature of tea. "You will have protection from my men."

"One of them was a woman," said Hannah, now removing the tea bag, adding milk, then turning again with arms folded and the mug resting in the crook of her elbow.

"Ma'am?"

"One of your 'men' is a woman, Brigadier. We women tend to notice such details."

"It is a generic term, ma'am."

Hannah looked to her right at the bright sunshine outline around the curtains. She wanted to be sitting thinking on Julia's bench right now, not feeling like a prisoner in her own home. Everything had been all right until 'help' had arrived. And what did those reporters want of her? She wasn't the news; get back to that spaceship, that's where things would be happening. She looked again at the Brigadier. She supposed it was not his personal fault. Maintaining her guard, she softened her tone a little.

"These 'men'. They are here for my protection, right?"

"Yes, ma'am."

"Not to stop me from leaving…"

"No, ma'am. You are free to leave any time you want to. However, I would strongly advise you against such action. The Minister has—"

"The Minister? Which Minister would that be, then?"

"The Minister has requested that you stay in your house until we understand the motives of the aliens. Plus it is for your own safety. Besides" —he gestured behind him towards the window— "I'm not sure you actually could leave even if you wanted to."

"No. Hmm. You have a point there, I guess. Still. One likes to have options."

"We will keep you informed of developments, ma'am. If you need anything from us, or if you have any difficulties or experience any…" He paused for a moment, searching for the right words. "Any after-effects, then just call me." He handed her a card which contained only a telephone number, then turned and walked out the front door. There was a brief flurry of flashes as he closed the door behind him.

Hannah sat on the sofa. Agnes immediately jumped up onto her lap, licked her hand once, then turned and sat upright on her knees as if she were atop a ledge overlooking the plains of the Serengeti. For the first time that morning, Hannah looked at the screen of her phone.

Twenty-five texts and eight missed calls, most of them from Gareth. So *that's* what it took!

Chapter 11

Ever Decreasing Circles

At the very moment that Hannah was pressing the 'call back' button and waiting excitedly to hear her son's voice, seven Army helicopters were taking off from Bristol Airport. They flew across Blagdon Lake and up onto the Mendip Hills. Each helicopter carried a world leader who was peering out across the morning, eagerly straining to gain their first live view of the spaceship. At last it came into view, hovering with a certainty and stillness that made it all the more foreboding.

The helicopters set down in fields adjacent to the one dominated by the spaceship, on the opposite side from the media enclosure. They landed far enough away from each other that one laser cannon from the spaceship would not be able to destroy more than one of the leaders at a time. There was no hint or suggestion that there was such a thing as a laser cannon, or even that the spaceship was armed, but information was generally thin on the ground, and security at presidential level was not about taking chances. The tenure as a world leader was a short one, however, and the fear of missing out on such a momentous occasion had proven to be far greater for the premiers than the fear of annihilation.

One world leader emerged gingerly from each of the helicopters. They were each accompanied by three men with wires coming out of their ears. At a gate to the field over which the spaceship hovered, David Armitage stood awaiting them. All the leaders walked towards him. His expression remained impassive as they grew closer. The Brigadier stood behind his right shoulder in his customary stance, legs apart and hands clasped behind the back.

The seven men and women approached David Armitage from their different directions at the same brisk pace, their three bodyguards fanned out behind each of them. It was as if they were performing at a local show as the synchronised world leader display team. With a sly glance to either side, the British Prime Minister quickened his step imperceptibly, hoping the others wouldn't notice and he would reach David Armitage first. The other leaders, half-expecting one of the others to make such a move, immediately upped their pace to match his. Next it was the US President who sped up further, expanding his giant stride to the full and reaching a pace just shy of a trot. The Japanese Prime Minister was forced to break into an intermittent run in order to keep up, sending her momentarily out in front of her bodyguards, who quickly resumed their positions relative to her as if connected by elastic bands. The Italian Prime Minister glanced continually left and right to ensure he wasn't going to be last, while the French President managed to continue his outward insouciance by extending the arc of his arms.

David Armitage stood in the middle of this ever decreasing semi-circle. The British Prime Minister arrived first, marginally ahead of the US President, who had attempted to sprint the last twenty metres but had only managed ten before needing to slow again to catch his breath. The German Chancellor skidded to a halt, while the French President toppled forward slightly, like a gymnast landing from a vault, before stepping back into line. The seven of them stood at approximately arm's length, forming an almost perfect semi-circle around David Armitage. The Italian and French Prime Ministers, whose helicopters had landed next to each other, exchanged a few words and a smile, and the Canadian Prime Minister swapped places with the German Chancellor in order to be next to the Italian Prime Minister. Only the US President stood perfectly still, his arms firmly folded. His bottom lip pouted slightly, and his face was set into the expression of a small child who has been denied an ice cream when they clearly felt that they deserved one.

"Right," said David Armitage, calling the group to order. "I am sure I do not need to remind you all of the serious nature of what is going to happen here this morning. Books will be written about the events of this day. So listen carefully. The woman, Hannah Siggers, has been thoroughly analysed." The Italian Prime Minister whispered something to the French Prime Minister and they both started giggling. They stopped when David Armitage rolled his eyes and then glared at them. He continued.

"She has been placed in quarantine, but at this point is showing no harmful side effects of having been in contact with the aliens. Nevertheless, we are taking no chances. You two" — he nodded towards the leaders of Canada and Italy— "need to go into that tent, where you will be prepared for entry to the spaceship. You will go through a detoxification programme once the meeting is over. We do not know if the aliens are armed or dangerous. The first thing we therefore need to do—"

"Hi!" came a bright voice from behind him. They all looked to see where it was coming from. An unfeasibly tall and slim woman was approaching them from the direction of the spaceship, dressed in a blue jacket, blue trousers and pink basketball boots. She was smiling broadly.

The Brigadier immediately drew his gun. "Halt!" he shouted. "Do not approach any further."

"Oh. Okay. Hey, look, I'm Rachel. You know, from the ship? No need to be pointing a gun at me. Come on, now, put it away." All the time her smile did not waver.

"All right, Brigadier," said David Armitage. "I think we are safe. Hello, Rachel," he said. "Our representatives will be ready to meet you and hear your demands shortly."

"Oh, we don't have any demands, silly. Just a request that we don't think you'll find too difficult to help us with. But I just popped out to let you know that we've run a load of tests and you don't need to bother with any of those detoxification procedures. We hold no threats to you, and you to us. We're all clear. Okay?"

"All the same, it is better to take suitable precautions," replied David Armitage, his demeanour unchanging.

"Oh, okay. It's completely up to you, of course. But we'd rather like to get on, you see. So perhaps we'll see if we can find someone else who can help us. Sorry to waste your journey. Byee!" Rachel waggled her fingers to wave goodbye, then turned to leave.

"Armitage," shouted the Italian Prime Minister, speaking quickly as he saw his place in history disappearing before his eyes. "I'm fine. I don't need to bother with all that." He waved his hand vaguely towards the wrong tent. The Canadian Prime Minister was nodding vigorously in agreement.

Rachel turned, her smile returning. "Ooh, that's great," she said, clapping her hands. "In that case, follow me! Ooh, and one other thing. Please release Hannah. There is no reason to keep her a prisoner – we carry no infections. Thanks!" She turned and walked towards the spaceship.

The Canadian and Italian Prime Ministers looked at each other, each took a deep breath, and they walked quickly until they were alongside Rachel. The others also walked forward, watching history being made. When the three of them were under the edge of the spaceship, they stopped, and then began to rise into the air. A door opened in the side of the spaceship, and they disappeared inside.

"God speed," said the British Prime Minister.

"*Ki o tsukete*," said the Japanese Prime Minister. "Go careful."

"Should have been me," said the US President.

It was said in his hometown that Marco Dominese had more front than Genoa. He had faced down countless ruffians, gangsters and corruption enquiries in his twenty-seven-year career in Italian politics. Among many other nicknames, he was known as '*il camaleonte*' – the chameleon. He liked to think of this as an affectionate reference to his somewhat bug-eyed stare when he was concentrating, but it had actually originally been coined for his constantly shifting political position to suit his career prospects. During his ascent he had been faced with accusations of: misuse of government funds; tax fraud; ordering the murder of political opponents; corrupting a judge; false accounting (twenty-three counts across his eight different businesses); extortion and bribery for political gain; money laundering; and child prostitution. He had survived them all.

Now, for the first time in his life, faced with Rupert the robot and two holograms of aliens sitting behind a desk on the spaceship, Marco Dominese was as utterly terrified as he had ever been. Just controlling his bowels was requiring great levels of concentration, and if it had not been for the determination not to embarrass himself in front of Olivia, the Canadian Prime Minister, he might well have let go.

Rupert stood – hovered – to one side of the large desk. Flanking the alien hologram that called herself Rachel was a man – a hologram of a man, Marco kept reminding himself – who was also in his mid-thirties. They sat with their hands folded on the table in front of them, and were smiling. In fact, they had not stopped smiling the entire time.

After arriving in the spaceship, the two leaders had been offered tea, two cups of which now sat on a low table in front of them, untouched. Marco and Olivia sat in high-backed, cushioned bucket chairs. For a moment, Marco had been reminded of a meeting early in his career with senior members of a particular family from Napoli that he would preferred not to have remembered ever again. A tiny drop of urine left his penis against his bidding.

He became aware that Rachel was talking and hoped he hadn't missed anything important.

"...these forms in order to not scare you," she was saying. "Our real bodies are in another room, away from your eyes in order that we do not shock. We are somewhat different to your human form. However, you may think of these people you see before you as the aliens with which you communicate."

"As you can imagine," said Marco, regaining the chutzpah for which he had gained a reputation, "we have a large number of questions. There is so much we would like to know. Where you have come from, about your culture, and so on. You are the first contact we have had with alien life. Prior to your arrival, we did not know if there was any life other than ourselves in existence."

"Yes, yes," said Rachel, waving a hand dismissively, "we can get to all of that. We'd be only too happy to help, of course we would. But first, I would like to know exactly what *you* are." She pointed at the two of them in turn. "On Earth, I mean. What are your functions? Where, exactly, do you 'fit in'?"

"Um, excuse me?" said the Canadian Prime Minister. Marco looked across at Olivia, who was putting up her hand as if to ask for permission to speak. "Hi. Um, if I may, there is one question I am dying to know the answer to. How can you speak our language? And with such fluency and subtlety?"

"Oh, that's easy," replied Rachel with an easy laugh. "We are a very advanced race. We intercepted some of the billions of messages that crisscross your planet every second and fed them into our computer, who analysed your language. When Hannah first spoke in English to us, our computer identified it and now translates our words into ones that you understand. It's a very... big computer, you see. Now, please. What are you?"

"I," said Marco, clasping his hand to his chest and bowing his head slightly, "am the Prime Minister of Italy, one of the major countries on the planet. And Olivia here is the Prime Minister of Canada. Along with five other leaders we make up the G7 council, which meets once a year to collaborate. You might say that together we are the closest thing to a leader of the planet that we have."

"And what does a Prime Minister of the country of Italy actually *do*?" asked Rachel.

"We are elected by our people to govern. We collect the taxes and we spend them in ways that bring maximum benefit to our people."

"Oh! I see," said Rachel. She turned to her colleagues in turn. "They are politicians! Simple administrators! Oh dear, no, that's not what we want at all. Sorry." She stood and walked around the table, beckoning for them to rise. "Thank you for coming, but, you see, we have a message that we need to get out to the most people on your planet possible, all at the same time. It really is so very important that we find the right messenger. We have people like you on our planet, and they lie so often that no one believes anything they say any more. So, you see, you are not the right people to get our message out at *all*." She was ushering them backwards, towards the door through which they had stepped only ten minutes previously. It slid noiselessly open, revealing the brightness of the morning casting its glow across the downs towards Cheddar Gorge. "Thank you for coming, really, but please send someone more appropriate, would you, please? Thank you, thank you."

Marco had been ushered furthest, and found himself on the edge of the spaceship. He glanced behind him and registered that the most notable aspect of what was outside was that it was entirely *below*. Olivia was still walking backwards as she tried to protest with Rachel, to suggest that they could be of assistance, and hadn't noticed that the doorway was now just a few steps behind her. Instinctively Marco tried to grab Olivia's arm as she took the final step out, a step which would surely result in her plunging to her death. To his relief she did not fall, but instead began to move slowly downwards, like a warm spoon sinking into a pot of honey.

With one last attempt to promote their credentials – which was met with a final "Thanks for coming and sorry to waste your time" from Rachel – he also took that extra step backwards. It seemed that the aliens had begun to rise upwards, before he realised that it was actually him that was now moving downwards.

He and the Canadian Prime Minister shared a contrite look as they descended. David Armitage, the Brigadier and the other world leaders awaited them below, stepping forwards and babbling with questions as they reached the ground. David Armitage put up his hand, and everyone fell quiet. Eventually, he simply said: "Well?"

"They didn't want to talk to us," said Marco, a significant pout now beginning to appear. "We were just dismissed by that woman. She said that we were mere 'administrators'."

"Aw, shit, you blew it," said the US President, wheeling around with arms flying outwards. "I knew you'd blow it. What an asshole."

"They didn't give us a chance!" protested Marco, flinging both hands outwards at a forty-five-degree angle like Jesus on steroids addressing the masses. "We barely said anything. They said they have a message they want as many people as possible to see." His arms were now flapping as if he was attempting to fly back up to the doorway. "Then they asked what we do. When we answered them, they said no one believes what politicians say, and told us to send someone else to get their message out."

"Well," said David Armitage. "At least that confirms that there is intelligent life on other planets."

All seven leaders shouted in protest. David Armitage waved at them to calm down.

"Enough already," he said. "Go and get a coffee, all of you. I have some calls to make."

Chapter 12

The Butterfly Collector

Torben gazed unseeing out of the window as the train trundled along the Whisky Belt towards Copenhagen. He had travelled the line hundreds, if not thousands, of times during his life and could describe many of the enormous houses that stood between the train and the coastline. Indeed, he had once attempted this feat at a student party. He had been swigging from a bottle of Tuborg on a two-seater sofa with a girl from class, feeling emboldened by the experience of being part of an actual real-life friendship group. He had described all the major houses up to Kokkedal station, at which point the girl he was talking to had risen to her feet and walked into the kitchen, and had not returned.

On this particular journey, the game of memorising the mansions had been pushed aside by far deeper ruminations. As every scientist knows, an experiment must be repeatable for the results to hold any validity. What inferences could be taken from the fact that the machine had not worked the second time? He was sure it was not broken – it had not been so much as touched since the first time. The thought that it was a machine that might be used only once had been analysed, just as he had analysed each individual part in his head, testing for whether it might need to be replaced. Again, he had come up with nothing. He could deduce no reason why Niels mark 23 should not have produced exactly the same effect the second time the orange button was pushed than it had the first time.

The issue of what effect that actually *was* had been filed away for future analysis in anticipation of the meeting with Professor Flensberg. Torben had stumbled half-blind through the theories of time and space, picking and choosing ideas that he did not truly understand, then building them into the machine. It was time to ask someone who might know what they added up to.

As he stepped off the train at Copenhagen Central Station, Torben scanned the platform for anyone who did not seem to have a good reason to be there. The morning commuter rush had dissipated, but as he walked onto Bernstorffsgade he found the old feeling of paranoia returning, just as it did whenever he spent time in the capital city. He looked into the faces of everyone who passed by, but quickly realised how difficult it was going to be to distinguish an ordinary person walking around the city from a Secret Service agent following him. It also struck him that he considered 'an ordinary person' to be someone who was not like him, which was a reasonable description of almost everyone he saw. Feeling exposed, he ducked into an art café on the concourse, and took time to compose himself over a black filter coffee with a pastry on the side.

His phone pinged: a message from his mother, with a reminder that a neighbour was turning sixty at the weekend. He hoisted the rucksack onto his back, chose a birthday card, and paid the bill. He walked out of the station towards the Niels Bohr Institute, the route taking him past the entrance to Tivoli Gardens and down Hans Christian Andersen Boulevard. The same route he had taken hundreds of times before when he had been a student of physics. Cyclists passed elegantly by, as much a part of the fabric of the city as remoulade with chips. As he crossed Queen Louise Bridge, Torben bridled at the pace of city life. He felt the pangs of the rising panic that made itself felt whenever he arrived in Copenhagen. It may well have appeared if he had gone to other cities too, but he had never been to any other cities. The towns local to him, Espergærde and Helsingborg, were familiar enough to give him comfort, not fear. Copenhagen's streets, however, never seemed the same two visits in a row, and the unfamiliar faces that whizzed past only made him realise how insignificant a cog he was.

Torben's parents would acquiesce to taking the young boy to Copenhagen at least once during the school summer holidays. The attractions of Tivoli were sufficient to trump the anxiety he felt when pulling into the train station. After a day spent on the Ferris wheel and bumper cars, Father would take them to an Italian restaurant owned by an old friend before they headed home. Every trip followed exactly the same format, just the way Torben liked it. He knew what was going to happen, knew that he was going to have a happy day, and knew that there was not going to be anything that he did not like. No surprises.

Even the years as a student had never quite made him accustomed to the pace of the city. He had found his way through, had quickly established new routines. The experience had taught him that it was possible to accommodate changes, to accept new influences by turning them into processes. It was during this time as a student at the university that someone had finally challenged the concept, so ingrained within him, of knowledge for its own sake.

Tilda had been the first person that Torben considered worthy of arguing with, a compliment higher than she could possibly have realised. She was studying chemistry and the opportunities for disagreements were limited, and so they had been forced to find other fields upon which to flex their argumentative skills.

"The trouble with you, Torben, is that you do not know *why* you are studying."

"I study for the love of the subject, Tilda. I study merely to understand. I wish to see under the carpet of the universe, to look inside the cupboard merely to see what can be seen." For his birthday in the summer before Torben started at university, his mother had bought him a series of books entitled *The Art of Conversation.*

Tilda had sat forward in her chair, leaning across the table in the Studenterhuset coffee shop as if being closer would be more likely to convince him of her argument. "But what is the point, Torben? What is it for? Do you not have dreams, hopes, ambitions? Do you not one day wish to make your mark on the world? All I live for is to discover a new element, or create a new compound with healing properties. Surely our lives are defined by the purpose we choose to give them? If you have no purpose, then you are merely accumulating knowledge like…like a collector of butterflies."

Torben shuddered slightly at the memory as he walked briefly through Fredens Park. He had suspected for many years that, at some point, he would be likely to make a friend. Everyone else did it – surely it would happen to him as well. He had analysed the process from all angles and finally concluded that it would need input on his part to allow such a flowering. He had seen potential friendships falter and wither due to his inability to offer anything other than information and loyalty, which he knew was insufficiently fertile ground on which to develop a series of conversations into a friendship. And now the moment had arrived; the great challenge had arrived.

With a deep breath, Torben had straightened his back and looked Tilda in the eye. Now or never. The moment had come to share his feelings.

"I *do* have a dream, Tilda," he had said. He had spoken quietly at first, barely audible, but had increased in volume along with his passion for the subject. "It is something I have never shared with anyone else ever before." He remembered noticing the flicker of excitement cross Tilda's face; he had found it strangely rewarding in return. Was this what having a friend felt like? Someone being interested in what you were about to say?

"All my life I have been alone," he had continued, becoming absorbed in the attempt to articulate what it was that he felt. "Happily alone. My parents were brilliant people who expected me to be brilliant also, and so I became brilliant. The local children thought me strange. I was bullied. I retreated into my studies, where I found joy. I do not, however, bear any resentment or animosity. No, it is pity that I feel, genuine sorrow for the world that I observe. People are only partly responsible for their own misery. I read science periodicals for the latest news on physics, but I see also the articles on climate change, on the future destruction of the human race, and I see our politicians unable or unwilling to do anything about it. And so I learn and I study in order that one day, maybe – just maybe – I may be able to invent something which will help a few people to see the world differently. I do not know how or what this will look like. I just know that I want to make a difference for *someone*. I wish to die being able to say that in my time on Earth I improved someone's life. I study for joy, but there *is* a purpose. It's just a little…" He had searched for the words, but his fluency had deserted him. "It's too big. Changing one person's life. It probably sounds preposterous."

As the words trailed away and the fog lifted from his eyes, Torben had once again noticed the room in which he was sitting. To his horror, he had seen that not only was Tilda listening to him, but so were people on neighbouring tables. One or two had given an approving nod or shrug before resuming their conversations. Tilda had stared at him as a zookeeper might observe two pandas that had finally worked out how to mate.

"There is hope after all," she had said through a smile so wry as to be revealing hints of self-congratulation. Then she had quickly returned to her default demeanour of couldn't-give-a-fuck, and he had realised that he was to Tilda what a mouse was to a cat.

Torben shook Tilda from his mind as he arrived at the Niels Bohr Institute. He paused in front of the humble yet imposing building with the red window frames and red-tiled roof, and prepared himself for the possibility – the likelihood – that he was about to make an enormous fool of himself in front of his mentor.

Professor Flensberg's secretary advised Torben that the professor was in the refectory and wondered if Torben would like to join him. Anxious at the lack of privacy, Torben dithered for a moment. Unlike the professor, the secretary *did* remember Torben only too well.

"The professor has a table in the corner, away from anyone else," she said in a soothing voice. "You'll be fine."

Torben thanked her and walked along endless white halls and down sterile stairs to the refectory. He spied the professor in the corner and waved before walking over. The professor stood up as he approached, and they shook hands.

"Shall we?" said the professor, pointing towards the line of students queueing for food. Torben did not remove his rucksack. They chatted awkward small talk as they waited, the professor enquiring as to what Torben had been up to since leaving university. If he had been surprised by the revelation that Torben's parents had emigrated to New Zealand, he did not show it. This led Torben to the sneaking suspicion that the professor was not really listening at all and was thinking of higher things, a thought that pleased him on several fronts.

They both chose a hot dog, Torben adding mustard and ketchup, the professor smothering his in fried onions. They added a drink (water for Torben, cola for the professor) and returned to the table. Torben took off his backpack and placed it by his side, hooking his leg through a back strap.

"So, Torben. Why the sudden desire to see me after all these years?" The professor took a large bite of his hot dog and waited while he chomped.

Torben placed his hot dog back onto his plate with considered gravitas and leaned forward. "I have invented a machine," he said in a whisper. "I do not know what it does, but I am pretty certain it was instrumental in the appearance of the spaceship that is in England." He leaned back, took a big mouthful of his hot dog and awaited questions, a large splodge of mustard landing on his chin.

"Right," said the professor as if this were exactly the sort of revelation he had been expecting. "Well. Where do we start with such a statement? What makes you think your machine made a spaceship appear, Torben? What is your evidence? Hmm?"

"Mmmm, mm mmm," said Torben. The professor held his hand up to indicate that he was quite happy to wait while Torben finished his mouthful. He scratched his own chin to indicate that Torben might want to wipe off the mustard and ketchup mix that had accumulated there. Torben picked up the napkin, wiped his chin, looked curiously at the evidence now on the napkin, jutted out his chin towards the professor (who nodded quickly), then began to describe what had happened when he pressed the orange button the first time.

"Then," he continued, "I saw the news bulletin about the spaceship, and it seems that it appeared out of nowhere, undetected by satellites or space probes, at exactly the same time as I turned on the machine. It surely cannot be a coincidence."

The professor smiled in a way that Torben had seen before, and his heart sank just a little further at the conclusion he anticipated the professor was about to reach. "Torben, I don't know what your machine did, but it seems at the very least highly unlikely that it caused a spaceship to appear. And I think that is being generous. Now, why do we not take a look at it and see if we can figure out what you *have* built?"

Torben opened the lid of the rucksack and put the machine on the table. The professor smiled when he saw the name written on the side. "This is your twenty-third version? Torben, what were you trying to make in the first place?"

"I was exploring. I have been applying theories in a practical way. I didn't have any specific purpose in mind."

"Well, what you described to me – what happened when you pressed the button and the machine did work – does give me an idea as to what might have happened." The professor wiped the hot dog grease from his hands, then lifted the lid of the box and peered inside. He gave a nod of grudging respect. "Okay, Torben, let's take this down to the lab and see what we can make of it. You never know. Maybe, just maybe, you have stumbled upon something very interesting."

Beaming so hard he felt his head might fall off, Torben put Niels mark 23 back into the rucksack, shoved the last of his hot dog into his mouth, and slung the rucksack onto his back. He followed the professor out of the refectory, a gooey splodge of yellow mustard clinging to his tie.

Chapter 13

Wealth

Darren Allison stepped from the helicopter and walked towards the greeting party like a lion approaches a group of hyenas gathered around a kill. He wore a black suit, white shirt and blue tie which were identical to the eighty-six other such outfits that were hanging in the wardrobes of his various houses around the world.

The man widely accepted to be the most successful business investor on the planet extended his hand to greet David Armitage. He allowed himself the merest flicker of a smile as David Armitage – the man whom the great and the powerful referred to as 'The Fixer' – gave the slightest of bows as they shook hands. It was not the extent of the bow that pleased Allison. It was the fact that it was involuntary. Everyone he met simply oozed respect for his record in having amassed an enormous fortune having started with nothing but a small fortune.

It was well known that David Armitage was able to organise quite literally anything that was physically possible. He had also been known on many an occasion to organise the seemingly impossible. And yet, for all his extraordinary influence, even he did not have the financial capability to bankroll putting a president in the White House. Darren Allison was one of the few people in the world who could trump David Armitage, and that had earned him an involuntary bow. It was worth every penny.

"Hello, David," said Allison in his southern American accent that could only be described with the word 'drawl'. "Pleasetameetcha once again." He nodded towards the spaceship that towered behind the reception group. "Sheh, that is quite a sight to behold right there, yes sir."

"Thank you for coming at such short notice, Mr Allison."

"Sheh, you kiddin'? Son, I have done many things in my life. I have achieved more things than most people even dream of. But being the man who meets the aliens and spreads their message throughout the world? Boy, this will be the cherry on top of a very considerable pie."

The Brigadier stepped forward and put out his arm. "Sir, we need to go through some formalities. Would you please step over to this tent and we can ensure that you—"

"Aw, come on, I'm not here to waste time," said Allison, pushing the Brigadier's arm to the side and walking towards the spaceship. "I'm here to meet aliens. If the goddam President of Italy can go in and out without catching a cold, so the hell can I."

"Well said, that man!" said a voice to his left. Allison turned and saw Rachel walking across the grass towards the group.

"How the hell does she do that?" David Armitage whispered to the Brigadier, who shrugged in response.

Allison held out his hand, then looked at it, suddenly unsure of how one greeted an alien. Rachel reached him quickly with her giant strides, then removed any potential awkwardness by grabbing his hand and shaking it vigorously.

"Are you the man to help us, I am wondering?" said Rachel.

"Sheh, you betcha," replied Allison in a staccato voice that surprised him. He realised that, for the first time in his life, he felt awkward and shy. The feeling was unfamiliar to him and was not welcome. He had met every single person he admired or who were his heroes – from the Pope to the Bee Gees and every step in between – and on each occasion the other party had been the ones who had stammered. Other people were nervous to meet *him*, not the other way around.

"Please would you follow me?" said Rachel, and she walked towards the spaceship at a pace that allowed Allison to quickly reach her side.

Two minutes and one disorienting ascent through the air later, Allison found himself standing alone in a large white room containing a large white desk, behind which were two chairs. In front of the desk was a third chair, presumably awaiting his own posterior. Rachel had excused herself momentarily when they stepped onto the ship, and she now reappeared from a door in the corner of the room that seemed not to have been there before. She led out a colleague, a man who seemed to trip over nothing before sitting heavily in his chair, and the short robot that Allison had seen in the videos that Hannah had posted. The fact that Rachel did not introduce the man told him all he needed to know about decision-making on the ship. Having sat in front of many thousands of company boards, the subtleties of power and decision-making were things for which he had developed a sixth sense.

Allison wondered fleetingly why the aliens had chosen different human genders in which to appear. Before he had a chance to develop the thought, however, Rupert the robot hovered to his side. Why was it that an entire spaceship floating above the ground was impressive, yet this little robot gave him the creeps? Maybe it was the strange colour that should be blue but somehow wasn't, or possibly the diamond-shaped eyes that seemed to be looking up at him even though there was only a weird glow where a pupil might be.

"This way if you would please, sir," said Rupert, its mouth flashing in time with the words as it led Allison toward the vacant chair. As he sat, the aliens smiled at him in unison. Nobody spoke as Rupert disappeared through the door in the corner of the room, returning seconds later with a glass tumbler one-third full of a dark brown liquid. The robot – Allison could not bring himself to refer to it as 'he' – offered the glass. Allison took a sniff, then looked up in surprise.

"Hine Talent de Thomas?" Rachel nodded. "Now that is one extremely fine cognac," Allison continued. "Mah dear, I am very curious as to how you may have come about a bottle."

"Rupert has many talents. Thank you for coming to visit us," said Rachel.

"Sheh, you kidding me? I'd sluff class every day to get this opportunity," replied Allison.

"Yes. Indeed," said Rachel. "Well, as I'm sure you have been told, we have a message that we wish to get to as many people as possible. So, before we proceed, please would you tell us: what are you?"

"Well, see, I'm glad you asked me that question. I happen to be the richest man on the planet."

Allison took a significant sip of the brandy, applied his favourite smirk, and waited. It was not often he got to make that claim, since everyone already knew that he was the richest man on the planet when they met him. It was invariably *why* they were meeting him. He was a man who literally needed no introduction. His brilliance at picking companies in which to invest had been proven over and over so many times that it was taken for granted. His books were bestsellers, bought across the planet by people who didn't have very much money but who wanted to become people who had a lot of money but without the tedium of hard work. The fact that not everyone who bought his books and followed his principles then became wealthy was not something that seemed to give rise to discussion. His latest book was titled *More Investment Secrets* although, for the six weeks during which it was compiled, he had given the manuscript the working title of *How To Get Rich Quick By Writing A Book Entitled 'How To Get Rich Quick'*. It had sold even more copies than its predecessor, *Allison's Investment Secrets*. The opportunity to inform someone that he was the richest person on the planet and see the awestruck look on their face was therefore not a pleasure he was ever granted. He savoured the moment.

That moment, however, grew first into a pause and ended up being a silence. He realised that the aliens had registered no reaction to his statement at all and were, in fact, waiting for him to continue. It was almost as if being the wealthiest person on the planet was not enough for them.

"I...*I* am the most successful investor on the planet," he continued, with emphasis on the personal pronoun. "I grew up in Utah and inherited a modest sum from my father at the age of sixteen, which I invested. I became the richest man in the world by using nothing but my acumen. I have sold millions of books worldwide and am revered across the globe."

"You have more money than anyone else on the planet,"

repeated Rachel. "Does this mean you have more money than you need?"

"Sheh, hoh yes," said Allison, mentally blowing on his fingernails and rubbing them on his lapel. "Many, many more times."

"Why?"

Allison opened his mouth to reply, then closed it again. He took a moment to gather his thoughts before reopening it. "Because I have been so very successful," he said. "As a result, I am one of the most famous people in the world, admired and respected everywhere."

"You are famous for taking more than anyone else?"

"Well, heck, I wouldn't put it like that. I have helped thousands if not millions of people to be successful."

"So, as well as taking more than you need, you have helped others to take more than *they* need?"

"As well as helping companies to succeed and do great things, make great products and services. And there is my charitable foundation which helps thousands of people. I have given more than a billion dollars to needy causes."

"Why do you just not take more than you need in the first place? Then those other people wouldn't be needy."

He poked a finger at the palm of his other hand as if underlining the point he was about to make. He began the lecture that he had given at a thousand black-tie dinners. "Well, that's not how it works, see. First you…" Rachel had stood up and was now walking around the table towards him, smiling and thanking him for coming to visit them. He continued talking, as if not registering that the aliens seemed to be done with him. "This is our system, this is how it works. I invest, I support people, and if it goes well everyone wins…" She was taking him by the elbow now and helping him to his feet; no one *ever* took him by the elbow. He stammered on, "…thousands of companies, and the charity, people read my books, and they…" Now he was approaching the door, Rachel guiding him. Eventually he stopped talking.

"Thank you for coming," Rachel said. "However, we want someone with a very broad appeal. The, uh, common touch. Who will be respected by everyone, not just other rich people and those who want to be rich. To get the message out so very widely. You would seem to appeal to a certain type of person. But thank you, really, thank you so very much for coming to see us." As she was talking to him, Rachel began to slowly disappear above him as Allison realised that he was now outside the spaceship and was slowly being lowered by the invisible lift. Shoving the humiliation he had just received into a dark and secure part of his psyche, he abruptly turned his thoughts to what he was going to say to the group eagerly awaiting him below.

Chapter 14

The Art of Implying

"So *that's* what it takes for you to call me, Gareth."

"Mum, thank God! Are you all right?"

"Of course I'm all right. Why wouldn't I be?"

"Oh, I don't know, just maybe perhaps because you posted a video of you on an alien spaceship last night. Where the hell have you been?"

"Since when have you been concerned about my where-abouts?"

"Mum, that is *not* helpful. This is not the time."

Hannah sighed quietly. It was the sigh of someone used to being found guilty of reacting to provocation. She settled into the role of her son's mother. "I've only just got home. After Rachel said I could go, I slept in a tent that the Army provided. They were worried about infection, so had me in quarantine overnight."

"Who is Rachel?"

"The captain of the spaceship. At least, I assume she is the captain. She *acts* like she is the captain. The other guy certainly isn't. Maybe they don't have captains. Maybe they don't have hierarchy."

"Focus, Mum."

"They brought me back home a short while ago. I think I'm a prisoner in my own home. So I made a cup of tea, fed Agnes, and called you. I think that brings you up to date on my life."

"You've been on a spaceship! You've met an alien and she is called *Rachel*! What is she like?"

"Well, that's what she said she's called. But then, I was talking to a hologram. I didn't see the real aliens. Apparently they are hideous or something, so they've taken human form to protect us.

I imagine this extends to their names as well. She's probably not actually called 'Rachel', but something unpronounceable. Perhaps 'Erchgertradum'. Or maybe her name is a smell. I don't know, they're aliens, for Chrissakes." Hannah recognised the weariness creeping into her bones and the irascibility that came with it. She took a deep breath as Gareth spoke.

"How can you be so calm about this? Me and Monique have hardly slept. An alien invasion, and my own mother was the first person they made contact with! I mean, it's just...awesome!"

"Right, a few things there, Gareth. Firstly, it is 'Monique and I'. Secondly, it's *not* an invasion. Rachel is very nice, actually, and they seem to have only friendly intentions. And finally, this is the first contact the human race has ever had with life beyond this planet and, as you point out, your mother was the one they first met. Surely you could think of a better adjective than 'awesome'."

"Monique and me were talking about it all night. She wondered if you might have been selected."

"Was she hoping I might have been abducted?"

"Really, though," replied Gareth, ducking the barb with practiced ease. "What if it isn't just a coincidence?"

"Oh, don't talk crap, Gareth. This isn't fate, there's no such thing. They knocked on my door because it was the first door they came to. You might as well ask why they came knocking on a door at all. I mean, if you were an alien landing on a new planet, how would you know which animal to speak to? To strike up a conversation with a human and not with, say, a sheep."

"Maybe they did. Maybe they took sheep form first, then realised their mistake when they tried to talk to them. I'm pretty sure sheep aren't very bright."

Hannah laughed. That felt better. "God, can you imagine the disappointment of talking to a sheep. I can't imagine they'd have much to discuss. Mulch? Dingleberries?"

It had been the two of them once. She used to tell little Gareth that they were a two-person army, just them against the world. Once Nana had gone, and her father – barely present during her life – had succumbed to his drinking, there had been a few years when it had felt like it really *was* just the two of them.

"So what are you going to do next?" Gareth asked.

"Next? What do you mean, next?"

"Mum, this could be amazing for you. Just what you need."

"Need? I don't know what you mean. I don't *need* anything."

"But you met aliens! This is your big chance! To make a difference."

"Make a difference? To whom would I want to make a difference?"

There are things that mothers can say to sons that sons can't say to mothers. Instead they learn the art of implying. The pregnant pause. Hannah never could resist.

"Gareth," she continued, aware that she was filling a gap deliberately left, "I do not have a mission, a destiny, and if I do have one it is not bound up with these aliens." She paused just long enough for the next line to be deliberate. "I cannot alter the future any more than I can alter my grandson's name."

"Mum!"

"Oh, relax, I'm only teasing. I'm just saying that the future will be what it will be. Everything is random. As proven by the fact that the aliens chose my door to knock on. I am the ultimate everyman, a proud nobody. I was before Rachel came a-calling, and I will be again. Just as soon as these stupid reporters leave me alone, that is."

The conversation turned to the events of the previous day, the resignation from the company, then meandered onto evergreen topics including Atticus and potty training, work, and life in Zurich, before they finally ran dry and said goodbye.

Agnes became the beneficiary of Hannah's good mood, lying on her back with legs akimbo. Hannah knelt and began to give the proffered tummy a rub that was as soothing to the giver as it was to the receiver.

Why *had* they knocked on her door? Of *course* it was just chance, not destiny, but it was a moment of chance that had happened to her, not to anyone else, and it all felt rather thrilling now she stopped to think about it. So *this* was what fifteen minutes of fame felt like. She allowed herself a moment to feel just a little bit special, even while simultaneously telling herself that it was all just silly and that she was no better or more deserving of the attention than anyone else.

She felt a paw on her leg, and looked down to see Agnes looking back up at her with that permanent expression of expectation. She took the Brigadier's card from the table, grinned and called the number.

"Yes, hello, Brigadier. You said to call you if I had any problems or needed help with something." She smiled at Agnes, who was now sitting looking adoringly back at her. "As you know, I am rather stuck inside with all these reporters and everything. I wonder if you could send someone over to walk my dog for me."

Chapter 15

Popularity

Unlike Darren Allison, David Armitage was used to being shouted at. Also unlike the man who was at that very moment pointing his finger in his chest and bellowing in his face, David Armitage didn't consider himself the greatest person in his chosen field. Indeed, he didn't consider himself the greatest person in the actual *field* in which they stood. He knew all too well the dangers of considering himself at all.

The greatest fixer that David Armitage had ever known was a man called Luka Dalic. Of Croatian descent, Luka had been around the business of sport since being forced to retire from playing for Palermo, in the second division of the Italian football league, with a torn anterior cruciate ligament. The perpetrator of the foul, a gnarly midfielder devoid of any real footballing skill who had only made it as far as Serie B due to his willingness to take a red card for the team, had suffered such a severe beating from assailants unknown three days later that he also had been forced to give up his professional career. The realisation that control over his future was as fragile as his knees had affected Luka deeply, although not as deeply as the realisation that he could get away with anything just by knowing the right people to call.

One of the first major jobs that the Armitage Foundation had secured was to ensure that the vote of the Olympic Committee went in a certain direction. Luka Dalic had been oiling those particular wheels for two decades, and when the two of them had first met, David Armitage had seen the man he wanted to become. Histrionics were not necessary when you had built yourself a reputation the size and breadth of Dalic's. Let others do the shouting. Let others lose their cool. And be there at the end to sort out the mess and gain the appreciation – in all its forms.

David Armitage modelled himself particularly on Dalic's brand of humility. It prevented many dangers inherent in the territory. This included displays of hubris such as referring to himself in the third person, as Darren Allison was doing at that very moment.

"Sheh, when Allison walks in a room, people know who he is, boy. Understand me? You don't bring someone like Allison to judge some pissant small-time cookery contest. When you call in a favour to get Allison, you'd better deliver on it, you understand me?"

"Mr Allison," said David Armitage. "I can only apologise. Had I only known that the aliens were going to treat you in such a clearly shabby way I would never have subjected you to such behaviour. Please accept my profuse apologies." He lowered his voice a little and leaned slightly forward. "I do have a little matter I would like to discuss with you, actually, which I think might make up for this rather, uh, unfortunate episode. An opportunity which I think may be apposite for your rather unique talents." By which I mean your obscene amount of surplus wealth, he thought to himself.

Mollified, Darren Allison made his way towards the waiting helicopter, leaving David Armitage free to focus on the next person he had lined up to visit the aliens. There was not much that could impress him these days. He had experienced everything that money could buy. Yachts the size of a shopping mall. Islands. And, of course, sex. Sex in all different flavours and colours, sex to pay for favours, sex which *was* the favour. He could use sex to buy two solutions at once. There was almost nothing for which sex could not be used either to give or receive as payment.

The only totally incorruptible person was the truly talented. The kind of person who would make it to the top of their chosen profession with or without favour. David Armitage was himself such a person, having refused many a bribe over the years, instead choosing to work solely on the basis of a professional reciprocation.

He therefore respected the quality in someone else. And there was no one he respected more for this quality than the pop superstar Bohemia.

He had tried to arrange for Bohemia to have sex with presidents, prime ministers, cardinals, CEOs and sports stars. He had even pretended that the Dalai Lama was interested at one stage, just to identify her weakness. A weakness did not, however, appear to exist. When she sang she seemed to be able to hit several notes at a time as she took a tune and turned it into something…well, something uniquely Bohemia. She was so extraordinarily popular as a singer, pop star and now, goddammit, as a movie star that she was beyond corruption. She had even named her last album *Corruption* in what must have been the ultimate private joke. She took her role as a hero to fellow black Americans very seriously and took great care not to disappoint them.

If he were pressed (if there was anyone who *could* press him), he would eventually be forced to admit that he was, in fact, deeply and irrevocably in love with Bohemia.

He walked to the other side of the field, where Bohemia was waiting for him, a broad grin lighting up her face like the aurora borealis. She knew, he knew she knew, and she knew that he knew she knew.

Her jeans were from an absurdly expensive designer label – her own. They included two large rips around the knees that had not been earned from time spent sanding a floor. A black leather jacket hid most of a baggy white T-shirt and super-strength black bra. Standing behind her were three enormous men in suits, wearing sunglasses that were so ubiquitous as to have become the minder's shibboleth.

"Bohemia, O light of my life," said David Armitage, clasping one of her hands in both of his. "Thank you for coming at such short notice."

She spoke in a voice so gentle that anyone who met her could only marvel at the contrast with the aggression of her singing voice. "How could I not have come? It is an honour that you even thought of me." She leaned forward and spoke so that only the two of them could hear. "Little did you know that meeting an alien may well have been the one item of leverage that would have worked on me."

"Nooo!" he mock-wailed. "Don't tell me that now! Ach, it matters not. I would never have used such a tactic even if I had known. My allegiance in this particular role is to a higher authority even than you, my dear."

"Is there such a thing?"

"It would seem so. Please." He held out his hand and began to walk towards the spaceship. She followed him steadily across the grass, without taking the hand. She had initially arrived in high heeled Tom Ford boots, which had immediately sunk into the Somerset earth. Her personal assistant had miraculously sourced a pair of Burberry wellingtons which, fortuitously, worked with the jeans.

As they walked towards the alien spaceship, David Armitage observed that, for the first time since they had first met, Bohemia looked nervous.

"So you are an entertainer?"

Bohemia stood on her own in front of the two aliens with their freaky little robot. They had offered her the seat, but she had chosen to stand. She was an imposing woman, and was not about to surrender that advantage lightly.

She had never imagined that she could feel so anxious. Even singing the national anthem at the Superbowl had been a walk in the park compared to this. Actual aliens! Right in front of her!

They didn't look very alien-y. They looked pretty much like your standard ridiculously tall human. Why would they make themselves so tall if they were holograms, she wondered. Maybe it was something to do with the hologram effect; perhaps it stretched you.

"Yes, I am. I sing, I dance, I write and produce my music, I act in movies. I also have my own range of clothing. I have been the biggest-selling performing artist in the world for the past three years in a row. I did a concert tour last year that sold tickets faster than any other tour in history. So if you want to get a message out to the people of the planet Earth, then, thanks to God, there is no one with a bigger reach than me."

"Great!" said Rachel, ever perky. "And how do you think your skills might help us to get our message across the whole of the planet? Because, you see, we really do need to reach as many people as possible with our message. It is very important."

"There is no one on the planet more popular than me. I am the most famous singer that there is. Perhaps that there has ever been."

"Yes, ha ha, that's lovely and everything," said Rachel. She was clearly the one in charge of the ship; the man next to her just seemed to sit there, smiling. Bohemia wondered for a moment if he was entirely all there. "But," Rachel continued, "you could be the most popular at something and still only be known by a few people. Do you see what we mean?"

"When I sing, people take notice," replied Bohemia. "When a new Bohemia album comes out, then—"

"Sorry, a new what?"

"Bohemia album."

"And you're Bohemia."

"Yes. And an album means a new group of songs that we put out at one time."

"Oh! I see!" Rachel looked at the man and rolled her eyes as if to say 'Silly us!'

"So if I put out a new album, then the world takes notice. I am definitely the person to get your message to as many people as possible."

"Well," said Rachel, sitting back in her chair. "Perhaps we should hear this amazing, world-conquering singing voice of yours then. Would you mind singing us a song?"

Bohemia smiled, took in a deep breath, and began to sing.

David Armitage knew that something was wrong the moment he saw the look on Bohemia's face as she slowly descended from the spaceship. The aurora borealis of her countenance had been replaced by a tornado, thunderstorm and monsoon combined. She stepped onto the grass and stomped past him, even the bodyguards struggling to keep up. David Armitage ran after her, managed to overtake, then tried to slow her down by running backwards with his arms out in front of him. But she marched straight past him without even looking his way.

He came to a halt and called after her. "Bohemia, wait a moment. What happened?"

Bohemia stopped abruptly. One of the bodyguards, who had been looking around for potential gunmen as he had been trained to do, failed to see that his charge had come to a halt, and continued past her for a few steps. Realising his error, he stopped, then took three large paces backwards.

Ignoring him, Bohemia turned and addressed David Armitage.

"They stuck their fingers in their ears!" she said to him, with words so measured and precise that he actually flinched. "I sang them *In Love and Crazy* and the woman – Rachel, is that her name? – actually stopped me halfway through. Do you know what she said, David? Do you? Hmm? She said 'Why don't you just sing the tune rather than using all those extra notes?' She said *that*! To *me*! I can only assume that they do not have music on whatever godforsaken planet they come from."

"Ah," said David Armitage.

"She said they need someone...someone with...with "universal appeal"! And then dismissed me! As if I *don't* have universal appeal! I told them, 'Dahling', I said, 'Dahling, you will not find anyone more popular than me in the entire universe!' Do you know what she did? Do you know?"

David Armitage shook his head very carefully.

"She ignored me!" screamed Bohemia. She glared at him, eyes aflame. For a moment he wondered if she might even be about to attack him. Instead she turned her head frontwards, in a gesture that left him under no doubt that he was no longer required, and continued her march towards the helicopter.

David Armitage stood watching the helicopter rise into the sky. He was not a man to be defensive. His assumed position was that his decisions could always be better, every problem was a learning opportunity. He thought of himself as the great white shark, always moving forwards, always on the hunt. Now he began to question his approach to the situation. He had one more person lined up to introduce to the aliens. If that didn't work, then maybe he needed to approach the problem from a different direction, to raise his sights a little. Perhaps there was an opportunity that he had not previously considered.

He spoke briefly to the Brigadier, who nodded in response and walked away to one of the many marquees and tents that now formed a village in the area underneath the spaceship. David Armitage, happier now he had other irons in the fire, marched towards the mess tent, where Keith Baracus was at that very moment sipping a coffee.

Chapter 16

Blinking Lights and Other Revelations

Rachel watched Bohemia step angrily out of the door to the spaceship and onto the invisible lift. The singer and actress had even managed to maintain her rage while simultaneously being scared of the drop that seemed to be below her. Rachel chuckled. In fact, she had chuckled every single time a human made that step. It would have been very easy to have placed the cage within the tractor beam as they would usually have done, but where was the fun in that?

She got up from behind the large desk, walked across the loading bay which they were using as a reception area and tapped on the white wall at chest height. A door-shaped segment of the wall glided aside, revealing another room of similar size. Whereas the makeshift reception area was furnished in what could be described, if one were feeling generous, as a minimalist fashion, this room was full of things that bleeped and winked. Desks, buttons, blinking lights and other revelations covered the lower half of the wall to the right, fronted by crew members variously prodding, rolling, listening, and cajoling the desks in front of them. Lined along the opposite wall was a series of screens, each with an identical bank of knobs on a desk below. A high-backed chair was secured to the floor in front of each station. Each of the screens was showing different events from around the planet, and watching the action on each screen were more crew members. Each was in human form, and each wore the same uniform as Rachel but of a colour somewhere past red but not yet purple. The exception was the screen where Clarence sat; his uniform was the same shade of sapphire blue as Rachel's own. He was at that moment sitting back with his arms folded, staring at the screen in front of him. He was no longer smiling.

Rachel walked behind his chair and leaned forward with her hands placed on the backrest. Clarence looked back and up at her briefly, then returned his concentration to the screen. They both watched Bohemia touch the ground outside the ship below them and begin to stride angrily across the field. She flew past the man who acted as if he was in charge of everything, who then ran in front of her, as if trying to calm her down.

"Huh." Rachel shook her head as though she were watching a pet fail to perform a new trick.

She turned her attention to the screens to her left. The first, with the words 'Los Angeles' written in white letters across the top, showed a series of images of people of various ethnicities throwing garbage cans into shop windows, followed by a group of white police officers who were gathered around a black man lying on the ground and were appearing to take it in turns to kick him. The next screen, headed 'Tehran', showed a large group of young men jumping up and down and shouting. An effigy held high on a stick was aflame. The next screen along, from London, showed a smaller group of people standing still, holding placards and singing. They looked mildly annoyed.

"It would appear," said Rachel to Clarence, "that our ancestors are reacting to the arrival of aliens in exactly the ways we feared they might."

"Oh boy, this is so depressing," Clarence replied, now staring at a screen to his right headed 'Paris', which showed a crowd of men with black scarves over their noses and mouths, throwing petrol bombs at riot police. "Is this really what we descended from? These people are…so…feeble. And yet aggressive. At the same time! Why is their reaction to what they think is the discovery of alien life to be so…*angry*?"

"This is just a theory," Rachel replied, "but I think it is something to do with the fact that they feel impotent. To have events happen to them which they cannot affect must be incredibly frustrating."

"But we do not have direct control in our time either. Yet we are not so angry as these people."

"No, but then we are listened to. These people are not. Imagine being told that you have a voice, but then slowly realising that the ear being turned your way is not connected to a brain, that it is deaf. Frustration leading to anger is the only logical outcome of such a system."

Clarence pointed at one of the screens to his right, headed 'Basra'. It showed tanks rolling across a dusty road and into a half-destroyed town. "This lot are still bombing the daylights out of each other. They are still arguing over which group of people owns which bit of land, even when they have just learned that there is life on other planets. Talk about a failure of context."

The two of them watched the images of protest and violence across the various screens from around the world. Their heads moved slowly from side to side almost in unison, and they sighed in sync.

"I've been reading some of their newspapers," said Clarence. "Some of the governments have restricted the movements of their people until they know how much of a threat we are. Lots of journalists are complaining about the loss of rights. The word 'freedom' gets used a lot."

Rachel stood, folded her arms, and shook her head angrily. "Rights! What does that even mean? An animal in the wild doesn't concern itself with freedom, it just cares about staying alive. They're not going to be much use to us if they think they have rights."

A series of flashes brought their attention back to the screen in front of Clarence. It showed Bohemia striding through a throng of reporters and journalists, cameras flashing as her security guards shoved the photographers out of her path.

Rachel tried to shake off the fug that she realised was enveloping her. "Any sign of our target? Of the box?"

"No," replied Clarence. "Not a sniff, I'm afraid. If we're going to stick with plan A, we still need to find someone to spread our message for us."

"I don't think these idiots are going to be any use to us." She pointed at the screen in front of them on which four men in dark suits, standing at the edge of the field in the afternoon sun, were engaged in animated conversation. One of them, the one in charge, was not talking, and broke from the other three to greet a fifth man, also in a dark suit. This man was much older than the others and had a face like a paper bag filled with cold porridge. He approached them with the air of a mill owner approaching his workers. "They are all so self-obsessed," she continued. "As soon as they know what the message is, they will forget about helping us to spread the word and think only of themselves. We need someone with a little... awareness. Only someone who doesn't want to be in charge is capable of being a true leader. This lot love the power too much."

"Well," replied Clarence, "we know this mission succeeds, otherwise we wouldn't be here on it. I still say we should ditch the subterfuge and take the direct approach."

"Let's not panic just yet. I'd still prefer to do this with as minimal disruption as possible."

"You call that minimal disruption?" laughed Clarence, sweeping his arms to indicate the screens in front of them. "People all over the planet are beginning to protest and riot."

Rachel placed her hand on Clarence's shoulder and patted it once. He looked up at her with hope in his eyes.

"This is nothing compared to what they'd be like if they knew the truth," she said.

Chapter 17

Moving Clocks Tick More Slowly

Torben stared at Niels mark 23 like a parent stares at their only child sitting on the potty for the first time. The early evening sun coming through the front bedroom window and across the landing gave the study a warm glow. Across the water Torben could see the island of Hven brightly illuminated against the darkness of the water.

Torben had visited the island just once, on a school trip. While his classmates had goofed around, happy just to not be in the classroom, Torben had discovered his first hero. The nobleman and astronomer Tycho Brahe had built a castle and observatory on the island in the late 1500s. For the teenage Torben, this absurdly romantic and heroic man became the idyll of what was possible through study. With his brass nose – the original having been sliced off in a duel following an argument over who was the better mathematician – resplendent moustache and pet moose, Brahe made science seem full of possibility and excitement. Even now, as he gazed across the sea, the spirit of Tycho Brahe seemed to be calling to Torben, encouraging him to believe in himself even when nobody else did.

He tried to imagine the fourteen-year-old Brahe staring in wonder, maybe even horror, at the solar eclipse of 1560. Already enrolled in the same University of Copenhagen that Torben had attended, which would have been surrounded by farmland at that time. Perhaps there had been a scream as a farm worker noticed that the sun was being eaten. Brahe would have looked up, following the trembling fingers. Initially blinded, he would have seen the sun disappear completely. Torben could only imagine the levels of panic among the uneducated people of Denmark at that time. The sun was a constant, it represented the future, the present, the past – it was everything, and now it was gone, the future now one of forever darkness. And then the extraordinary relief as it began to reappear, and along with it the realisation that life is so fragile, so dependent upon a burning ball in the sky, that the concept of control is an illusion invented by ourselves in order to cope with an unknown future. Our lives being carried on invisible tides, destination unknown by anyone or anything.

But Brahe was unsatisfied with this conclusion of uncertainty, and so dedicated his life to studying astronomy. Was this his way of trying to regain the feeling that he had some sort of predominance over his future? To understand is to wrestle back control, to swim against those tides. Is this why we study? To be master of our destiny – or, at least, to continue the illusion that we are.

Professor Flensberg had been unable to work out exactly what the machine did, or what had happened when Torben pressed the orange button for the first time. He *did* admit that much of the theory that Torben had put into making the machine was sound, and that there was every possibility the machine did do *something*. It may or may not have been linked to the appearance of the spaceship, but the professor had to admit that the coming of an alien spaceship did mean that all previous assumptions about what was possible in the field of science were now, at best, open for re-evaluation. For Torben, to have gained a modicum of respect from his astrophysics professor was something of which he had only dared to dream. In those many hours of deep concentration, soldering and reading, it had been the professor who had been in his thoughts, the equivalent of the parent to be shown the child's picture. To have received even a guarded approval in return had been sufficient to allow Torben to declare to himself that the machine was a success.

Torben had left the professor with his address and they had parted, agreeing that Torben would return to his office in a week's time.

Now, however, he needed to decide what to do next. He, Torben Christiansen, a name familiar to no more than a dozen people, had created something genuinely new. He had – he paused for a moment, hardly daring to use the word – invented something. He was convinced it was connected to the arrival of the spaceship; the coincidence was too great. He just needed to work out what to do next. He wished he could speak to the woman in the video – Hannah – but the very thought made him want to sit down and not stand up again. If he felt pangs of anxiety travelling to Copenhagen, how would he feel travelling to the United Kingdom?

The sound of female laughter came through the partially opened window of his study. He involuntarily shrank back into his chair. The noise was all too familiar. Freja and Clara were sisters who had lived in the house next door, which was one of the oldest on the street. The girls – they were women now – must have returned home for the weekend for their father's birthday celebrations. He listened to their excited chatter as he had done so many times before. They seemed to be walking down to the jetty; perhaps they were planning to take their small dinghy, *Fossegrimen*, out into the bay for an evening paddle.

Slightly older than him, their existence had, for Torben, been in equal measures heaven-sent and the work of the devil. The family had moved into the house when the girls were in their early teens and Torben was himself approaching that impossible age. For them, he had barely existed. For him, at least for a short period, nothing else had except them. They had seemed to be demons in angel form, sent to the Earth with the express instruction of creating passions within him which he would not be able to express or satisfy.

Torben leaned forward across the desk and peered left towards the sound of the voices, over to the garden next door. He spied the two women through the bushes that formed the border between the gardens all the way down to the shingle beach. They were walking away from their house and slowly down the lawn, chatting as vibrantly as one might expect from two sisters who hadn't seen each other for several months.

He jumped back from his desk, sending the chair scraping backwards across the wooden floor. Running quickly downstairs, he stopped briefly at the back door to put on his sandals, then went outside, closing the door behind him as quickly as being quiet would allow. He could still hear the voices, now slightly more distant. His house was set closer to the bay than his neighbours' but was still some forty metres from the shoreline. At the end of the lawn, a snaking path made its way down the final slope to the water's edge.

Torben ran, crouching, across the lawn and on behind the bushes. He could hear their voices, much closer now, moving slowly towards the top of the pathway which zig-zagged down to their own allotted section of beach. The bushes gave way to a low wall as the scrubby slope to the beach began, and his crouching became more extreme. Rather than follow his pathway, he kept close to the wall to ensure he was not seen, scratching his ankle on a rock as he did so. He reached the bottom, listened, then, assessing that the two young women had taken a turn away from him, made the final jump onto the stony beach. Then he took two steps to his right and straightened just enough to see over the wall. The sisters were just about to turn back towards him. Quickly he stood up straight, folded his arms, and stared out across the bay with what he felt was an enigmatic posture.

The sisters didn't notice him at first. They walked along their own little beach towards their jetty, engrossed in conversation, then he heard the nature of the footsteps change, away from the crunch and roll of the stones and rocks to the lighter tone of flip-flops on wood. If they went along their jetty towards *Fossegrimen* he would miss his chance. Cursing, he unfolded his arms, turned, and called "Oh, hi!" in a falsely surprised tone which broke in the middle, starting high and ending low. He cursed briefly, then waved and smiled as they turned and saw him.

Clara gave a mini-wave back, and the two of them stepped back from the jetty and walked over to him.

"Hello, Torben," said Freja, sharing an identical expression with her sister, as if meeting their bank manager. "Haven't seen you for ages! How are you?"

"Oh, I'm okay." Torben replied as if he didn't much care either way. Then, realising he may have overdone the insouciance, continued, "Well, very good, actually. How long are you both back for?" He wanted to ask whether they were still living in London and Copenhagen respectively, if they had boyfriends, whether their lives were working out the way they had expected them to when they were aged thirteen, if the flats they lived in had balconies and if they sat on them at night drinking white wine and smoking cigarettes while reading poetry, how they coped with the crushing normality of life, if they had boyfriends, and whether they would both like to come over for dinner that evening. Following the unwritten rules of their relationship, he had instead begun with the only topic allowed to him: the details of their visit.

"Just a few days," replied Clara, then lowered her voice to a conspiratorial whisper. "We don't come back enough, but, to be honest, we can only cope with it when we are here together. Give each other support, you know!" She nodded back up the slope towards the house. Torben smiled and supported it with a knowing nod, even though he knew of no more delightful people than Freja and Clara's parents.

"So what does 'very good actually' mean, then?" asked Freja with a conspiratorial wink. "Not like you to be so positive. Are you up to some mischief, Torben?"

Torben felt his hairs stand to attention with the thousand thrilling intimations of the question. He attempted to adopt the attitude of a man in a bar who had placed one arm against the wall next to his head and was leaning against it, swirling ice around a glass of bourbon with the other hand. In reality he stood stock still, as if all his mental capabilities were being kept occupied by his mouth.

"Oh, nothing really, just something I've been working on," he replied. Noticing that, while Freja continued to feign interest, the sparkle in Clara's eyes was already dimming, he quickly continued. "It's a machine. A sort of beacon. Into space, I think."

"A space beacon? Whoah!" said Freja. Her expression made his heart sing. "That sounds seriously cool. What does it mean?"

"How can you 'think' you have made a space beacon?" Clara asked him the question in several ways at once. In addition to the spoken words, she simultaneously folded her arms, leaned back slightly, and raised an eyebrow. The overall impression was one of being interrogated by a cat.

When he had eavesdropped on the teenage girls in their garden, gossiping about their days at school, Clara had been the serious one, urging caution. Torben had seem himself most in Clara: methodical, careful in her decision-making. He had always imagined Freja to have been his favourite, her attractiveness and exuberance so easy to love, but it was Clara who returned to his thoughts unbidden, like something organic, ingrained. It was she who inhabited him. Freja would bring him joy in his thoughts, Clara brought about an almost exquisite sorrow.

"Oh, it's still in testing," Torben said quickly. "I know it works, I'm just, um, just not sure exactly what it does." He laughed casually, as if he had just tossed off yet another bon mot. Freja looked around her briefly, as if she had heard a duck which was mildly more interesting to her than the conversation in which she was presently engaged. Worried that he might be losing their attention, he said, "Did you know that a moving clock ticks more slowly than a stationary one? It's, uh, all to do with string theory. Time travel and all that."

"Well you've always been into astronomy and physics, haven't you?" said Clara with a shrug. She was looking at him as if he were a normal person. He felt a surge of confidence that made him wary. She turned her head towards her sister, then slapped her on the arm. "Hey, maybe it's a machine that sends signals to aliens! Maybe it brought that spaceship to England!"

"Torben Christiansen, the man who brought the aliens to Earth," said Freja, laughing. "Imagine! And we could say that we know you!" She nudged her sister, who joined in the giggle.

Just for a moment, time stopped still. Outwardly Torben was smiling gently back; inwardly he was a swirling mass of delirium. His father, who would spend mealtimes reading a book, had only ever given him one piece of advice about the opposite sex. "The objective of the female is to trap you. The objective of the male is to let them." Given that his father had only ever dated one girl, whom he had then married, Torben had treated this advice with a certain wariness. This may have been a contributing factor to a sexual history equally as barren as his father's. And yet now here were two of the objects of his desires during those impoverished years actually lifting him up towards a possible pedestal.

"Mind you," said Clara, "that assumes they turn out to be *good* aliens. If they end up killing us all we might not be so grateful to you!"

They laughed at each other again, elbows clashing. For one joyous moment he realised that they were laughing with him, not at him. He allowed himself a momentary release of mirth. They were all actually laughing together! As the chuckles died away, he wondered at what might have been and, more importantly, what could be if his machine turned out to be what he thought it was.

"Well," said Freja, breaking the silence that Torben hadn't noticed was accumulating, "we're off for a little trip round to the harbour. Nice to see you again, Torben." The two women walked away, waving to him, recommencing their private conversation. Torben turned and floated back towards the house.

Returning to his desk, Torben gazed blankly at Niels Bohr. The framed photograph stood next to the one of his parents. The picture of Niels was in portrait mode and housed in a grey leaden frame of loops and curls, whereas Mum and Dad were landscape and in a black modern frame. Niels was twice the size of his neighbour and therefore dominated the tiny gallery. The photograph was of Bohr as a young man, his features already lumpy, with slicked-back hair, thick lips, and eyebrows well on their way to becoming heavy. Torben saw wisdom and inspiration behind the eyes; the comfort and safety of science, where unknowns became known and surprises were greeted as a challenge. When he had first heard Bohr's most famous quote – 'Prediction is very difficult, especially about the future' – it had brought a light to bear on Tycho Brahe's lifelong dedication to understanding what was beyond his reach, and had shown him a pathway by which he too might attempt to throw a lasso around his own destiny. Torben had finally understood what his place in the world might be. It had brought to an end the brief obsession with the sisters next door – or at least had put a lid on it for a while. His was not to be wasting time staring at girls. There was little point in trying to change what already was, and even less point in trying to change what would be. No, for Torben, understanding was the only goal he needed. Through understanding came knowledge, the bridge between the two being insight. If he could only continue to accumulate knowledge, he might eventually develop wisdom as the dots became joined.

Talking to Clara and Freja had affected him, however. No, he needed to be more honest. Being *listened to* by Clara and Freja had affected him. To think that they might actually be proud to tell people that they knew him. The effect of their brief attention had been euphoric – he felt light, full of air and possibilities. He might even have used the word 'flippant' if not for the fact that he had never felt it before and did not possess the words to describe such a feeling. All he had ever wanted was to find someone to whom he might make a difference. Science could change the future, but to combine science with the humanities was to focus on the microcosmic changes that could combine to create real change. This, ultimately, was what Tilda had taught him, bringing together the various strands of his youth into a realisation that, when it arrived, seemed to have been there all along, hiding in plain sight: that science was nothing without love.

He had not begun building the machine with a view to making something to help anyone; he had simply wanted to try out some of the theories that he had read about and thought he understood. He had had no one to test his understanding against, no one to mark his work and tell him whether his understanding of the theories was sound. He could only build the machine and see where this took him, and not wonder at the big prize that he so desperately sought.

Yet the driver of the recognition of others continued to stand shyly in the wings. He *did* want, if not to be loved (that felt like too high a hope), then to be appreciated. Maybe it was his, as yet, uncapped capacity for love that had made the difference. He grinned ironically at his own scientific approach in trying to understand himself.

There was no denying that the theories he had used in Niels *were* sound; Professor Flensberg had told him as much. The machine was built on hypotheses that did not always relate to each other, and yet placed together they made...what? He felt like Fleming staring at his Petri dish, knowing that the unexpected result created an opportunity for discovery, but not yet having worked out what the discovery actually was.

He turned to look again at the white box. If Niels *was* somehow connected with the arrival of the spaceship, then this little machine could be of historical importance. Suddenly he felt that having Niels mark 23 on the table, out in the open and for all to see, was reckless and absurd. He needed to be more careful, more circumspect, until he found out what purpose Niels served.

He looked around the sparsely furnished room for a hiding place. The bookcases lining the wall to his right inspired no suggestions, nor did the sofa to his left. His mind wandered onto the landing and into his parents' old room, then back out to the bathroom, and on downstairs through the hallway and into the lounge. There it was! A hiding place so obvious he felt slightly embarrassed at not having thought of it before.

Torben carried the white box down to the lounge and placed it on a sofa. He dragged the rug back, revealing a trapdoor. Lifting it revealed a small room, just a few metres square, which had been built in the early days of the German Army's occupation of Denmark. Torben enjoyed the cool stale air that wafted upwards. Then he climbed down into the cellar, reached up, and brought the box in with him. He placed it on the floor of the cellar, climbed out, closed the lid, and replaced the rug.

Chapter 18

Influence

Keith Baracus was Australian by birth but international in attitude. Starting with only a small fortune, by the time he was forty he had amassed homes, businesses and mistresses all over the world. His media empire included the most prominent newspapers and television channels in every one of the top thirty largest economies in the world. He had long ago realised that the key part of the famous Abraham Lincoln quote was being able to fool some of the people all of the time, as long as the number of the 'some' was big enough to win the election. One-third seemed to do the trick, generally.

The Baracus empire was so great, its tentacles so ubiquitous, that it was said that no leader of a Western country could make a major decision, such as leaving a trading bloc or starting a war, without first getting his clearance. He was the 'Bigger Picture' being referred to when one politician would comment to a colleague, "We need to focus on the bigger picture."

Now in his eighties, Baracus had spent a lifetime collecting politicians the way others collected trading cards in the school playground. A neoliberal from the very moment the free markets had worked in his favour, he vigorously defended the right to a free press while simultaneously abusing that same privilege. His newspapers and television stations were filled with either negativity or triviality, and were consequently hugely popular.

The only person who wielded greater influence in the world was David Armitage. The Pope came a distant third.

Baracus had contacted Armitage the moment that the news of the alien spaceship had reached him, which was a few seconds after Hannah had posted the video. He had made the call on his 'Armitage phone'. Sitting in his New Halifax office, he had picked up the brown leather briefcase, pulled out the power cable, and placed the case on the desk in front of him.

Inside was a rack of thirty-four mobile telephones mounted on charging pods, which were connected to the main battery unit. Each phone had a twin which was permanently on the person of either one of the heads of Baracus's companies or the head of a political party. Oh, there had been one or two newly elected premiers who had attempted to rebel and refuse, but the suggestion the next day in that country's bestselling newspaper that details were emerging of a rather unpleasant college initiation ceremony usually brought them into line. And if that didn't work, David Armitage would always supply the final pressure. It was extraordinary the amount of information that man had gathered.

Baracus was a keen vexillologist, and therefore each phone the twin of which was in the pocket of a country's leader sat inside a case emblazoned with that country's flag. At the top left was a phone that bore no flag. This was the one that he had eased out of its black foam surround. He had pressed 'speed-dial 1'. The memory bank of each phone contained only one number.

His voice was thinner and higher-pitched than people expected it to be from a man who wielded such power. Many books had been written about his life, but none had quite managed to pinpoint – or decide upon – what drove him to accumulate wealth so far beyond a level that he could enjoy. Had they heard the seventeen-year-old Keith Baracus speaking in exactly that weedy voice as he pleaded with the captain of the Aussie Rules football team not to hit him again, they would have begun to understand. That the story never made it into one of the many biographies was testament to just how far his influence reached.

The conversation with David Armitage had focused around the importance of the news reporting about the arrival of the spaceship being filtered by Mr Baracus personally. Should the intention of the aliens be in any way unfriendly, then it was essential not to cause alarm. It had been agreed that Mr Armitage was to keep Mr Baracus personally apprised of developments, and they were to agree which news agencies were to be told what and when. It was the sort of agreement reached by two people who had silently settled on a joint agreement of Mutually Assured Destruction.

A few days later, when news came that there was a message to be spread and the aliens wanted to speak to whoever was best placed to spread it – well, naturally Mr Baracus had offered his services. A few other commitments he really couldn't get out of would delay his arrival at the site by a day or so, but rest assured, Keith Baracus would be there to provide the answer.

And so it was that he now found himself rising into the air as if on an invisible elevator towards the open doorway of a spaceship. His fourth wife, Hiroko, held onto his arm. They had married three years ago. She was actually his nurse but they had got married as a cover for her having to be with him at all times. For the first time in many years he felt the excitement of the deal, the buzz of adrenaline – or was it testosterone? – that had once been a standard part of his working day. These days there was so little left to conquer that he had to construct ever more extravagant deals, until he was taking over businesses with a bigger income per head than some small countries.

There was no risk these days, that was the trouble. Sure, there were thrills to be had from influencing elections or toppling governments, from the wielding of power. But the real buzz, from the threat of danger, of losing everything – that had long since gone. He had felt the slow chipping away of his personal power as he entered his eighties, but that had soon been snapped back once those who thought he could be circumvented had been put firmly back in their place. His son and daughter would take over the business on his death (not a day before) and they were his eyes and ears.

For the first time in many years – decades, in fact – he felt a tingle in his tummy. He was actually going to meet aliens. He was going to be the one person on the entire planet who would take the message that the aliens had brought and spread it across the globe. Every single person who inhabited this planet would know his name. The ultimate goal, the one that he had dismissed as not being feasible, was actually going to be achieved by him. He felt heady for a moment as his eyes reached the lip of the doorway, and he held onto Hiroko's hand just a little tighter.

As the invisible lift stopped, he could see inside to a large white room. Standing a few paces back from the door was a lady dressed in exactly the sort of blue trouser suit that he would have expected to see. It was as if the aliens' research had consisted entirely of watching early episodes of *Star Trek* TV shows. It was also hard to believe that this was a hologram. He looked around the room behind the image, shape – whatever it was – that he was to call Rachel, in the hope of seeing some clue as to the true nature of the aliens. All he saw was a room devoid of furniture, except for a desk at the far end, in front of which were two chairs and behind which sat one other hologram alien-type person. Hovering behind Rachel was the robot that he had seen in the video; it seemed a great deal stranger in the, well, *not*-flesh. It didn't do a great deal, but just hovered around waiting to be instructed. Baracus was very much used to the presence of such individuals.

"Hi!" said Rachel, brightly. "Do come in. Do you need a hand?"

"No, I do not," he said, more sharply than he had intended. Then, in a softer, winning tone, "No, thank you. I am fine."

"Please," said Rachel, leading them to the chairs in front of their desk, her smile neither faltering nor flowering. She went at their pace, and only when he was settled and Hiroko made it clear she was happy to stand just behind her husband did she join her companion on the other side of the desk.

"So," she said brightly. "Tell me why you are the best person to spread our message to the world."

"Ah," said Baracus in his whiny mid-Pacific voice. "That's easy. I control half the world's media. I own newspapers and television channels all around the world. There is nobody who can come even close to the amount of news that they control. The editors of my papers print what I tell 'em to print. The producers feature the stories I tell them to feature. If you have a message you want to get out to the largest number of people, I'm the man to do it for you." He stopped, pleased with himself. Never a man to waste words, he knew he had said all he needed to say. He smiled at this hologram woman in much the way an anaconda smiles at a wounded baby goat.

"Aha," said Rachel. "I see. A question, if I may. If your media outlets report on the issues that you tell them to report on, that presumably means that your readers, viewers and listeners know that they are only hearing about the things that you choose that they will hear about, and presumably from the angle that you also choose. Would that be correct?" That smile again. It never changed. Boy, she was good.

"I do not censor any of my editors or producers."

"Censoring means preventing something from being published. But if they know what you want, they presumably don't need to be censored." Baracus opened his mouth, but Rachel continued. "Would that be correct? Please understand, we are not here to criticise. This is your business. You can make it work in whatever way you want to. However, as we need this message to be understood by as many people as possible, we don't want to use a mouthpiece whose integrity is tainted by the ego of its owner. Do you see?" Rachel rose from her seat. "Thank you *so* much for coming, though. We very much appreciate you taking the time out of what must be a very busy schedule, what with all those papers and TV stations to be running."

Baracus did not immediately register that he was being shown the door. He had not been told that a meeting was finished for some forty years. *He* was the one who ended meetings. Only when Hiroko put her arm under his to help him to his feet did the realisation dawn on him that he was not going to be the one to take this message to the world. He opened his mouth to protest but, for the first time in forever, he found no words for the situation. The face of the alien was as impassive as that of an airline employee informing passengers of a delay, offering the hope of help and assistance that was never going to be forthcoming. He almost expected her to apologise for any inconvenience caused.

Even more slowly than they had arrived, Keith Baracus and his wife left the spaceship.

Chapter 19

Humility

Hannah recognised Keith Baracus as he was helped out of the decontamination chamber. She was walking with the Brigadier to a Land Rover which would take her to the spaceship. She also recognised the thunderous sneer on the face of the octogenarian media mogul as being the reaction of someone not used to being treated in the way that he had clearly just been treated.

The two of them stopped as they passed each other. Here was one of the most powerful men in the world, literally just a few feet away from her. A man capable of affecting elections, and with a history of doing so. A man so wealthy that he could purchase Hannah's house, give it immediately back to her for free, repeat that exercise every day for twenty years and not have to make a single change to his life. A man so powerful that prime ministers and presidents would sacrifice members of their own party in order to appease him.

And yet here was this supposedly omniscient individual standing and staring at Hannah, clearly wondering – nay, *demanding* to know why *she* was being led in to see the aliens when *he* had just been told his talents were not required. He was a man whose spoken sentences were peppered with italics.

He looked down at her as if he had trodden in something unspeakable. "What the fuck are you?" he asked in his thin Australian voice.

Hannah glared at the media baron with the eye of an astringent teenager. "I'm just something who doesn't give a fuck what you think," she replied, and walked forward, ducking through the plastic hanging screen and striding out into the open field. The Brigadier scuttled out a few moments later trying to conceal a smirk, and quickly reached her side.

"Hannah," he said, easily falling into line with her stride, "I do not permit myself many moments of levity. My position brings with it such responsibilities that you cannot even imagine. The look on that old bastard's face, however, is likely to provide me with moments of mirth for many years to come."

"Always hated that power-crazed little shit," Hannah replied. "Imagine knowing that the entire course of human history would have been better if you had not been born."

"I am uncertain that Mr Baracus would see things that way."

"Only because no one has ever told him."

"Indeed. Now, if we can just slow down for a moment, I need to brief you on the forthcoming negotiations with the aliens. If we could—"

Hannah stopped abruptly. The Brigadier took two extra paces before reacting, then he also stopped, turning to face her. Hannah took an extra step forward. She had to reach upwards in order to poke the Brigadier in the chest.

"Let's get something clear here," she said. "I am not under your command. I do not take orders from you or anyone else. I will do what I want to do, when I want to do it. You barge into my house this morning and tell me that the aliens asked to speak to me. To *me*. Which means that not you nor anyone you represent will tell me what I have to say or do. Are we clear with each other, Mr Hot Shot Army Man?"

"We are on the same side, Hannah."

"There *are* no sides. Do you not get that? We are not being invaded, we are not at war. Frankly, the very last people who should be allowed to be the first point of contact with aliens are politicians or soldiers. Why is it that the first reaction is to send in the Army, huh? Why not bring in a funfair, show the aliens how we like to have fun? Bouncy castles. Or clowns, or dancers, or singers. But no, you men have to get out your guns and tanks. It is only because you are such a load of bullies that you get to dictate what the rest of us do. And then, when they ask to speak to someone influential, who do you decide to send? Businessmen and media tycoons! Shit, you men are so myopic! You only see the world in terms of what you can control! Now, get out of my way and let us see where a bit of old-fashioned feminine freewheeling gets us."

The Brigadier paused for a moment, uncertain, his expression belying the fact that he was not used to his orders being questioned.

"But," said the Brigadier, stumbling over his words. "But we have a narrative to follow. A line to stick to."

"No, *you* have a line to follow. All my life I have been put into a position where I have literally no possibility of making the right decision. Well, that's finished. I'm not going to make any decision, I'm just going to listen. I'm not going to try and control this one. I'm just along for the ride. Let's see where it takes me, eh?"

Hannah thought she saw a twinkle in the Brigadier's eye and one side of his mouth threaten to make a break towards a smile. Then he licked his lips as if attempting to suppress the potential outburst of an emotion, his face regained its impassive hang and he stepped to one side. Hannah nodded at him, then continued her stride towards the spaceship.

Rachel had appeared in the doorway and was grinning down at her. Without pausing, Hannah walked into the beam and rose into the air. As she reached the door, Rachel stepped aside and extended her arm in an invitation to enter.

Hannah walked past Rachel and straight over to the chair. She stood behind it, leaning against the back, as Rachel walked around the desk and sat down. Hannah hadn't noticed Clarence was even in the room, but now he was standing behind Rachel. Rupert the robot hovered silently in the corner.

"You summoned me," said Hannah, not sitting. "How can I help you?"

"I have a question for you," said Rachel. "I am wondering whether you might be able to help us."

"Okay," said Hannah, "but I have a question for *you* first."

Rachel nodded to indicate that that would indeed be acceptable. Hannah resisted the urge to point out that she had not been seeking permission. She looked at Rachel, who was smiling at her like a dog who thought she heard the word 'walkies' but wasn't too sure, then stepped around the chair and sat down. She steeled herself to maintain her bad mood in the face of such affability.

"I've been locked up in my home for a day," she began. "I don't like that very much. But it has given me a chance to do some thinking, and I want to check a few things. When we first met, you said that you were a hologram, and that your real body was on the ship. You also said that your real form would be shocking for me to see, which is why you are in human form. And yet you travelled up the lift thingy outside. You are also really good at non-verbal communication. Have you been studying us humans or something? Cos just being a hologram wouldn't make you know how to act like a human."

Rachel continued to stare at Hannah, head tilted, her beatific gaze unchanging. Clarence shifted his weight slightly.

Hannah did not wait for an answer. "And I was also wondering about the night you came to my door. How did you know to knock on the door? Is that, like, a universal etiquette thing? Cos that seems a bit weird to me. And how can holograms knock? And I haven't even touched on the whole speaking our language thing. Why aren't you speaking Spanish, or Chilean, or sheep? For aliens in hologram form, you've got this being human thing pretty well nailed. How come?"

Rachel looked at Hannah in the same way that a vulture might look at another vulture. She shifted her head to tilt on the other side. Then she sat up straight, as if having reached a decision.

"Hannah," she began, "we have asked you back here because we wonder if you might be the right person to deliver our message. You posted two videos out to the world, and as a result all these supposedly important people have been coming to see us. If you have that level of reach across the world, then maybe you would be able to get our message to as many people as we need it to get to. So, do you think you might be the one to spread our message?"

"I don't know," replied Hannah. "What is the message?"

Rachel broke out into an enormous smile and clapped her hands several times, like a small child promised an ice cream. She looked up at Clarence, who nodded enthusiastically like someone agreeing to a particularly brilliant plan. Rachel turned back to Hannah.

"Hannah," she said, standing. "There is something I need to tell you. First, though, I need you to promise me something. That you will keep what I am about to tell you a secret for as long as we ask you to. Can you do that? Can I trust you?"

Hannah, shrugged. "Sure, of course." Seeing the serious expression on Rachel's face, she continued "Yes, absolutely, you have my promise."

Rachel beamed. "Wonderful! Now we can answer your question about us. Please, come with me." She walked over to the corner of the room, opened a door that Hannah had not realised was there, then turned and invited Hannah to follow her through.

"Wait," Hannah said, still standing behind the chair. "Is that the room where your real alien forms are? Am I about to get freaked out? I'm not sure I'm ready for this."

"All is fine," said Rachel, in a voice of marshmallows and buttercups. "Please. Come."

Hannah walked gingerly across the room towards the door, her stomach twisting and turning. As she got to the door, she leaned forward, her instincts to look inside outweighing those telling her to sprint in the opposite direction.

The room was approximately a quarter of the size of the main reception area. A long cocktail bar ran along one side, with pink bar stools lined up in front. The wall behind the bar seemed to be a giant video screen showing a tropical paradise. Either it was a very advanced version of a 3D screen or the rest of the spaceship was actually a beach and the Caribbean Sea. A long, furnished pink leather bench lined the wall opposite the bar, and in the middle were several low tables on which a few bowls held an assortment of snacks. Bohemia this bar area was a dance floor, and towards the far corner was a pool table. At one end of the bar stood a monitor showing the empty chair that Hannah had occupied until just a few moments ago.

The furnishings of this mini-nightclub were absorbed rather than seen, however, as Hannah's attention was more immediately drawn to the seven figures who were seated variously on bar stools and along the bench. They were all in human form, they were all Caucasian, and they were all dressed in the same outfit as Rachel and Clarence, but of a colour which, had she been forced to name in order to win a speedboat, she would have called puce. One particularly tall man stood behind the bar, polishing a hi-ball glass. They each wore the same welcoming smile as if it were part of their uniform. Hannah felt as if she had walked in on a meeting of the management committee of the regional section of a religious cult. Clarence walked around Rachel and Hannah and sat down on the end of the bench, to the smiles of the others.

He looked round at everyone, ensuring he had their attention. "This is Hannah," he said to the crew.

"Hi!" they chimed in response, almost in unison. One or two of them even gave her a little wave.

Hannah looked at Rachel blankly.

"I think we need to talk," said Rachel, taking Hannah gently by the elbow and leading her to a vacant stool at the bar. "Would you like a mojito?"

Chapter 20

The Antidote To Humanity

As Rachel spoke, Hannah drank aggressively at her cocktail. As the monologue came to an end, Hannah downed what was remaining in one gulp. Still staring at Rachel, she handed the empty glass to the tall barman, who started the process of making a second drink. Everyone else sat in silence, Rachel with her benevolent countenance, the rest of the crew leaning slightly forward on their bench seat waiting for a reaction. Hannah continued to stare blankly.

Once the mint was mashed and the ice was crushed, Hannah took the second drink, and this time took a large gulp. As if shaken roughly awake, she turned to the bartender – or Dan, crewmember responsible for supplies, as Rachel had just introduced him – and said, "This is actually a very good mojito."

"Thank you," replied Dan from behind the bar. He threw a worried glance at Rachel, who gave a reassuring wink in return.

"So…shit, where the heck do I start?" said Hannah. "So… just how far into the future have you come from?"

"Quite a long way," replied Rachel.

"Oh, come on, don't be coy. I'm sitting drinking cocktails in a spaceship which has time-travelled from the future."

"We are from the year 2384," replied Rachel. "We have travelled back three hundred and sixty-six years to be here."

"But I thought it had been proven that time travel is not possible? Because if it was, we would already have met someone from the future? Or my grandfather would have killed Hitler's grandfather. Or something like that." Hannah took another deep sip and nodded at the glass in appreciation.

"That is not how time travel operates. It works rather like a telephone works for you. To speak to someone over the telephone, you first need someone to answer the call. Well, time travel is the same. You dial a moment in time – literally, a second in time – and hope that someone gets the signal and answers. We have been working on the technology for many years now, and have only just managed to dial the correct time. Someone finally took the call, so to speak, which created a link, enabling us to travel back in time to now."

"Wowsers. And you're definitely not aliens? You're sure about that?"

"Definitely not. We are humans, like you."

"But you can't be human. You're too…nice."

"Well, we are a bit more than just human."

"I knew it. Are you some weird mutation of humans and cute fluffy bunnies?"

"No. We are Canadian."

"So, sort of a 'yes', then." She held her right arm out to the side in the direction of Dan, winking and nodding towards the now empty glass where she wanted a drink to be. "So then why did you pretend to be aliens?"

"Ah."

"And," said Hannah, pointing at Rachel with her left arm, "if time travel works like telephones, who the heck did you call? And what planet did you come from? And, for that matter, why did you arrive hovering over fields in Somerset, rather than London or the White House or something, like aliens always do in the movies?" The questions were starting to come to Hannah thick and fast now, and she struggled to stop herself from blurting everything out in one long stream of 'what-the-*fuck*-ness'.

"Ah," repeated Rachel. She looked around at her crew lined up on the bench, who gave her a variety of supportive winks, nods and smiles. "This is the awkward bit." She paused as Hannah seemed to be distracted by watching Dan preparing her third mojito. She leaned forward and tapped Hannah on the arm, who turned and focused again on Rachel. "You see, in eighty years' time, all life on planet Earth will be wiped out. It will be the sixth mass extinction. The last one was the dinosaurs, and the next one is now." Rachel watched Hannah anxiously to see how she was taking the news.

"Oh, is that all? Just the end of humanity as we know it. I thought you were going to say something serious." The third mojito appeared in front of her. Hannah waved her finger in Rachel's general direction while bringing the cocktail to her lips with the other arm. "To be fair – shit, that's good mojito – that is actually the most believable thing you've said so far. When, according to you, is this going to start?"

"It already has. Do remember we are from the future. The wiping out of all life on the planet Earth started when humans hunted the dodo to extinction. It will be complete with the extinction of humanity, in around eighty years' time." Rachel paused. "We thought pretending to be aliens might deflect attention from our real purpose, so we wouldn't scare people." She looked down at the ground with the manner of a schoolgirl who had tried to help the teacher but had instead dropped the books into a puddle.

"Well, that didn't work!" said Hannah. "Where's your proof about life on Earth ending in eighty years? A biggie like this should really have a bit of proof, you know." She tried to cross her left leg over her right, then gave up and tried to return her heel from the bar to the stool. She missed, slipped off the stool, stood up, then sat back down again. At no point was a single drop of mojito spilled.

"This knowledge has been handed down from generation to generation by the first settlers on our planet. It is a matter of history. At least, for *us* it is history. For *you* it is destiny." It occurred to Hannah that Rachel had the ability to deploy a tone of voice which performed much the same function as 'bold' did to a line of text. It turned conjecture into statement, opinion into fact, and supposition into declaration.

"This, therefore, is our mission," Rachel continued. "We have travelled back in time to select a small number of people, take them to a planet – our planet – which can support life, so that the human race may continue."

"Wait, let me get this right. You have come back from the future to take a few humans and dump them on a distant planet for them to evolve into...you?" Hannah handed her once again empty glass to Dan, the arm a little less steady than the previous time. He looked at her enquiringly as he took the glass from her wobbly hand at the second attempt, and she nodded vigorously in reply.

"That is correct," replied Rachel. "We activated the machine and travelled back in time. Our mission is to pick up two thousand people – the pilgrims who will become our ancestors." She spread her arms and hands in a minor fashion, as if to offer a slightly abashed 'ta-dah!'

Hannah eyed this person sitting opposite her. She felt like a passenger in this conversation, as though it was happening *to* her, rather than her being a part of it. Maybe it was the mojitos, or maybe it was the unreal nature of the conversation. She decided to stop trying to retain any form of control and just to let go. She asked the question she would have asked if this had happened when she was a small child. The honest question that she really wanted to know the answer to.

"What is it like to travel through time?"

Rachel squelched her lips together, then pushed them to one side of her mouth. "Pretty uneventful, to be honest," she said, acknowledging the disappointment of her statement with sad eyebrows. "There is no song and dance, no fanfare. One minute you are standing in one place, then suddenly you're still standing in the same place but everything around you has changed. In fact, it was so much of an anticlimax that our engineers built in some light shifting, so that you at least felt like something special was happening. Big events need a big entrance. A red carpet, or a fanfare. Even bad things – the last meal, or someone shouting 'Dead man walking' at you. Things need to be announced in order to have the appropriate gravitas, for people to notice. You don't want to sleepwalk into major change, you want to take in the signs so that you can prepare yourself."

"When you travelled back in time, three hundred and whatever years, you would still have been on your own planet.

Then how did you get here? There are no planets that can support life for gazillions of light years from here."

"The spaceships are fitted with teleportation drives. They are the very latest model, you know." For a moment Hannah thought Rachel was actually going to blow on her fingers and rub them on her lapel.

"Wow, so you can teleport? Cool! Can you teleport me to Switzerland? Now? Well, after I've finished this, obviously." She took a sip to underline her point.

To Hannah's surprise everyone in the room laughed, as if sharing a private joke. "No," said Rachel, grinning. "You can't teleport individuals! We realised that around one hundred years ago. We did try it, of course, with animals, but it was rather... messy. We could not find a human volunteer to test the system."

"And yet this spaceship teleported here with all its inhabitants?"

"Oh, we can teleport organic matter if it is inside a ship fitted with a teleportation drive. Think of it like a cake tin. If you pick up the cake tin and move it from one place to another, you're only moving the tin box, yet the cake inside is also travelling the distance."

"I'm pretty sure that doesn't fit with any of our known principles of physics."

"We are from three hundred and sixty-six years into the future, Hannah. If you go back three hundred and sixty-six years ago from now, people thought the Earth was flat."

"Certain people still do. They're all over the globe." Hannah laughed in a staccato burst. "All over the globe! Ha ha!" She took a sip and turned to Dan the barman. "And, by the way, these are just getting better and better! I haven't been this funny since I was on gas and air!" The barman grinned like a child being awarded a star. "So, Mrs Spaceship Captain Who Is Not An Alien After All, tell me something. All of us on this planet is going to die. Are going to die. And you're from the future. No problem. You're taking some settlers to a new planet far far away. Roger that. But why did it take you three hundred and sixty-six years to get round to it?"

"Knowing that something is preordained can tend to make you a little lazy," said Clarence helpfully.

Rachel picked up the story. "It didn't seem to matter when we actually built the time machine and came back. We knew we would do it, because we existed. Of course, it took a long time for the population of the new planet to stabilise – several generations. Then no one really bothered about it for the next two hundred years or so. We had the machine that originally received the message, and we needed to build the transmitter, but it just didn't seem that important.

"After a while, some philosophers began to suggest that if we never built the time machine transmitter, we might actually cease to exist. So the government set up a task force to look into the matter. It actually took them a month just to find the receiver, which had been put into storage. Then research into how it worked began, which took a further thirty years. They were completely stuck until eventually they realised the key component was living matter. Discovered it quite by accident, as it happened, when a spider crawled into the machine before they turned it on one day. Once they knew how the receiver worked, they could start work on the unit to send out the signal, the transmitter. That took another twenty years. Until finally..." Rachel spread out her arms. "We have arrived."

"Either these mojitos are really starting to kick in, or I am beginning to understand this. I even think I've worked out what this message is that you want to spread across the planet. You need to find the box, right? The receiver thing." Rachel nodded. Hannah was waving her arms around expressively now, and yet still managing to keep the majority of the cocktail in the glass.

"So you need to get hold of this box, but you want to do it in a way that does not start a full-scale worldwide panic. Fair enough. Nobody wants panic." She put the glass on the bar forcefully to underline her point. She looked into the glass, then looked again at Rachel. "So you take the box and the colonisators...colnisators... colonisatorists...people who are going to live on the new planet off with you in your spaceship. Which means tha...waidasecond. How many people did you say are going to come with you?"

"About two thousand," said Rachel. Then, in response to Hannah's askance look around her, "We have two more spaceships ready to come. Big ones."

"Ah, you didn't mention *that!*" said Hannah, momentarily losing her balance on the stool. "Mind you, two thousand. That's not much, many, is it? So, Mrs Lady From The Future, here's the big question: how are you going to decide who gets on the ark – I mean, the ships?" She passed the glass once again to Dan who, upon receiving an almost imperceptible sideways nod of the head from Rachel, began making another mojito, except that this time the bottle of rum had been sidelined in favour of a different, unmarked bottle.

"I'm not sure we are too concerned, Hannah," Rachel replied. "Although it would be really neat if you were to be one of them."

"I'm sure I'd love to. But we'd need to take my son and grandson if we did. I'm not going anywhere without Gareth and Atticus."

"Atticus?"

"Yes, Atticus. Don't go there. I did once, and it got a bit messy."

"What about Atticus's mother?"

"Oh yes, of course. She'll probably have to come too. I guess. It all needs a bit of taking in, this news."

"First, however, we have a job for you to do. This message we need to get out. We need to find the person who took the call," said Rachel. "We need that box."

"But surely you know who made the time machine?"

"No one knows. We do know that the first settlers were brought from Earth, and the receiver was with them. But for some reason the person who invented it was not recorded. Early records are rather sketchy. They, eh, had other things on their minds, it would seem. In time our scientists were able to begin work to develop space travel. Then they got started on the time machine transmitter. It was developed from the receiver that came to our planet from Earth in the first place. That is why we need to trace the person; we need that machine to go with the pilgrims."

"There's one thing I don't understand," said Hannah, rocking unsteadily forward on her stool and stabbing the air with the finger of her left hand vaguely towards Rachel, while simultaneously stretching her right hand out behind her and, without looking, grabbing what she assumed to be another mojito that Dan was offering to her. "You find this person that invented the machine, the receiver, take him or her to colonise a virgin planet, and they could just make the transmitter. Easy. You obviously do find the machine, otherwise you wouldn't be here. And if you find the machine, you must find the guy who invented it. So just take them with you. Simple. Except you don't. You don't even start work on it for a few hundred years." Hannah looked drunkenly at the ground. "I'm a bit lost now, if I'm honest."

Rachel looked sad. Hannah did not notice, instead concentrating on the new cocktail.

Rachel watched Hannah for a moment before continuing. "Since we started working on the machine, we have been engaged in a philosophical debate about who we take from the planet. Many thought that we should bring back only the greatest people. Then we had an argument about what defines greatness. The most successful people in every profession, perhaps. Others wanted the most caring, loving people. If the human race is going to have to start again, they said, then we may as well take a group which leaves behind the sins of greed and corruption."

"And does that work out?" asked Hannah, furrowing her brow in trying to select the correct tense. "Do you…did you pick the right people?"

"That's the fun part!" said Rachel. She leaned forward, a grin spreading as if she were about to deliver the punchline to a rather convoluted joke. "For us, the future has already happened. Whatever we do *must* be the right thing, because we are standing in front of you right now. So" —Rachel spread her arms with glee— "it doesn't actually matter *what* actions we take, or which people come with us. Hah, you should have seen the look on the face of that Baracus man when I told him we didn't need him. Priceless!"

Hannah eyed her coldly. "Am I among the people you take?"

The grin slid from Rachel's face. "We, um…we don't know," she replied.

"What about this receiver inventor person?"

"I'm sorry. We just don't know. We have no records of those first settlers."

"Damn, I feel sober all of a sudden."

"That's the antidote," said Dan from the bar. "That last cocktail. I used antihol instead of rum. It's an antidote to alcohol. It means you can get really drunk, then sober up instantly."

"Wow, that could have saved me a few disastrous evenings." Now completely clear-headed, Hannah mentally rehearsed the idea of her being the person to spread the message to the world, to be the one who found the machine. To hold a place in history. She might be the answer to a pub quiz question in years to come. She allowed herself a moment to try on this new apparel, this revised definition of herself. It felt like a good fit. This was a person she could be, someone who could help people from the future to… No, that was too far. The ending of humanity, travelling to distant planets, that was still too much to take in. It was enough that a knock on a random door happened to be at her house, and that she could now help these people. It wasn't destiny, or fate, or changing the world, or making a difference, because the future was already set. As Rachel had said, they knew they were successful, because they existed. So she, too, could allow herself to be swept along by events, knowing she would succeed. The challenge, however, was to make sure that Gareth, Atticus and Monique were on that ship when it left.

"Okay," she said to Rachel, "I'll help. Your secret is safe with me. Let's find the machine, with a minimum of fuss. But on one condition. My son and his family are among the settlers that you take with you. Deal?"

Rachel had sat up brightly for a moment, but now sagged again. "We will do our best, but I can make no promises." Hannah looked at Rachel through narrowed eyes. "We simply don't know who makes it," she protested, "but I promise we will try our best. You get the box and your son and his family to your house, and we will get them all onto the ship."

There really wasn't much alternative. If she refused to help these time travellers, then they might announce the real reason for their mission to the world. That would indeed cause panic, and Gareth's chances of getting out of Switzerland would be greatly reduced.

"Okay. Tell me, what do you know about this person?" asked Hannah, turning back to Rachel. "How are we going to find the inventor of this time machine?"

"It should be easy. We know their name, as it is written on the side of the receiver. We need to get a message to someone called Niels Mark, who is aged twenty-three. Can you somehow get a message for that person to get in touch with us via you, without it being obvious?"

"Couldn't you just sit here and wait? As you say, you know you'll get the box somehow. Circumstances will surely bring it to you."

"We could. But we don't know how long that would take. And…" Rachel paused for a moment, and Hannah saw fear flash through her eyes as she looked at her crew for support. She looked like a scared child for a moment, not the blasé, relaxed character she had been portraying.

It occurred to her that she hadn't thought what sort of world these people had come from, or what the future might be. Was society different in the future? Were there still wars? Did people still argue over who owned which bit of land? Or had the reality of humanity going from eight billion people to just two thousand been sufficient to put an end to the experiment of collective individual self-interest resulting in the common good? Had the mistakes from Earth been learned by the settlers? Or had they been forgotten in the ensuing years?

"This mission is the first of its kind," Rachel continued. "We've been living on the ship for several years now, as our colleagues tried to find the right moment that the receiver was switched on. We have been away from our families, knowing we could be sent back in time at a moment's notice. We…" Again she glanced at her crew. "We'd really like to make sure we get home safely."

"You have a family too?"

"Yes, a husband and an eight-year-old son."

Hannah looked at Clarence, the number two who didn't actually seem to do anything but follow Rachel around. Then at the rest of the crew, who now seemed to be so small and scared. At least she knew the future was a good place, that it was all worthwhile. It must be, she thought, bevause these seem to be good people. And if these are the ones sent back for such a crucial mission, then perhaps the future might not be such a terrible place as the science fiction movies suggest.

She jumped down from the stool and took her phone out of her pocket. "Is there anything else about the box I should know?" she asked.

"Yes, a sentence is written on the side of the box. It has become one of our most well-known proverbs. 'Prediction is very difficult, especially about the future.'"

"And our authorities don't know about this box and what it does?"

"It doesn't seem so. They haven't mentioned it."

Hannah walked back into the main room. Clarence followed, Rachel delaying for a moment in the cocktail lounge to speak to the crew.

Reaching the middle of the room, Hannah held the phone up in front of her and hit 'record'.

"Hi, world! Hannah here again, on the spaceship. These aliens are *such* nice people! Say hi!" She panned the phone round to Clarence, who gave an awkward wave. Hannah turned the phone back on herself. "See? Adorable! They've got loads of cool stuff on the ship. They can get you drunk and get you sober again all in the space of ten minutes! Now, I know you want to see more weird stuff, but I need to get a message to someone. Niels Mark, are you there? You're aged twenty-three, and I have a simple question for you. 'What is difficult?' Send your answer to me as a direct message to this account. Okay, guys, more news from the spaceship soon. Say bye!" She swung the phone back to Clarence, who gave the same awkward wave. Rachel had joined them, and also waved as she walked out of the cocktail lounge. Hannah turned the camera back on herself. "I love these aliens! This chap is second in command and is actually called Clarence! Imagine, an alien called Clarence!" She stopped recording, stabbed a few more times at the phone, then, having sent the video out into the world of social media, put the phone back in her pocket.

She looked at Rachel and grinned. "And now: we wait," she said. "Damn, I've always wanted to say something like that."

Phase 2

Jockeying For Position

Chapter 21

Prediction Is Difficult

Torben sipped at a drink that he would not have described as being coffee had the global café chain notice board not advertised it as being so. He was still plucking up the courage to take a bite from the item on the plate that had been described on the menu as being a sandwich. He was aware that, unlike in Denmark, a sandwich in the United Kingdom consisted of two pieces of bread, not one, but he hadn't expected them to be quite so firm.

He stared out across the Bristol Airport lounge at a large group of young women crowded around a table in the bar opposite him. They were wearing identical T-shirts with a variety of insulting nicknames on the back. One of them was wearing a tutu and a unicorn horn. They were all drinking pints of lager and the table in front of them was festooned with empty glasses, which suggested they had been drinking for most of the evening. He felt as though he had entered a different dimension, not just a different country.

Like the rest of the world, Torben had seen Hannah's new video within minutes of it being posted. Unlike the rest of the population of the planet, however, Torben's own world had collapsed around him as he listened to her words. 'Niels Mark, aged twenty-three.' Niels mark 23. It surely was not a coincidence. His machine had indeed been the instrument that had brought the alien spaceship to Earth. It had not only worked, but had turned out to be…well, he still wasn't quite sure what function the machine served. He just knew it put him at the heart of what was potentially the most important event in the history of the entire human race.

And then Hannah had turned the phone a second time to show the two aliens.

The moment he saw the face of the woman in the background, he knew he was involved far more deeply than he had previously dared to suspect. He had seen her face for only a moment, but he knew instantly. The face of the alien woman was the same face that he had seen in the bubble when he had operated the machine.

The questions quickly became overwhelming. How did they know about the machine, about Niels? The only time it had left his house was when he had gone to see Professor Flensberg. Had *he* told someone? Had he secretly known what the machine was all along and made some telephone calls?

But if that was the case, then why had the PET, the Danish internal security service, not already bashed his door down? Or was it the FE, the foreign intelligence service? Which would be responsible for aliens? Surely aliens counted as being a foreign power? You couldn't get any more foreign than not of this planet, surely? One thing he knew for sure was that, when Professor Flensberg saw the video (this was a 'when' not an 'if', as it was inconceivable that he would not see it), a normal reaction would have been to get in touch with Torben straight away. The fact that he had not received such a call immediately, and the additional fact that his front door remained on its hinges, meant that there was a third option. Not only had the professor not contacted Torben, he had, for some reason, not told the authorities. What this third option could be he didn't like to think about, and yet he found himself thinking about nothing else.

You are getting paranoid, Torben said to himself, before reminding himself that he had invented a machine which had somehow brought an alien spaceship to Earth and that any level of paranoia was therefore probably not enough.

Hannah, on behalf of the aliens, knew of the machine, and wanted him to get in touch with them. But they had done so in a roundabout way, by referring to what was written on the side of the machine rather than referring to the machine itself.

This surely meant either that they had been told of the machine, and interpreted 'Niels mark 23' as being a name and age, or else that they had actually seen it. Which, of course, was impossible. Which, in itself, left only one possibility.

He had invented a time machine.

If this were the case, he could understand why they had sent out the cryptic message, and not just told the authorities. They had said they wanted to speak to 'Niels Mark', and had not mentioned the machine at all. Which meant that they did not want the world at large — or, more specifically, the authorities — to know about the machine.

He needed to tread carefully and move quickly. He sent the word 'Prediction' as a direct message to the account. Instantly he got a message back from Hannah asking him to send a message to a number. He did so, and she immediately called him back.

"Hi," she said brightly. "So, are you Niels?" She sounded as though she had put the call on speaker.

"No," he replied. She really did believe that it was a person. His degree of paranoia rose another notch.

"Oh," she said. "Hmm. So was that a guess, then?" He thought she sounded disappointed. He recognised the tone.

"No," he said. "but I need to know what it is you are really looking for." His English was halting but otherwise excellent, stemming from a childhood watching *Battlestar Galactica* and *Doctor Who* with subtitles.

There was a moment's silence on the other end of the phone, and Torben imagined Hannah checking with the alien before she spoke again. "It's a white box. A machine. With the name 'Niels Mark' on it, and his age, twenty-three."

"That's not a name," said Torben, with a level of irritation in his voice appropriate to a person who has spent a lifetime not being understood. "Please look carefully. The word 'mark' is not capitalised. The machine is called 'Niels'. After Niels Bohr. I've been working on the machine for many years, and this is my twenty-third attempt. So the box is called 'Niels'. Mark 23."

He heard a lengthy laugh coming from a woman other than Hannah, along with various exclamations he could not quite make out.

"And what is the full quote?" asked Hannah.

"'Prediction is very difficult, especially about the future.' It is a famous Niels Bohr quotation. But I do not understand how you know that sentence if you did not know that the word 'Niels' on the box referred to the physicist?"

"Because that saying is written on the side of the box, of course."

Torben felt his stomach lurch and he fought to control the excitement from his voice. "Ah, yes. Of course. How silly of me."

"Okay, we are convinced. You have the machine with you?"

"Yes. But...I...I'm not sure...I'm not entirely sure what it does. Can you tell me?"

"You're the inventor but you don't know what it does? Oh, that's a good one! We'll tell you everything when you get here, not on the phone. We need you to get it to us. But, and this is important, you must do so without anyone knowing."

"Why? What is going on?"

"I'll explain when we meet. Does anyone else know about the machine?"

"Only one person."

"Do you trust them?"

Torben paused. How to answer such a question? He had not trusted anyone for as long as he could remember. Could he trust even *her*?

"I don't know," he answered. "I thought so, but now I'm not so sure. This has made me, kind of – I don't know the word for it. *Vagt*. Scared and uncertain."

"Wary?"

"Yes, that is it. I am very wary of everyone right now. And I'm a bit freaked out, to be honest."

"That's okay, uh...hey, what's your name?"

"Torben."

"Okay, Torben, my name is Hannah. I'm a bit scared too, so don't worry, you're not alone. I'm currently standing on the bridge of a spaceship, so I know exactly how you feel. 'A little bit freaked out' barely covers it. Can you get yourself to Bristol?"

"Yes, I think so. I already checked flights, and I can be with you this evening."

"Good, because somehow we need to sneak you and that box onto this spaceship. For reasons I can't get into on this call, we want to keep knowledge of your box to just us, okay? I will meet you at the airport, so you text me when you know what time your flight will arrive. Do you have money?"

"Yes, I have money. Should we, um, I don't know, take more precautions, do you think? If it might be dangerous. Perhaps we should change phones or something."

"If you want to, Torben, but I think you're worrying unnecessarily. I won't tell you too much over the phone, but at the moment only I – and now you – know about the connection between your box and the...aliens. Rachel has got things totally under control. You'll like them, they're lovely peo...alien beings."

He bought a ticket online for a flight to Bristol leaving later that evening. Retrieving Niels from its hiding place in the cellar, he placed it in the middle of a rucksack and packed his clothes around it. Realising he had forgotten something important, he then unpacked Niels again, and set it on the bed. He went back to his study, pulled open the drawer in which he kept stationery, and stared at the array of different coloured Sharpies lined up neatly. He took out a black pen, then ran back to the bedroom and stared at Niels, trying to decide what to do.

He knew the expression 'Prediction is very difficult, especially about the future' only too well; it was Niels Bohr's most famous quote. There was only one thing not right. The expression was *not* written on the side of the box.

He unclicked the pen and approached the machine. Then he paused, his eye twitching. An idea arrived. A test. A way to find out for sure if this really was a time machine. He put the lid back on the pen, put the box back into the rucksack, and put the pen into a side pocket.

Next, he put a few shirts and some underwear into the rucksack, on top of the box, stuffing a towel down the back so that it would be more comfortable to carry. Hoisting the bag onto his back and locking the front door behind him, he scurried to the train station, looking around him all the way. He changed at Copenhagen for the shuttle to the airport, where he purchased a new phone. He texted his flight number to Hannah then sat nervously in the terminal for six hours.

And now here he was, sitting in a café in Bristol Airport, waiting to be picked up by Hannah.

Chapter 22

When You Act Like a Predator, They Act Like Your Quarry

Somewhere, in a theoretical laboratory, those infinite monkeys are still sat in front of their infinite typewriters.

If this theory were to be put to the test in the form of a live experiment, it would raise a number of questions. Some of these would be of a practical nature. For example: how much time would need to be set aside (presumably an infinite amount of time)? How would you house the animals, or would they be out in the open? Is each monkey typing at the same time, or one at a time? Presumably there is an infinite number of people checking what the monkeys are writing. Some of the issues would be more ethical; for example, would it be appropriate to strap the monkeys to their chairs in order to stop them running away? Would one monkey with one typewriter who types for infinity produce the same result as infinite monkeys typing for one day?

The issue that Professor Flensberg wrestled with on his train journey from Copenhagen to Humlebæk was more to do with the output of the experiment. The implication of there being an infinite number of monkeys is that the monkey that achieves the works of Shakespeare could be literally any of the monkeys to make the attempt. It might be the 15,000,000,000,000th monkey to attempt the feat that succeeds.

Also implied, however, is that the specific monkey would be random. It is therefore just as possible that the very first monkey to make the attempt would be the one to succeed. And, if this were the case, would the conclusion to the experiment be that *every* monkey is able to write the works of Shakespeare? Or that Shakespeare was, in fact, a monkey?

Torben *was* that monkey. To the professor's knowledge, no other person, academic or otherwise, had attempted to put together a machine made up of a random collection of astrophysics theories as Torben had done. As soon as he had seen the latest video on the spaceship which had mentioned Niels mark 23, the professor had known that this reclusive, geeky, somewhat irritating former student of his had succeeded in creating something that only the writers of science fiction had previously considered possible. The professor had not deduced exactly how the machine worked, but he *was* convinced that it had brought a spaceship to the planet Earth.

Immediately the video had finished playing, he had moved to pick up his phone to call Torben. He had checked himself, however, wary of doing anything which might prove to have a permanent effect on the course of events. He had then sat in his chair – or, more accurately, he had knelt in his chair – and stared out of the window over the skateboarders in the Fælledparken park and on to the suburbs of an overcast Copenhagen.

Professor Flensberg was as phlegmatic as one might expect from someone who had spent half of their twenty-year working life teaching students with unrealistic ambitions and the other half producing research papers which were only ever read by people who were producing their own research papers. He knew the game – every paper he produced included the same conclusion: that the results of the research were ultimately inconclusive and required additional funding.

During the course of these studies, he had, on occasion, been asked to present his findings to various branches of the Danish government. The professor was a firm believer in scientific research for scientific research's sake, but he was also grounded enough to know that he had to continue being paid a salary. Research papers that begat additional research were his currency. He let others worry about possible uses of the ideas; as long as he had a research grant application about to be accepted, he was happy.

One such presentation had been to a row of impassive, besuited men, in a windowless room at the top of a small office block in the Østerbro district. He had been unsure of the success or otherwise of the presentation – the men had given no reaction at the time. He had, however, returned to his office with a business card in his pocket. It had belonged to an elegant man in his late fifties who had followed him out of the building. He had handed the card to the professor with the enigmatic instruction that it was to be kept safe and used "only in case of the sort of emergency that would prompt you to call a number given to you by a person like me." The card had been as black as the man's suit on both sides and had borne no name – simply a telephone number in silver numerals. When asked for clarification, the man had merely said: "It is like being in love. You'll know if it happens." The card had sat ominously in the drawer of his desk ever since.

Surely there was no more appropriate time to take out such a business card than on discovering that a former student had accidentally invented a spaceship-generating machine? And yet...

The man in black had been effortlessly intimidating. During the presentation he had looked rather bored, asking just one question, relating to the practical application of the research. There had been eight of them round a large boardroom table, and he had been the only one to push his chair back and stretch out his long legs. He had worn no tie, and his skinny black jeans ended up in brown leather boots. There had been an insouciance about him which was unnerving.

Professor Flensberg had opened the top right-hand drawer of his desk, moved aside the photos of his wife and children that he kept meaning to get framed, the box of sea salt for adding to his lunchtime sandwich, and assorted receipts for expenses long since unclaimed, and taken out the mysterious business card.

Feeling the weight of an unwanted responsibility, he had dialled the number, realising as he did so that he had no name, no one to ask for. The phone on the other end of the line had rung once, then a low, nicotine-ridden voice had answered.

"Yes, Professor Flensberg. How can we help you?"

"Hello, can I speak—wait, how did you—?"

"What can we do for you, professor? Has something come up?"

The professor had gone on to explain about Torben, and Niels mark 23, the white box. The man at the end of the phone had not spoken, leading to the professor saying a little more than he had intended. He had realised that he was nervous and was gabbling a little, and had stopped mid-sentence.

After a few moments of silence, the voice had spoken again. "Thank you, professor. This is of great interest to us. Indeed, it may well be of national importance. The whereabouts of that box is our number one priority. This is what we require you to do. You say you know where Torben lives?"

"Yes."

"Good. Do exactly as I say. Travel to his home. When you get there, knock on the door. If there is no answer, ring me again. If Torben does answer, assess the state of his mind, then ring me again. We can have a helicopter there to pick you both up within minutes of you calling me. Do you understand?"

"Yes, yes, of course," the professor had stumbled. "I...I won't let you down."

"Excellent. Goodbye."

And so he found himself on a train to the village of Humlebæk, a place he knew only because he had once visited the Louisiana sculpture park. What am I doing, he wondered. Why am I making this journey – and for whom? He was certain that the person on the end of the line was an FE agent. Did that mean that he was himself now a spy?

He would often gossip with university colleagues, over a lunchtime sandwich, about their various research presentations. They would compare the mysterious audiences, with the prevailing conclusion being that the government was very interested in their activities. These suspicions were heightened when the professors attended international conferences. At such events, academics from around the world gathered to publicly discuss great ideas and innovations, and to privately share stories about how the CIA, MI6, Mossad and all the other secret agencies were keeping a very close eye on their research. Each of them suspected the others of reporting these conversations to their own Secret Service agencies. They then returned to their respective hotel rooms, where they called their wives and partners to inform them that yes, it was a very interesting day, but they were unable to reveal all that had been discussed with their peers from round the world in case someone was listening.

Looking around the train carriage, Professor Flensberg wondered if one of his fellow passengers might actually be an FE agent, tailing him in order to discover the location of the mysterious white machine. The young mother with the sleeping baby was dismissed, as were the elderly couple reading. Three seats away down the train was a woman in her early thirties wearing a black polo-neck sweater. Her blonde hair was shaped into a bob and then tied behind her head in a tight bun. She was reading something on her phone – or at least, pretending to – and had a small compact rucksack on her lap. In truth, the professor was a little surprised that she was so obvious. If one were to look around the carriage as a child's game and decide who might be a spy, she would be chosen every time. Still, it made him feel more comfortable to know that he was being accompanied on this mission.

The woman looked up from her phone and caught his eye. He smiled at her, enigmatically, crookedly, from one side of his mouth only, raising the eyebrow over the opposite eye at the same time. The woman continued to stare at him, then went back to her phone. Smooth, thought the professor. Not a flicker. She is good. Very good.

At that same moment, in a small office above a second-hand record store in the Østerbro neighbourhood of Copenhagen, a sixty-three-year-old man named Lars, who was feeling too old for this kind of thing, made several telephone calls. The first was to his contact at the telephone company, from whom he obtained the last number Professor Flensberg had called, thereby obtaining the name 'Torben Christiansen'. He then arranged for a recording of all calls Mr Christiansen had made in the last day to be sent to him. His next call was to his contact at the broadband supplier, from whom he learned that Mr Christiansen was at that very moment booking a flight from Copenhagen to Bristol. The penultimate call was to his counterpart in Bristol to make him aware of the developments.

Satisfied that the arrangements were in place, Lars made the final, and most important, call. It was not one he had expected to ever make, and the prospect made him pause for a moment to rehearse what he was going to say. Eventually he dialled the six-digit number that every operative knew off by heart. The phone rang once before it was answered by Security.

"Yes," he said in reply to the first question. "This is an emergency." Pause. "Sixty-five." A further pause as he listened to see which of the twenty different security questions he would be asked next. "Arch Stanton." A further pause. "Cheese sandwiches." A longer pause, with a sigh as he had passed the test. Finally, he was put through to the man with whom he had never expected to actually speak.

The voice he heard next was as chilling as its reputation had led him to believe. "Hello, Mr Armitage," he began. "Yes, I have located the item that was referred to in the video from the Hannah woman. It is a white box. The words do not, in fact, refer to the name of a person called Niels Mark, who is aged twenty-three, but to the words written on the side of the box. It is called 'Niels', after a Danish physicist, and it was the twenty-third incarnation. Hence 'Niels, mark twenty-three'." He smiled as he heard a chortle from David Armitage, then immediately corrected himself. He stood up in order to better concentrate. This was not a call in which to make a mistake. Armitage asked him a question.

"A man called Torben Christiansen," he replied. "It appears he invented a machine but he does not know what it does. He has spoken with the Hannah woman and is bringing the box to Bristol. He will arrive at the airport at twenty-one hundred hours and Hannah is to meet him. Yes, I have already spoken to the local operative in Bristol." Another question. "From the Torben's old university professor, one of my sleepers. I have sent him on, what do you call it, a wild goose chase. Thank you, sir. That is most kind, sir. I will, thank you, sir."

Lars hung up and slowly placed the telephone on the desk before slumping back into his chair. For fifteen years he had been secretly working for the Armitage Foundation, laying down the framework by giving his card to a myriad of people who might one day prove useful, each card with its unique number and catalogued in a complicated filing system of his own devising. And now it had all been worth it. David Armitage himself had said a significant bonus would be in his pay packet this month. He had heard rumours about such bonuses; they tended to be for life-changing amounts. It was one of the ways that the Armitage Foundation kept its operatives sharp. He allowed himself a rare smile, and picked up his personal telephone to suggest to his wife that they might go out to a restaurant that night.

As Lars was completing the most important telephone call of his life, Professor Flensberg was mistakenly thinking he was making contact with a spy on a train, and was travelling to Humlebæk to meet Torben.

Torben, however, had been stepping onto the bus that would take him to Copenhagen airport. Several hours later, he would be sitting in Bristol Airport, nervously waiting for Hannah.

Chapter 23

The Geography of Hope

The area directly in front of the entrance to Bristol Airport is bordered by a concrete blockade. The entrance is barriered, and manned by a security guard. Only pre-registered taxis and police cars are allowed to enter this area. Had Torben been aware of this restriction, he would have been alarmed to see the barrier rise and a large four-wheel-drive vehicle with blacked-out windows drive into the area without needing to stop and report to the security guard. Had he been able to see inside the vehicle, he would have seen two men of unfeasibly large stature occupying the front seats. One of them had spoken with his counterpart, Lars, in Copenhagen some hours earlier.

In the rear of the car sat the Brigadier, arms folded, staring at the entrance to the airport terminal. He took a phone from the pocket of his uniform and pressed '1'. As it autodialled, he placed it to his ear.

"Well?" said David Armitage. No preamble, no salutations.

"I can see him," the Brigadier replied. "He is waiting to be picked up, as they arranged."

"Does he have the box?"

"Not that I can see, but he does have a big rucksack. Presumably it is in there."

"Right. When she picks him up, follow them. I don't know what that box does, but if it is so important to the aliens, then I need to have it. Intact, you understand? Understand? In. Tact."

"Yes sir. Should I—?" He looked at the screen. Mr Armitage had already hung up.

*

158

The drive from the top of the Mendip Hills to Bristol Airport takes around thirty minutes if taken slowly to enjoy the open countryside. The fields and moorland disappear as the road descends into Burrington Combe. They are replaced by rocky valley sides populated sporadically by goats, who stare disparagingly at groups of pot-holers as they make their way to squeeze through the tiny entrance to Rod's Pot.

Hannah eased the car down the winding road, past the yawning black entrance to Aveline's Hole, the cave situated next to the road. As the result of a lifetime of habit, she glanced to her right to check whether the bear that 'lived' in the cave was at home, a game she had played with Gareth from the very first time he had been able to see out of the window. She smiled as she remembered him sitting in the front seat, straining against the seatbelt to see out of the window as he tried to spot the fictitious animal lurking in the dark depths of the cave.

She glanced for the hundredth time in the rear-view mirror to check if she was being followed. The Brigadier had returned her to the cottage in a large and inevitably black Range Rover. The short drive had been accompanied by a gentle interrogation. He had asked one basic question, but in many different ways, each time receiving the same bland response. No, she didn't understand the video message either, she had just done what they had asked of her, and if you want any more information, go ask Rachel.

Hannah had called her son the moment that she had stepped inside her house and shut the front door in the face of the Brigadier. Gareth had again been greatly relieved to hear from his mother. She had told him to pack for a very long trip, just in case. It had not been the easiest of conversations – she could hear Monique starting to panic in the background, wanting to know what was going on, who were these aliens, what did they want. Gareth had begun to ask his mother the sort of questions that she had promised Rachel she would not answer. Eventually Hannah had forced herself to end the call, before she could tell Gareth everything she knew.

Then she had received the message from Torben, and they had agreed that he would get to Bristol Airport, where she would meet him. Her only challenge now was how to get there without the combined might of the British Army, Navy, Air Force and media becoming aware.

The remainder of the afternoon had been an endurance. The video clips were now on rotation on the news channels, and she had paced the house with the remote control in her back pocket ready to mute the sound the moment that her face appeared on screen, as quick on the draw as a young cowboy with a point to prove.

The news reports from around the world had been addictive. One government after another declaring their position on the spaceship, as if it had anything to do with them. Protests and riots, demonstrations of peace and welcome. The human race seemed to be reacting to the arrival of the spaceship by splitting into different groups then fighting with each other to be heard by the very groups they had just split from. Everyone striving to prove to everyone else that they were the most right. It was as if the presence of outsiders had caused a mass search for identity, but no one could agree on which was the correct identity. Some wanted a military reaction before the aliens opened fire; others wanted a peaceful response. Some resented the government and the Army being the ones to make contact; others proposed themselves as the ideal group to be representing humanity.

There were commentators who thought that this was a signal that the world was ending; others who hailed the arrival of aliens as a bold new beginning. Hannah was the only one who knew that they were, in fact, both right.

She had spoken several more times with Gareth, to check that he was packing and that they had booked a flight. As of the two o'clock call, they had not. Frozen by the enormity of the situation, of something so completely unknown and uncharted, they too had found themselves glued to the rolling news. Only Hannah's remonstrations had awakened Gareth to the fact that something serious was up, even if she could not tell him exactly what it was. He had called her at six p.m. to say that they had booked seats on the first flight available. Unfortunately, this was not for another two days. Far from ideal, but as it was the only option, then she would need to tell Rachel to wait.

At eight she had informed the soldier posted outside her door that she needed to speak to the Brigadier. To her surprise, the soldier had immediately called him on a VHF tactical radio. He had handed her the handset.

"I need to take my car out," she had said. "Can you tell these soldiers to force the media camped outside my driveway to let me out?"

"Where do you need to go?" the Brigadier had replied.

"To the airport. I am picking up my son and his family. They are coming home, to stay with me. You know, given what is going on and everything."

"Would you like us to escort you? You are the most famous person on the planet right now."

"No, thank you, but you could make sure nobody follows me. No paparazzi on the back of motorbikes, no helicopters with cameras."

"Hannah, you have my word that you will not be followed. I will personally see to it."

She drove past the Rock of Ages, the crevice in the cliff where the Reverend Augustus Toplady had sheltered from an electrical storm and had been inspired to write the hymn as he cowered against the rain. History was everywhere, the past packed with events both of note and of inconsequence. It was hard to keep up sometimes, to filter only the events that could be of use. The Burrington pub, to which she had taken Julia the first time she had visited. She smiled as she drove, remembering her lover's face as she had taken her first sip of local Somerset cider. The pleasant surprise of the initial taste, the first pint going down so quickly, Julia ignoring her warnings as the second followed, then the trip home after a third pint, culminating in having to help her into the house and to kneel by the toilet for two hours.

The past seemed to be all around, judging her decisions and actions. The events of the future are driven by the actions of the past, but she could never acknowledge this truth or allow it to change her approach to life. The implications for the decisions she had made, for the decisions she was going to make, were just too great. The idea that Gareth had moved his family because of her and not despite her was too much to contemplate. As she spent dark nights on the sofa with Agnes, her thoughts would drift away from Atticus to a slowly dawning realisation that it was for her own protection that she had placed a wall between herself and her past. A wall which moved at the same pace as she did and which, once breached, would not be rebuilt.

As if the judgements of her past decisions were not enough, she now had the judgement of the future as well. The human race was blindly running towards its own destruction. Atticus might get a life, but his children – her great-grandchildren – would not. Could she mourn for progeny she would never meet? Could she feel blame for something that she could not affect? Does being part of collective responsibility result in collective blame? Does this disbursement of blame mean everyone is equally responsible for everything, or that each person is given a tiny slice of that responsibility, as if to rob it of its power?

As she pulled off the main road into the airport, she felt a moment of futility. The day spent watching news channels had, she realised, been emotionally exhausting. Of all the billions of people on the planet who were transfixed by the greatest story of the century – perhaps of *any* century – Hannah alone possessed the context. The *real* reason why the ship had arrived. That they were not aliens, but humans from the future returned to save humanity, which was merrily careering towards mass extinction. Here was one fuck-up that was never going to be tidied up, explained, sorted, justified, tied into a neat little bow and put in the drawer marked 'Not My Fault'. The human race was about to be lost, and no blaming of other people was going to change the result.

But what could *she* do? She was only one person on a massively crowded planet. And, of those people, she would place herself in the bottom quartile of those who wanted to be in charge. She was just one of several billion people all taking no action because they thought it would make no difference. The biggest impact on every election and referendum is made by the people who thought that their vote wouldn't matter. Why should she be the only one to accept culpability?

The rise of freedom of choice had come hand in hand with the loss of collective responsibility. The slogan for the age seemed to be 'That's a really terrible thing I've just read about. Someone should do something about that.' What could one person do in the face of such mass intransigence? And if it was the future, what was the point in even trying?

With so many unanswerable questions occupying her thoughts as she drove to the airport, Hannah did not stop to consider why the Brigadier had agreed so readily to her making the trip.

Hannah left her car in the short-stay car park and hurried up the steps towards the Arrivals hall. No car had followed her to the airport, as the Brigadier had promised. What Hannah did not know was that this was because the Brigadier already knew where she was going, whom she was meeting, what flight he was on and what colour trousers he was wearing. Never having been the centre of an internationally coordinated surveillance operation run by the very best agents lured from Secret Service agencies around the world, she did not notice the five people who watched her walk from the car to the terminal. She failed to notice: the car in the restricted zone in front of the airport; the woman buying a newspaper; the man studying the Arrivals board; the man pretending to have a conversation on his phone; and the woman serving insipid cups of coffee and overpriced brownies.

There was, however, only one skinny man of average height with blonde hair, black glasses and an orange rucksack, looking extremely worried, sitting in the Arrivals hall. Hannah walked over and sat down in the vacant seat next to him. His knee was pumping up and down nervously.

"Torben?" she asked.

"Yes. Hannah?" He did not turn to look at her but spoke through the side of his mouth.

"Yes. You're…you're not what I expected."

"Oh," Torben replied as flatly as was possible when trying to move one's lips as little as possible. "I'm sorry. I…what were you expecting?"

"Oh, I don't know. Just someone a bit more…well, a bit more 'Viking', I suppose."

"It is true that no one has ever suggested that I look like a Viking," Torben replied. "Could we leave now, please?"

"Sorry. Of course. We can talk in the car." She stood, uncomfortably aware that several people were pointing her out to their friends.

"You walk on and I will follow at a distance." He still had not looked at her.

"Oh, Torben, come on, you're being paranoid. No one is out to get you."

"If this machine does what I think it does, then we are in great danger. Please walk out of the airport now."

Hannah shrugged, then stood and walked out of the airport. A woman ran up to a man, they embraced, and then they too walked out. Had Hannah been paying as much attention as Torben had been, she would have noticed that the woman had not in fact just emerged from the Arrivals gate but had, moments before, been studying the periodicals lining the shelves of the newsagent's.

Torben stood and walked out into the night. He followed with failed nonchalance as Hannah trotted back down the steps, across the road and into the short-stay car park. His eyes darted left and right as he looked for any movement in the bushes or behind the parked cars. He waited in the shadows as Hannah went to the pay machine. He watched her walk across the car park, get into the car, turn on the ignition and drive around the one-way system until coming to a stop by the pay station. Still Torben detected no movement as he tried his very hardest to be invisible. As if propelled by a pinball flipper, he suddenly broke for cover, running across the tarmac. He ripped open the back door, threw his rucksack into the back seat and dived in after it, reaching back to slam the door shut.

"Go!" he shouted. "Go, go!"

"All right, keep your hair on," Hannah tutted, then pulled away, with Torben peeping behind them over the back seat. She pulled up at the barrier, paid the ticket, drove onto the exit road and on out to the main road. They turned right onto it, soon catching up with a car being driven at a consistent ten miles per hour below the speed limit.

"See anything, Mr Bond?" said Hannah, watching for an opportunity to overtake.

"My second name is Christiansen," replied Torben in a voice so deadpan that Hannah suddenly wondered if 007 was a thing in Denmark. "I am not sure. There are many cars behind us now, so it is not possible to tell if any are following us."

"Oh, for Christ's sake," Hannah said under her breath, then, to Torben, "You're being paranoid. Look, I'll prove it to you."

The road straightened for a short distance and no traffic was coming the other way. Hannah dropped down a gear, then suddenly pulled out to overtake the car in front, pulling back in just before the road turned left downhill. She accelerated on down the hill.

"Shit!" shouted Torben, as he watched three black 4x4 Audis break rank from behind them and attempt to overtake the whole queue of cars. The first one achieved the feat, but the other two were forced to pull back in to avoid cars coming up the hill against them.

"Holy crap, you *aren't* being paranoid," said Hannah. "Strap in."

As Torben rolled around the back seat, Hannah took a sudden right turn into a lane lined with cottages, accelerating as she did so. A car coming up the hill beeped his horn as she turned in front of him, the male driver making a gesture with his hand that Hannah did not need to see in order to understand the message. Torben watched that same driver slam to a standstill as the foremost black Audi attempted to copy the turn and instead smashed sideways into the front of the now-stationary vehicle. The Audi reversed, leaving bits of both cars scattered on the road, and accelerated violently in pursuit of Hannah and Torben.

Having gained some four hundred metres on the chasing cars, Hannah pressed a speed-dial number on her phone. She switched off her lights, following the road out of the tiny village by memory and moonlight, then turned suddenly right into a lane so small that grass grew down its middle.

"Hello? Hannah?" said a voice over the speakers in the car. "What a delightful surp—"

"Ted, don't ask me why, just open your electric gate now. Right now, Ted. Go go go!"

"Oh, what? Um, right, okay."

Hannah accelerated up the hill. She took another turning left up a private road. An absence of moonlight across the road ahead suggested gates, and Hannah drove directly towards them. A moonlit vertical line appeared as the gates started to open. Hannah did not decelerate.

"Um, Hannah..." said Torben as they got nearer and nearer to the gap that was widening almost painfully slowly. "I don't think... We're not going to... Oh. That was close."

Hannah skidded to a halt on the gravel drive in front of the main door to the house just as it opened. A tall, stocky man appeared, his body – that of someone who was once Army-trained – silhouetted by the lights in the house. He stepped forward, filling the doorway with his rod-straight back and broad shoulders, flicking a switch as he did so. Light flooded the outside of the house and revealed the man to be greying at the temples and carrying a face full of concern. Hannah wound down her window.

"Ted, shut the gates! And turn off that fucking light! Now now now!"

"Okay, will do. Blimey, Hann-*ah*." Ted reached inside and turned off the light, then pointed a remote control at the gates, which slowly began to shut. They could hear the revving of an engine coming from the lane up which they themselves had just travelled. Across the fields they saw the headlights of a car coming their way. It sped between the houses that were dotted up the lane, slowing abruptly at the gate of each one, then fast ahead again. They watched the gates to the driveway closing achingly slowly as the car drew nearer. Another roar, and the car reached their house just as the gates clicked shut. A bright beam of light appeared from the end of the driveway and flickered around the wooden gates, then the car roared quickly away again.

Ted looked at Hannah in the moonlight. "I know I said drop in any time, old girl, but I never thought you'd take me quite so literally. Thought you were currently busy being an internationally famous friend to aliens." He had the voice of an auctioneer and Hannah almost felt it booming across the countryside.

"I'll explain in a minute, Ted. Can I hide this?" asked Hannah, jerking her thumb towards the car. "And do keep your fucking voice down, would you?"

"Oh, sure, sure," said Ted, only a few decibels lower, unfazed thanks to a skin which seemed to be thicker than that of a deaf rhino. Another click of the remote and the garage door opened. Hannah drove slowly, slowly, the crunch of the gravel under the wheels seeming to echo across the valley. She and Torben got out of the car; he held his rucksack tightly. Nobody spoke again until they were inside the house. Ted turned the latch, shutting the door like a teenager arriving home in the early hours of the morning. He allowed the latch to slowly turn and lock, then, the house silent around them, he swivelled on his heel on the carpet. They listened together for a moment, straining for the sound of pursuing armed men in high-performance cars. Eventually, Ted looked up at them both and smiled.

"Well, you do know how to make an entrance, old girl," he bellowed. "Wowsers."

Hannah and Torben took an involuntary step back. "Thank you, Ted, you literally may have just saved our lives. But please, your voice is like a foghorn. Keep it down for a minute, would you?"

"Righto," said Ted in a whisper that was the equivalent volume to Hannah's voice when she was calling Agnes for dinner. "Sorry. All those years as a chorister." He directed that last comment directly to Torben. He led them both through the hallway, past a grandfather clock that looked as if it had been placed there a minimum of a century previously. To Hannah and Torben's surprise the song of a common garden bird, possibly a blue tit, came from the clock. It seemed to be announcing the time as being nine o'clock. Ted walked on into the lounge without comment, inured to the unusual chime. He turned and addressed Hannah. "And, ahem, the 'we' is...?"

"Oh, sorry, Ted, this is Torben," said Hannah, entering the

lounge. As on the previous three occasions she had been in the room, she found herself wondering if there was a snooker hall from the 1970s that was missing its soft furnishings. Black and red were the prevailing colours, leather was the main fabric of choice, and 'functional' had clearly been the main brief. Vertical blinds over the far wall hinted at a patio door behind. "He is from Denmark and seems to be of great interest to persons unknown and, as yet, untrusted. Torben, this is Ted. He is one of those tossers who made a pile in London because of his public-schoolboy connections, then says he 'downsized' to the West Country by selling a one-bed flat in Knightsbridge and using the money to buy this five-bedroom house which the locals couldn't afford. We drink in the same pub on occasion, and he's been trying to get into my knickers for the last three years, so far succeeding on only one occasion."

"'So far'!" Ted beamed at Torben. "Did you hear that, Torben, old chap? 'So far'!"

Torben looked perplexed at this foreign creature in front of him, then turned to Hannah.

"Do you English make a joke out of *everything* that happens to you?" he said.

"I'm afraid so," she replied. "It's our coping mechanism. It gets less annoying the more you live with it."

"So what happens now? What do the aliens want to do with my machine?"

Hannah turned to Ted. "Ted, I need something medicinal. Some of that special bourbon you keep, maybe. You too, Torben?"

"I would like a glass of milk, please, if that is possible."

"Great, so that's a glass of milk and a large something with ice in it, and if you could take about fifteen minutes getting it, that would be ideal."

"Ah," said Ted. "I see. Gotcha. On it like an Easter bonnet. Leave with, will sort. Drinks on their way, served with a side order of privacy. Understood." As if he had not made it clear enough that he had got the hint, he tapped the side of his nose before turning and leaving the room, closing the door behind him.

Torben finally relaxed his grip on the handle of the rucksack, placing it carefully on the burgundy carpet and leaning it against one of the two black leather sofas. He sat down while keeping one hand on top of the rucksack. Hannah sat back on the opposite sofa, a low table of smoked glass with curved steel legs separating them. Torben stared at her expectantly. Hannah saw before her a scared young man who was used to being one of life's passengers, but who could now be filed under the category 'Should Have Been More Careful What He Wished For'.

Hannah sighed. "So. Torben. This machine of yours. What do you know about it?"

"I know it has something to do with the arrival of the spaceship. And I do not think the people on the spaceship are aliens. I think they may be humans from the future. Which means Niels may be some sort of time machine. I think the humans from the spaceship may want to take my machine back into the future with them. I also think that there are some people who do not want this to happen, but I do not know why."

"Wow," said Hannah. "You do speak seriously good English."

"Thank you," replied Torben. "Although it is only ever the English who are surprised at how well foreigners can speak their language."

Hannah opened her mouth to reply, then changed her mind. Instead she chose to stick to the issue at hand. "You are right, Torben. They are humans from the future. How did you work that out?"

"The quote from Niels Bohr. 'Prediction is very difficult, especially about the future.'"

"Yes. It's written on the side of the box."

"Yes. And I'll wager that it is in *your* handwriting."

As Hannah's mouth hung open in preparation for the arrival of a response, Torben stood and untied the top of the rucksack. The black pen he had put in at the last minute fell onto the floor. Torben placed it on the table. He started to take out clothes and place them on the floor. Then he reached both hands inside the rucksack, grasped Niels around the bottom, and began to pull.

Suddenly the door opened and Ted entered the room backwards.

"Ho ho," he said loudly, turning to reveal that he was holding a tray carrying a large tumbler containing rum and coke that rattled with ice cubes, a glass of milk and a large bowl of crisps. "Only me, won't say another word, thought I'd give you your drinks before I leave you in peace. Thought you might be a tad peckish. Here we go."

Torben hurriedly shoved Niels back into the rucksack and, not taking his stare from Ted, grabbed blindly at the pile of clothes. He used a pair of purple boxer shorts to conceal the top of Niels as Ted approached the table.

Hannah jumped up, moving swiftly from one shocked state to another. "Ted, for fuck's sake," she shouted. "What bit of 'fifteen minutes' don't you understand? Give me that." She took the tray and put it onto the table.

"All right, old girl, all right. Only being hospitable." He looked like a scolded puppy that knew it had done wrong. Hannah put her hand on his arm.

"Ted," she said in a voice ever so slightly more friendly. "Thank you very much. Now, would you be so kind as to fuck off?"

"On my way. Not another peep. I'll hide in the old kitchen. Just shout if you need me."

Torben, still crouched over his rucksack like a dog guarding a bone, did not take his eyes off Ted as he walked out of the room. Only when the door clicked shut did he straighten and face Hannah.

"Can you trust him?" he asked her.

"I've no idea. Now, what do you mean, that writing on the box is in my handwriting? I've never seen the box before."

Torben once again took the clothes from the rucksack and carefully placed them, still folded, onto the floor. Then he took out a bulky item wrapped in towels. He set it onto the table and removed the towels.

Hannah looked at the side of the box that was facing her. 'Niels mark 23' was written neatly in the top right-hand corner. She stood and leaned first to the left then to the right. Next, she leaned over to look at the side facing away from her. Finally, she lifted the box.

"There is nothing written on it," she said. "Nothing other than the name. I don't understand."

"The quote is not on the box because it is not written yet," said Torben. "If this *is* a time machine and these *are* humans, then they *must* be from the future, not the past, *because* the quotation is not written on the box yet. So, if time travel is really possible, let us give it a test." He held out his hand and offered Hannah the pen. "You write the quote on the machine."

"Me? Why me?"

"I don't know. Why not? I would just like it to be someone other than me. To have someone else – what is the word, *engageret*, um – committed to this story, to this future. At the moment it is only me who seems to be linked to this machine. I would like someone to join me in whatever is happening to time. Given that you have met the time travellers, it seems appropriate that it be you."

Hannah looked at the pen in Torben's hand for a moment. Then she took it from him. The words 'Permanent Marker' were written on the side. There was, indeed, something permanent about what she was being asked to do. If Rachel was to be believed – and, given that she had explained the story of the future of humanity while they had been standing on a giant spaceship hovering fifty metres above the ground, Hannah was inclined to accept her story of the future – this white box played the most pivotal role in the colonisation of a distant planet which ensured the survival of the human race.

"Okay," she said. "All right, I'll do it. What's the phrase again? I don't want to get it wrong!"

"I think you'll find you cannot get it 'wrong'. The logic of time will not allow it. But the expression is 'Prediction is very difficult, especially about the future'. It is intended to be ironic."

Hannah gave him a withering glance of only medium intensity given the mitigating circumstances, then began writing at a speed which would ensure she did not think about the fact that this box would become the most famous box in the history of another world.

As she handed back the pen, her head snapped towards a faint noise from the hallway. She uttered an obscenity that even

Torben's excellent grasp of English would have failed to identify.

"Get that box back in the bag," she said, standing quickly and walking to the blinds at the back of the room. "Now." Torben jumped to his feet and, recognising the urgency in Hannah's voice without the need for questions, did as he was told, shoving the clothes on top. He swiftly tied the cords at the top of the rucksack and, swinging the bag onto his back, followed her out of the patio door and into the garden.

Chapter 24

The Prospect of Immortality

David Armitage surveyed the accumulation of power that was both sitting in front of him and watching from afar. In addition to the political and religious leaders who had made the trip to see the spaceship for themselves – or rather, whom he had summoned – there were forty other individuals and their entourages sitting in their offices around the world, staring at a screen and awaiting his pronouncement. These included political leaders of some of the second-tier countries such as Australia, owners and CEOs of newspaper and television channels, founders of social media platforms, and a former captain of the England football team and current fashion model. It was late in the evening in the United Kingdom, but for many of those on the other side of the camera it would have been the middle of the night. It was a casting call of influence and ego which had the collective power to make things happen anywhere across the entire planet. And it was awaiting *his* instruction.

Rows of chairs had been hurriedly assembled in one of the larger white marquees that formed a second wave surrounding the spaceship. They were now filled with the Armitage A-listers, a group of people every one of whom would have been the centre of attention of any other room they walked into. Each had come scuttling along as soon as they had received the 'code white' message on the phones that he had provided for them. And now they sat chatting noisily before him. Even David Armitage had never before seen such a demonstration of his influence. He couldn't deny that it felt good.

He surveyed the scene laid out below him. The Prime Minister and Chancellor of the United Kingdom sat next to each other, each with their arms folded, looking away from each other; still not on speaking terms ever since the former had refused to resign to allow the latter to take the top job on the date that they had agreed many years before. The presidents of the USA and Russia, chatting excitedly with each other like two schoolgirls seeing each other for the first time after the summer holidays. Keith Baracus and his two idiot sons. The young King of the United Kingdom and his wife, who seemed to have been virtually stapled to his side since the coronation, as if terrified of the weight of history that she had married into. Twelve of the wealthiest people in the world, each one male and old and white and ugly and sitting with a beautiful wife a minimum of thirty years their junior. The heads of the Army, Navy and Air Force of the United Kingdom, who sat apart from each other on the edges of the seating area in an almost perfect equilateral triangle. The Pope and one of his cardinals sitting in the front row, hands on knees, looking at David Armitage expectantly. The archbishops of Colchester and Halifax lounging on the back row, glancing around, arms slung over the back of the seats next to them as if they were at the back of the school bus. Three of Hollywood's highest grossing actors, each wearing sunglasses. The CEOs of the six biggest companies in the world. Added together, these people represented the greatest assemblage of power and influence ever to be gathered in one place in the history of the planet. And not one of these people would be sitting in those seats if they had not been put there by David Armitage himself.

He gave the microphone in front of him a single tap then, satisfied, began his address. "Gentlemen," he said in a voice of sunshine and chocolate, then paused to gain their attention. When the hubbub in the room had subsided, he added: "And ladies." He smiled towards the queen consort. What was it about the entitled that made them so damned fascinating? He turned a glare towards the archbishops and pointedly waited for them to stop whispering to each other before he continued. "Thank you," he said, with a hint of sarcasm in their direction. He thought he saw the Archbishop of Colchester give an insolent shrug. The

British Prime Minister had insisted on adding some of his own establishment to the G7 leaders. As David Armitage had himself insisted on the Russian President being there, he had reluctantly acceded to the Prime Minister's request. It was his country, after all, albeit temporarily. Nevertheless, David Armitage made a mental note to do something about that Colchester.

He turned on his smile and projected the benefit of his personality across the room. "Thank you all for coming at such short notice. I confess I never thought I would need to issue a white message, and I do so now only after great consideration. I would like to update you with what we know, and I am sure, once you have heard what I have to say, you will all agree that the situation does indeed deserve this level of emergency.

"As you know, the aliens have told us that they have a message, and we have spent the three days since their arrival on our planet trying to find a person acceptable to them who will deliver this message. This has not been successful. They have rejected every person we have offered to them, despite each and every person we offered being, if anything, over-qualified for the role."

"Damned fucking rude they were, too," said Keith Baracus.

"Quite," said David Armitage in a tone devoid of interest. He perked up as he returned to his theme. "I think we should stress that the aliens have shown no signs of aggression or taken any action to give us any concerns whatsoever. They just – well, float there, not really doing very much.

"Now, as I am sure you know, yesterday the aliens met with the woman with whom they had their very first contact: Hannah Siggers. Although we do not know the outcome of that conversation, she was in the spaceship for just under one hour. She then posted a second video on social media. This was rather more mysterious than the first, asking for someone called Niels Mark to get in touch, adding a cryptic message about something being dangerous. Our agents immediately located the three individuals in the world who bear that name, tapped their phones, checked their bank records and personal histories, and had them followed. None of these three individuals made any effort to contact Hannah.

"I then received a call from one of our operatives in Copenhagen. He had been diligently following our processes for fifteen years of contacting all the important people in the city—"

"Yes, yes, David, we know how good you are at your job. Please get on with it, there's a good chap," said a voice from the back of the room. David Armitage raised an eyebrow at the Archbishop of Colchester. The Archbishop of Halifax stuck an elbow into the ribs of his colleague.

"Hmm. Anyhow. Our operative in Copenhagen had identified a young man who, it would seem, had answered Hannah's call. This young man seems to have invented some kind of machine. This machine would appear to be connected with the sudden appearance of the alien spaceship. Niels is the name of the machine. This young man is currently in our custody, as are the machine and Hannah Siggers."

A murmur of excited chatter greeted this latest revelation. David Armitage raised his hands to bring calm and quiet back into the room.

"I propose to confront the aliens," he continued. "I would like Douglas, Sergei and Davis to join me." The heads of state of Britain, Russia and the USA all tried their best not to look like the boys who got picked first for the school football team. Two of them succeeded. "We have the Army and Air Force on standby" —he nodded towards the heads of the British Army and Royal Air Force, who nodded back, as the Admiral of the Fleet folded his arms— "although I do not expect any trouble. The rest of you need to be on hand to mobilise any influence that we may need to bring to bear. I will wish to reconvene this meeting as soon as we know the real purpose of these aliens arriving on Earth. Now, are there any questions?"

Suddenly everyone started shouting at once, aside from the British, Russian and American heads, who sat smugly, leaning back in their chairs with their arms folded.

David Armitage waved both arms up and down, indicating that everyone should sit down and calm down. "Okay, okay everyone, settle, settle. Kyoko, you were sitting quietly with your hand up. What question do you have?"

The Japanese Prime Minister stood and gave a small bow. "If you please, may we have a little more information for our people? I know that we are not the only country where there is unhappiness. Our newspapers demand information. People are not turning up for work, they sit looking at their phones awaiting news, they are thirsty for news, but we have nothing to tell them. Please, in order to keep peace and order, may we have something to tell them?" She bowed again and sat down. The Italian, German and French premiers shouted their agreement.

David Armitage stood impassively, hands clutched behind his back. He was on the verge of shouting 'It's your time you're wasting, you know' when they finally started to settle. He opened his mouth but realised that one of the Hollywood actors had nudged his sunglasses to the end of his nose and was peering over them while talking to the wife of the founder and CEO of the world's largest data-tech company. Realising he was the only one still talking, the actor pushed the glasses back with an index finger and lounged back in his chair.

When all was quiet, Armitage resumed.

"Tell your people that the aliens' purpose in visiting our planet is entirely peaceful. One might even describe them as being charming." Keith Baracus gave out a loud snort. David Armitage continued. "Although their message has not yet been made clear, they are being extremely helpful. Everyone should go on with their lives, carry on as normal, and we will give further news as soon as it is available. Now, if you will excuse me, I need to meet with the aliens."

He turned and walked out of the tent through a flap behind him which was being guarded by two very large men in black suits. He ignored the calls and shouts behind him. The British, Russian and American premiers jumped to their feet and ran after him. They caught up with him as he entered another marquee, the closest to the spaceship.

"What's the plan, David?" asked the British Prime Minister, already breathing hard.

"The plan, gentlemen," he replied, "is to take back control. To get ourselves into the driving seat. Just follow my lead, understood?"

The three premiers nodded while simultaneously jogging to keep up with David Armitage's stride. As they walked out of the marquee, the Brigadier and five other soldiers appeared at their sides. The group walked across the grass, their feet becoming wet with the night dew.

The Brigadier whispered something into David Armitage's ear. Armitage cursed in response.

"Well, just find them!" he replied, without attempting to lower his voice. The Brigadier wheeled away from the party.

The four men rose on the invisible beam towards the spaceship, leaving the soldiers on the ground below them. The US and Russian Presidents whispered excitedly to each other. David Armitage looked at the British Prime Minister, who grinned nervously back at him. He was reminded once again that these people were merely men, only children at heart. Few men or women have characters of sufficient resilience that they can withstand the pressure on their ego when handed great power. Only he, by staying in the shadows, had been able to cope with the extraordinary responsibility that came with the power and influence that he had built up over the years, and which he now wielded like a benevolent dictator. And surely only he, as the ultimate architect, was suited for taking that extra, tiny step out of the shadows to accept the burden of ultimate responsibility.

As they neared the level of the doorway to the spaceship, they could see Rachel standing inside waiting for them. She stood in what they were now recognising as her customary pose, arms held straight at her sides and a welcoming smile plastered onto her face with a degree of sincerity so bright it could surely not be believed.

"Hi!" she said as they stepped into the spaceship. Her head snapped to an almost forty-five-degree angle and she beamed. "I don't recall asking to see anyone?" These words were spoken with lashings of sugar and candy floss, like the opening salvo of a custard pie fight. David Armitage felt his loins gird themselves. He had taken on far bigger battles than this in the past and emerged victorious. He was not about to be beaten now by an alien, even if it was an alien projecting itself as a hologram of a rather imposing human being.

"Good evening," he replied, the three premiers lining up beside him. "My name is David Armitage." He put out his hand. Rachel smiled back, ignoring the outstretched hand, then turned and walked towards her desk. She stopped in front and rested her bottom against it, to face four empty chairs that had been lined in a row. Rupert the robot was hovering around at the back of the room, having placed the fourth of the chairs. It then moved towards Clarence, who was standing with his hands behind his back, legs shoulder-width apart. Rupert rotated and hovered next to Clarence and placed its own hands behind its back even though it, unlike Clarence, had the option of withdrawing them inside of its body. The two of them emitted an air of two bizarre bodyguards, in contrast to Rachel's attempts at informality.

The four men walked slowly across the lounge area of the spaceship in a V formation. They stopped in front of the four chairs. As David Armitage did not sit, so the three world leaders also remained standing. Rachel addressed them, leaning back against the desk.

"Well," said Rachel, the smile unnervingly fixed into place. "How can I help you gentlemen?"

"I believe we may have something you want," said David Armitage, sitting as he spoke. The premiers also sat. "We are willing to give it to you, but first we must know the real reason for your being here on our planet. You have come for a white box. We wish to know what it does, and why it is so important to your race."

"White box? What white box?" That smile. Impenetrable.

"Come now, please don't patronise me. I have had men tailing Hannah, and she has met a young man carrying a white box. They are now in our custody. What does it do, Rachel?"

Rachel stood, thoughtfully. She moved to her left in order to walk around the desk and take her seat behind. As she went past David Armitage, he stretched out a leg. Rachel's front foot hooked behind his calf, and she stumbled forward for a moment. She paused, glaring down at Armitage. If she had been wearing a tie, she would have straightened it at the knot before continuing around the desk.

The Prime Minister of Great Britain and the President of the United States laughed like schoolboys watching a wedgie. The Russian President, however, glared. He stood, pointing at her accusingly. "What is this?" he shouted, switching his angry stare from David Armitage back to Rachel. "You are supposed to be a hologram! How can a hologram trip over an object? What is this?"

Clarence's arms came from behind his back. Rachel's eyes darted left and right. "I...we...I am a hard light hologram," she said. "We are, uh, able to touch and feel."

"Oh yes," said the Russian President, walking around the desk towards Rachel. "You certainly are." Rachel tried to take a step backwards, but the Russian President grabbed her head with both hands.

Clarence took a step forward and at the same time a door opened to the side of the room, revealing the gaudy interior of the bar. Several other aliens ran out, including one man holding a cocktail shaker in a threatening manner. The Russian Prime Minister took them in with one glance, keeping hold of Rachel as he did so. "Ha! I knew it!" he shouted. His thumbs moved to touch lightly on the top of her eyeballs. "Do not move or I will take out her eyes! I have done this before to my opponents. Do not think that I will not do it!"

He again addressed Rachel. "I know what you are. You are not aliens at all. You are human. You will now tell us the truth of why you are here, or so help me..." He began to push down with his thumbs, and Rachel's arms started to flail.

"No, please, it's okay. Stop, stop, this is not necessary. Please," Rachel shouted. "I will tell you everything. It's not difficult, just stop."

The Russian President sneered as if trying for one last moment to decide whether to show mercy, then his hands flung aside as if Rachel's head had given him an electric shock. He took two steps backwards, breathing heavily, and allowed his arms to slowly return to his sides, his chin high and chest puffed out, like a gymnast having executed a perfect dismount. Rachel dropped backwards into her chair. Immediately Clarence and several of the crew members ran over to her.

The Russian President walked slowly back to his chair. He looked at the three other members of the boarding party, who were now staring at him. He shuffled his feet, a little abashed, then leaned across and said, in a whisper, "I was, uh, how you say, bluffing her. About the eyeballs. Just scaring a little bit. You know." He nodded as if to confirm his own statement.

"Sure, sure," replied the US President, his eyes still wide. The Prime Minister of Great Britain suddenly found it necessary to look anywhere in the room except at the Russian President.

David Armitage sat back in his chair with his arms folded and surveyed Rachel and her crew in the way a lion regards a herd of gazelle, the barest of smirks playing across his lips before he spoke.

"Now, Rachel," he began. "Let us tell you a few truths. Number one: I do not believe that you are capable of posing a threat to the planet Earth. Nor, indeed, to any of us sitting here in front of you. If this spaceship were armed and you intended at some point to use force then you would have given us a demonstration by now. As even the most simple-minded politician knows, it is not violence that rules but the threat of violence."

The US and Russian Presidents nodded sagely, before the Russian President suddenly realised what he was agreeing to and rested his chin between his thumb and forefinger. The US President continued nodding.

"Given this," continued David Armitage, "and given the extraordinary amount of weaponry and firepower currently aimed directly at this vessel of yours, I think it is time you told us the truth, don't you? The truth of why you are here, where you have come from, and, perhaps most interestingly, who is Niels Mark – and why is his name written on the side of a white machine? Pray tell me, Rachel, what does this machine do?"

Rachel regathered her wits and sat slowly upright in the chair, placing her hands on the table in front of her, fingers intertwined. "Your threats of violence are as disappointing as they are un-necessary," she said. "*You* will not harm *us*. You will perpetrate no acts of violence against us. You are merely bluffing. I know this to be true. Because we" —she gestured to her colleagues with the sweep of one arm— "are from the future. We live on a distant planet and have travelled across time and space. We have come to *save* you. If you harm us, then we cannot complete our mission. And the fact that we are here proves that we do, indeed, complete our mission. So, you see" —she now leaned back in *her* chair— "you cannot harm us."

It was Rachel's turn to pause, and David Armitage found himself unable to answer for a moment, frozen as a wrestler in a headlock. Unable for the first time in a very, very long while to come up with an immediate response, he gestured for Rachel to continue.

Rachel tilted her head slightly, her benign smile now re-established in its default position, and began. "Your planet has a virus. It is called humans. The Earth is in the process of ridding itself of this virus. Overpopulation, carbon fuels, plastic into the oceans, the constant decimation of forests and the animal kingdom. This process will culminate in a mass extinction of life on Earth in around eighty years' time. It will be the sixth mass extinction to have taken place in the planet's history. The Earth has purged itself before, and it is about to do so again. Just in the two days we have been on Earth, some four hundred species have become extinct. It would therefore seem that this process has already started.

"We are, in fact, human. This small crew you see before you, plus two other spaceships ready to join us, are here from the future – thanks to that white machine you speak of – in order to take two thousand pilgrims to a new planet and thereby ensure the continuation of the human race. The fact that we are here talking to you now is the proof that this plan works. Given that you therefore cannot harm us, please, put away your silly little macho posturing, and talk with me sensibly about how we are going to get two thousand people onto our ships without causing a mass panic among the people of the Earth. Starting with you giving us the white machine that you say you have come into possession of."

A quiet borne out of the crashing arrival of reality descended upon the room. David Armitage was furiously working out the ramifications of what he had just heard. Previous experience of dealing with concepts too big to contemplate told him that he needed to break the issue down into its constituent parts. In order to achieve this, he needed to deploy the skill he had utilised most effectively in the early days of building his empire. He needed to play for time.

"We will provide the white machine when the appropriate time arrives," said David Armitage. "Think of it as my...security. We now know that you cannot leave as long as we have the box. In the meantime, it is getting late. You must be tired. We will leave you now and visit again in the morning, when we can discuss arrangements for your exit. Such as who it is that you will be taking with you."

David Armitage stood and the other three men immediately followed suit. They left the spaceship in the same formation in which they had arrived.

When they touched back onto the ground, David Armitage strode out of earshot of the other three men and took out his phone.

Somewhere only a few miles away, the Brigadier was sitting in a large black 4x4 Audi with blacked-out windows, staring at what looked on the outside like a small cottage, but which he now understood to be a pub. His phone buzzed. He held it to his ear and heard the voice of David Armitage ask him: "Do you have them in sight?"

"Yes," he replied.

"Do they have the box?"

"Yes."

"Good. I want that box, and I want it now. Understand? I'd prefer the other two alive as well, but it's not completely essential, as long as I have that box."

"Sir." The Brigadier put the phone back into his pocket.

Chapter 25

The Sum Of Our Experiences

Torben studied the pint of cider that Hannah had placed in front of him. It held neither the colour nor consistency of any liquid that he had previously encountered. He lifted the glass to eye level, better to examine the strange shapes floating in the beverage. Lowering it, he looked around at the soft furnishings and sofas, then blinked at Hannah with an expression that suggested he had thirteen questions but could not decide in which order to ask them.

Hannah shrugged in response. Torben's reaction was not unusual for first-timers, both to Somerset scrumpy cider and to Dotty's pub. They would often wonder aloud if they had accidentally walked into somebody's lounge. In a way, they had.

An hour earlier they had been sitting in Ted's front room. Hannah had heard the clock in the hallway announce nine thirty with the song of the common chiffchaff. It had been immediately followed by a barely audible, but definitely manly, grunt of surprise. They had exited out of the patio door barely thirty seconds before five large men dressed overwhelmingly in black and carrying automatic weapons had burst into the lounge. Those thirty seconds had been just long enough to allow the fugitives to duck through the leylandii, over the fence at the back of the garden, and into the field behind Ted's house.

Hannah knew the highways and byways around her house for several miles thanks to her daily walks with Agnes. By the time the five men and Ted had set off in serious pursuit, she had led Torben at a run across the field, over a stream by way of an old railway sleeper that now served as a bridge, down the old Wells to

Bristol road which was now an overgrown track, finally ducking into a footpath hidden by a bush. Ten minutes after their escape they had been walking at a good pace in a direction ninety degrees from their pursuers.

After a brisk and somewhat paranoid walk, they had arrived at Dotty's. Now aged in her nineties, Dotty had opened her pub from the front room of her two-bed house when she retired from a career in the civil service. It was situated in the middle of a terrace of four houses, located on the very edge of a hamlet. Established several hundred years earlier by Quakers, the village had had no existing watering hole, and so when Dotty's had opened in the late 1980s it had quickly attracted a small crowd of dedicated regulars. Dotty had run her establishment with an iron hand, which the clientele had secretly loved. The swear box alone had produced sufficient donations to purchase a minibus for the local Scout troop. Hannah liked to sit in the corner with a pint and a book, but occasionally succumbed to a riotous lock-in. She was undecided as to whether Dotty's overbearing nature was the reason the pub barely survived or was why it attracted the punters that it did.

In 1994 Dottie had declared that, as fifty years had passed and she was now freed from the Official Secrets Act, she could admit that she had been a codebreaker at the secret military base at Bletchley Park, working on translating messages intercepted from the Japanese Army. Her tales of wartime exploits became the stuff of legend. Every month the fifty-year rule had passed like a receding tide, revealing more secrets to the delight of the patrons. In time Hannah had begun to wonder if the stories might have been coming from Dotty's fevered imagination. The friendliness with which Dotty pulled her particular pint had seemed to wane over time, the suspicion growing that Dotty had spotted Hannah's rolling eyes as yet another ripping yarn was revealed. The two had settled into an uneasy peace, which meant that Hannah's visits to this pub had become less frequent.

"Cool as mustard, that one," said Hannah, nodding towards Dotty. The landlady was perched on her stool behind the home-made oak bar, bent like a vulture on the back of a playground bench. Once in a while she picked up her phone in her arthritic hands and stabbed at it, as if she were trying to kill a chicken as slowly as possible.

The only other occupants in the pub at this late hour were: a couple Hannah had not seen before occupying one corner, he with his pint of beer, she with a half pint, each staring at different parts of the room in silence; a man sitting in another corner reading a book, with an enormous Saint Bernard dog lying at his feet; and an elderly farmer seated across the bar from Dotty and at right angles to it, with a purple nose, a pint of beer and a whisky chaser. A metal sign which read 'Bill's Throne' was nailed onto the wall behind his head.

Hannah watched carefully as Torben nervously put the pint glass to his lips. His expression turned from fear to pleasant surprise.

"It tastes like fruit juice," he said, before heading in for a second slurp.

"Scrumpy," Hannah replied. "It's hardcore cider."

"Hardcore?"

"Yeah, as in, it's for the dedicated cider drinker. What do you think?"

"It's really good. Is it supposed to be this cloudy?"

"Oh yes. That mainly comes from the rats that fall into the open tanks. Helps give it that lovely tangy aftertaste."

Torben's smile melted away as he saw that Hannah was not laughing.

Their walk across the moor had slowed to a talking pace, once they became confident that they were not being followed. Hannah had enquired as to Torben's history, starting with his childhood. In Torben, however, she had met her match, failing to penetrate far enough even to provide a foothold on which to base further enquiries. Torben had learned to inure himself to the ambivalence of others. As they walked, he had slowly turned the tables and begun to probe Hannah, using the simple technique of not saying very much. To her surprise, Hannah had discovered that she rather enjoyed the unburdening experience of talking about herself, and was soon telling Torben about the impact of

Gareth on her young life, how she had struggled to adjust after he left home, and the happy times with Julia. She had told half-truths when explaining the relationship with Monique, and had failed to resist passing comment on the suitability of the name 'Atticus'. She had rounded off the tale with the current uncertainty as to her own future, given her recent change in employment circumstances and the fact that Gareth had moved to Switzerland. By the time they reached Dotty's, she had felt that the entire arc of her story had been revealed, and at the same moment had realised she still knew very little about this quiet young man who might just have changed the course of history.

Torben placed his glass back on the table and peered at Hannah as if she were a formula on a blackboard. "Why do you not just go and visit your son and his family? If you would like to see them more often, why not just see them more often?"

"Torben, I do love your scientific and, if I may say, somewhat male view on life. It is, however, not as simple as you make out."

Torben shrugged. "Surely that is up to you. It has always seemed to me that we are the sum total of our experiences. That means we can be wrong, if our experiences result in us reaching misleading conclusions. If I conduct an experiment one hundred times it only needs to fail once and the whole thesis fails. And yet after just one experience we assume that everything will always be that way. It is not logical to *not* have an open mind. Just because one action caused one outcome does not mean the same action will cause an identical outcome if repeated. It would be more scientific for you to go to your son, behave differently than you have behaved before, and see if you get a different outcome."

"Do you always see everything so annoyingly simply?" Hannah asked.

"Yes. It is one of the reasons why I have so few friends." She was unsure how to react for a moment, until he let out a short laugh. The noise reminded Hannah of Agnes chewing a chicken bone. She was beginning to reach the conclusion that Torben was not used to laughing. Indeed, the smile that lingered after the laugh had dissipated looked so out of place on his face that she wondered if the whole performance had been staged in order to cover up the fact that he had been telling the truth and that he did, indeed, have no friends.

"Do you still live with your parents?" she asked him.

He made a noise from the back of his throat as if he were attempting to expel a small insect. After it continued for several seconds, she realised that he was, in fact, full-on chuckling. He had an extraordinary ability to show the external signs of mirth without ever actually committing to the emotion.

"No," he eventually replied. "Though you are not the first person to have made that assumption. They are in New Zealand."

"New Zealand? Why are they there? More to the point, why aren't *you*?"

"They are marine biologists. They went to Auckland as part of a research trip, and stayed. Did you know that nearly all species of sea turtle are classified as endangered? Once they are gone, there is no getting them back." Torben left a pause sufficient for Hannah to wonder whether he had been referring to the sea turtles or his parents. "My parents are trying to make sure they do not disappear. And to do that, they need to be in New Zealand." He stared at his drink for a moment before abruptly returning his stare to Hannah. "And, for the same reason, we need to get my machine onto the spaceship. How are we going to do that, Hannah?"

"Rachel told me to get the box to my house. I had planned to just drive us back there, with you hidden, but Ted's betrayal seems to have put a stop to that. Dotty will be closing up soon. They – whoever 'they' are – are presumably scouring the countryside looking for us."

"We must also assume that whoever those men were, they also know about Niels. Do you have any way of contacting Rachel?"

"Um, no."

"Did you not agree a plan?"

"No. Seems a bit daft now, but they just seemed, well, pretty confident that I would succeed. I didn't think I'd be chased by men with guns. I've not exactly been in this position before, you know."

Torben opened his mouth to reply but, instead of flat Danish tones, the room was filled with a loud squeaking of hinges from the large oak door to the pub which seemed to suffer from a heightened sense of the theatrical. Ducking under the mantle, Ted entered the room. He walked over to where Hannah and Torben were sitting, hooked his fingers around a three-legged stool from an adjacent table, dragged it across the concrete floor and joined them at their table in one fluid movement. The Brigadier had followed him through the door but remained there, standing with his hands clasped behind his back.

"What ho," Ted said as he joined them. "Mind if I join you?"

Hannah glared at him. "Ted, you utter tosser. How did you know we were here?"

"Hey, steady on, old girl," he said, looking genuinely hurt. "When you turned up in a bit of a pickle I thought it a bit thick, given that you'd been on the interweb and all that, so gave some old chums a call. Had to adhere to the old loyalties, you know. And, frankly, their reaction was so damn strong it seems I did the right thing."

"How did you know we were here?" asked Hannah again, in a voice of impending thunder.

An involuntary flick of his eyes towards Dotty gave Hannah the answer. "Come along, you two," Ted said, "we've got some cars outside. All very relaxed, no need for any unpleasantness. Just some chaps who want a little word, that's all. No biggie. Hm?" He stood and hovered over them as they looked at each other. Hannah shrugged, and the two of them stood. Torben started to pick up his bag, but the Brigadier strode over and grabbed the handle.

"I'll take that, thank you," said the Brigadier.

For a moment, Torben resisted. He looked at Hannah for guidance, but she could only shrug helplessly. He let go, stood, and stomped towards the door.

Ted continued to face Hannah, waiting for her to follow Torben towards the exit. Instead, she went to the bar. She removed a five-pound note from her pocket and pulled the swear box towards her, glaring at the old lady, who was focusing all her attention on cleaning a glass. She pushed the fiver through the slot, not letting go.

Hannah leaned over the bar. "Once in the service, always in the service, eh, Dotty?" she hissed. Then she pushed the note into the swear box. "Well, fuck you." The old lady did not look up.

Hannah turned and stormed out of the door and into the road, where the three black Audis were waiting. The Brigadier handed the rucksack to one of the men in black, who strapped it into the back seat using the seat belt. Torben was pushed into the rear of the second car and received the same treatment. The door to the third car was being held open for Hannah by Ted.

She walked over, smiling forgivingly at him. Without breaking stride, she veered at the last moment before having to duck into the car, and instead swung back her leg and brought her foot as hard as she could up into Ted's crotch. He made the sound of a football being punctured by a combine harvester and slowly sank to his knees, turning the colour of tea when someone had forgotten to take out the tea bag.

Hannah leaned over the crumpled body. "That's what you can do with your loyalties," she said. "And don't call me 'old girl' again, you poncified prick." She stood briefly to watch her erstwhile lover slowly curl into the foetal position while still standing, then slowly collapse onto his knees. Only when satisfied that he had fully received the message did she climb into the back of the car.

Chapter 26

Our Nature Lies in Movement

"This is un-be-fucking-lievable!" shouted the President of the United States, walking from one side of the tent to the other and back again, arms flailing along the way. "What idiots! What total assholes! A mass extinction! How could they be so stupid as to let this happen? Why did no one see what was going to happen? How could the scientists be so stupid? God, it makes me want to puke."

"Uh, sorry, *Mr* President," said the Prime Minister of Great Britain, who was the only other person in the room who had not yet sat down, "but – and with the greatest respect to your position of office – what the very fuck are you talking about? May I remind you that it was *you* that cancelled the international climate agreement that we had all agreed to?"

"I acted upon the advice of the scientific information I was given," shrugged the President.

"If I may be so bold as to correct you, you acted upon the advice of the scientific information that you asked for."

"Those scientists were unanimous in their opinion that climate change predictions were incorrect."

"Yes, that is true. They were unanimous. Both of them. So that was two experts denying climate change, two *thousand* experts confirming it. And you chose to act on the information from the two because that gave you a better chance of securing donations for your election campaign."

"Fuck you, you limey shit! My advisers consistently told me that this was the appropriate course of action given our objectives."

"Your advisers were chosen by you to achieve your objectives of improving your own business interests!"

The President of the United States stopped pacing at the point at which he passed the Prime Minister of the United Kingdom, and took a fast step forward to stand nose to nose with his transatlantic peer. He pointed a quivering finger into the ruddy face of the man he had personally approved as leader of his party.

"Don't you dare fuck with me, son," he said. "I was elected by the people of the U S of A to represent their interests. It is my duty to make America great again. That is what my people demand."

"Great? Great! Compared to *what*, exactly? And what is the point of being great if we're *all going to fucking well die?*"

"Gentlemen, please," said the President of Russia from his chair. "This is not being helpful. The three of us have been through so much together. Let us not start arguing at this most crucial of moments."

"Sergei is, of course, right, as he always is," said David Armitage, joining the three leaders through a flap in the canvas. They were in a room within a room, the white canvas walls rising vertically and then stretching overhead. There was only one entrance and exit, and it was guarded by two soldiers, even though they were within a compound which itself was guarded. David Armitage was not a man who ever took chances. "The others will be joining us shortly. We need to agree a plan. Or, to put it more exactly, I need to tell you what the plan is that you are going to agree to."

"Plan?" said the American President, having now resumed his pacing. "David, you need options to be able to plan. It seems to me there are only two options here, and one of them barely qualifies. We either stay on the planet in the knowledge that we will die, or we travel to another planet. Christ, I can barely believe those words just came out of my mouth." He ran his fingers through his artificially golden hair, then surreptitiously glanced at his palm to check for hairs.

"It is true that the enormity of what we have just heard is difficult to comprehend," said the British Prime Minister. "Given that, how can we be sure that they are telling the truth?"

The American President turned to face his counterpart again, this time with his hands on his hips. "Because they are in a goddam spaceship," he shouted, "and they are from the future! Plus, I ain't about to sit around waiting to find out!"

"There are two issues that face us," said David Armitage in a voice that had poured plenty of oil over troubled waters in its time. "Clearly, the four of us will be on those spaceships bound for a new planet. You have my word on that. Once you have each had time to accept this inevitable fact, you need to decide who you wish to accompany you. There are one thousand, nine hundred and ninety-six places to fill. That's a pretty long list I need to complete."

"*I?*" said the British Prime Minister.

"Yes, Douglas, 'I'. Other than ourselves and a few selected others who will form the new government, the remainder of the pilgrims will be people who are best placed to ensure our survival on this new planet. I will, of course, discuss practicalities with Rachel to ensure we have the best spread of skills. Then there are the animals to take, provisions and equipment. I have much to do."

"I, uh, guess we will need a lot of fertile young women," said the American President. One smirk and one raised eyebrow turned his way. "What?" he said, spreading his arms out in feigned innocence. "I'm only being practical."

"We will, indeed, need fertile young women. And fertile young men as well, remember. I have already made the arrangements to start populating the list with suitable individuals with appropriate skills."

"Hold on," said the American President. "You haven't told anyone else about this, have you?"

"Davis," said David Armitage with withering condescension. "Do I tell you how to win an election? No, I do not. I do it for you. So please, trust me to do my job." The American President shrugged in the face of an unanswerable truth. David Armitage continued. "Now, listen, there are two key issues we must address. Firstly, Davis is right that this must remain our secret for as long as possible. Widespread panic could destroy any chance we have of getting away on that spaceship unmolested. Rachel understands.

It is the very reason why they pretended to be aliens when they arrived. It is why they are hovering just out of reach. So choose your loved ones carefully, tell them to pack for a long trip, but do not tell them that life on Earth is doomed. Do we understand?"

The three men nodded in agreement, happy just to have secured their places on the ship.

"What about the woman Hannah?" asked the British Prime Minister. "And that Danish boy? Are we sure they know nothing about the true nature of the mission?"

"We don't know for sure," said the POTUS. "That Rachel woman could have told her."

The Russian President shrugged. "Why not just make them disappear now? It is easy enough, no?"

The American President laughed bitterly. "Oh, Sergei, why must you always be so impulsive?"

"We can keep them isolated. Hannah is favoured by Rachel. We do not want to create an issue should she wish to speak with her again," said David Armitage. "It just needs the three of you to keep this secret for as long as it takes to be ready to leave. If we achieve this, then we can populate the new planet with the people of our choosing and become the leaders of the new world. Are we in agreement?"

The three men nodded enthusiastically.

"And what is the second issue you referred to?" asked the Russian President.

"Ah, that is a much easier matter. It is one that you can leave in my hands. It is simply a matter of what lie we tell the world. Starting with your political peers, who will be so eager to hear how our meeting with the 'aliens' went. This is an area in which, I'm sure you gentlemen would agree, I have somewhat excelled over the years. Now, it is shortly after midnight, and I for one wish to be fresh for what promises to be a long day tomorrow. I have a *lot* of organising to do."

Chapter 27

All the Time in the World

Hannah awoke in a cot bed in the corner of a large square tent which appeared to have ambitions to be a marquee. In addition to her bed, the tent was furnished with a table and two chairs. Next to the bed was a clothes rail, on which hung her own clothes. She was wearing cotton pyjamas that had been provided for her. Next to the clothes rail was a wooden chair on which she could see clean underwear, still in the packet.

After a few moments of reorientation, she looked over to the entrance of the tent. She could make out the outline of a figure through the canvas, standing in the way that one might expect an armed guard to stand. She quietly slipped out from underneath the blanket and crept over. She pulled the flaps of the tent aside marginally, the threaded rope that held the canvas door together allowing a little give, and peeped out through the gap. She saw a female soldier, facing away from the tent, holding a gun against her chest.

Hannah returned to the cot and quickly changed into her clothes. Last night she and Torben had been driven to the camp near the spaceship. They had been forced to hand over their phones and had been given a meal. More specifically, they had been given a menu from which to choose a meal. She had chosen the duck chasseur (which had tasted sublime), accompanied by a half-bottle of Merlot that she had to admit was considerably better than her normal fare. They had then been separated. Hannah had been brought to this tent, by which time it was nearing one am. Realising how tired she was, she had had no other choice but to succumb to her captivity, and had quickly fallen asleep.

The new morning brought fresh determination, however. A rebel needs something to rebel against, and she found a spring in her attitude as she considered her options. Clearly, finding Torben was top of the priority list, quickly followed by finding the machine. He seemed to be a gentle soul, unlikely to have experienced anything like this before. Given that she had also never been kidnapped before, there was no reason why she should be any better at dealing with the situation than he, but she felt certain that that would turn out to be the case. One did not need to have experienced something to be able to deal with it; one just needed a certain…attitude.

Just the sheer invasiveness of what had happened made her furious. They had been abducted by, she presumed, the Secret Service, taken to a secret camp and…fed very well and given nice wine. Given the indignance she was trying to build, she put those last points to one side. All that mattered right now was that she was being held prisoner in a camp, as, presumably, was Torben.

She considered her options. The first was to overpower the guard; however, she quickly realised that, even if she had been able to take the gun, she had no idea how to use it. She briefly considered the idea of slitting the guard's throat from behind, but revulsion appeared even before the realisation that she owned no weapon that could achieve such a feat. Besides which, the tent was within a larger camp. Escaping from this little tent would only leave her with a far bigger challenge.

She crept over to the entrance again, knelt and peered out. There were tents either side of hers and opposite also, forming a road. From behind the soldier's legs she could see two men in black suits walk along from the right then turn, one holding the flap of the door open for the other to enter, giving her a glimpse of what looked like a briefing room. She put her head out a little further and looked left, seeing more tents and more people walking with purpose, in the uniform of either a soldier or a Secret Service agent.

"Good morning, ma'am," said a friendly voice from above. Hannah looked up to see the soldier smiling down at her. The voice carried a genial Scottish brogue seemingly at odds with the status of its owner. "'Tis a lovely day. Would you like some breakfast?"

Hannah withdrew her head quickly, pursed her lips decisively, then stood. She began to remove the large wooden buttons in the canvas from their loops. The soldier leaned her gun against the canvas of the tent and started to do the same from the outside. In a moment the two were face to face with each other through the widening gap. The soldier smiled awkwardly.

"Everyone loves camping, eh?" she said through her grin.

"Humph," replied Hannah.

"You were a sleepy head. Must have needed a good rest, eh?" The soldier's head nodded cheerfully a few times as if agreeing with herself.

"Um, yes. I guess I did." Had she really entertained the idea of slitting this woman's throat a few moments ago? Hannah checked herself. Toughen up, girl, you've got a job to do. Find Torben, find the machine, get onto that spaceship, work out how to get Gareth and family there as well.

Hannah stepped out. To her surprise the soldier did not immediately pick up her gun. Hannah eyed it for a second, wondering if she could get to it first.

"Sooo," said the soldier slowly. "What are you up to now then?" The words suggested a threat, but the way they were spoken was more akin to a mother enquiring after a bored child during the summer holidays. "Anything I can help with? What about that breakfast? It's over there." She pointed to the large tent which Hannah recalled coming out of last night. The soldier looked at her. "You'd better hurry though, they've almost finished. You and your big sleep! Ha!"

Hannah stared at her in disbelief for a moment. "What, you mean I can just walk over there? You won't try and stop me?"

"Me? Nooo. I was just here to make sure no one tried to get into your tent last night. You're world-famous, you know! There are crazies surrounding this camp, more gathering all the time. Can't take nae chances. Go on now, off to breakfast. Your mate is already there. He'll be waiting for you, I expect."

"Can I have my phone back, then?"

"Ah, that's nae for me to say. I'm just frontline." She leaned forward as if sharing a private joke. "Cannon fodder! Ha ha!"

Hannah backed slowly away from the soldier, who was still grinning while simultaneously nodding in the direction of the mess tent. When she was sure that this wasn't an elaborate trick, Hannah turned and strode quickly into the tent. It was empty except for two chefs, washing up in an extended kitchen area out to one side, and Torben, sitting on his own in the middle of a long trestle table. With his elbows on the table, his fingers on his head and a mug on the table in front of him, he looked as if he might have been attempting to communicate with his coffee. She went quickly over to where he sat. He looked up and grabbed her hand as she put one leg over the bench and sat down opposite him.

"Hannah!" he said. "I am so happy that you are safe. Are you okay? What have they been doing to you?"

"Well," Hannah replied. "It's a bit odd. They've…they've been really nice."

"Nice?"

"Yeah. It's been like staying at a newly-opened bed and breakfast in Devon run by a retired couple from Yorkshire. What about you?"

"Hannah, we are prisoners here. It does not matter that they have been nice to us. They have stolen Niels."

"Excuse me, madam."

Hannah looked up to see a short, hirsute man wearing a chef's outfit. He had bushy sideburns which joined onto a bushy beard, and thick black locks of hair crept out from underneath his toque blanche. He would have been about the same height as Hannah standing up, if you measured him to the top of his chef's hat. He was wiping his hands in a white Army tea towel which seemed to be attached to his apron.

"Um…yes?" Hannah replied.

"I was just wondering. Will you be wanting something to eat? We've started prep for lunch, but I can whip you up a scrambled eggs and smoked salmon if you like?"

"Oh, well, yes, that sounds lovely, thank you."

"On sourdough?"

"Um, well, yes, I suppose so."

"Cracked black pepper and sea salt?"

"Okay."

"Coffee or tea? We've got Earl Grey, Darjeeling or builder's."

"Builder's would be fine, thank you."

The chef backed away, still wringing his hands. Hannah turned back to Torben, who was glaring at her.

"What?" she said to him. "I'm not going to turn down salmon and eggs now, am I? Have you not eaten?"

"Well, yes, but just a little rye bread. And a bowl of chia porridge. But I did not order that – he just brought it to me. Said his wife's second cousin is Danish. It was very nice, actually. But what are we going to do, Hannah?" He leaned forwards. "We have to get Niels back, and we have to get him to the spaceship."

"'*Him*'?"

"Hannah! Please focus!"

"Okay, let's assess our situation. We're not exactly held at gunpoint, are we? Have you tried just getting up and walking out?"

"Well, no, but…but they *brought* us here at gun point. *And* they have Niels!"

"And I need to get Gareth onto that ship."

A voice interrupted them from the other side of the room. "She's right, you know. You *can* leave any time you want to."

David Armitage stood in an entrance to the mess tent opposite the one by which Hannah had entered. He was dressed mainly in black – trousers, jacket and waistcoat – offset by a white shirt with button-down collars. Hannah suspected he slept in black silk pyjamas. He walked over and sat on the other end of the bench, a few metres along from Torben. He sat side-saddle, undoing the buttons on his jacket as he settled in. Hannah could imagine that he rose each morning at five in order to spend an hour in the gym. Which, she further guessed, was in one of the wings of whichever of his houses he happened to be staying in. And they were probably all laid out the same. She found herself despising his world. He was in a demographic of one, which was reason enough for her to take an instant dislike to him.

"No one is stopping you," he continued. "You can just walk right out of the camp. Go on home, Hannah, my people will give you a lift. Torben, we'd be delighted to take you back to Bristol Airport. You can be on the next flight back to Copenhagen. Our treat."

"I'm not going without Niels," said Torben. "What have you done with him?"

"Him? Torben, Niels is a machine, not a person. And 'it' now belongs to us."

"No!" Torben slammed his fist on the table. "He is mine! I made him!"

David Armitage looked at the young man, not so much unmoved by the outburst as totally indifferent to it. "Torben, do you have any idea what you have made?" he asked.

The young man steeled himself as if he were a teenager standing up to his overbearing father for the first time in his life. "He is a time machine. But I don't really understand how he works. I just followed logic."

"And do you know why the aliens want the machine?"

"They're not aliens, they're humans. And no, I do not know why."

"Well, *I* do. And so do you, don't you, Hannah?" David Armitage turned to look at her, and Hannah felt something inside her wilt. Whoever this man was, he carried the air of someone whom people obeyed on an extremely regular basis.

"You do?" said Torben to Hannah. "Why did you not tell me?"

Hannah hung her head for a moment before looking Torben in the eye. "I made a promise, Torben. To Rachel. And a girl always keeps her promises, right?" She went to put her hand on his arm, but he moved it away. "Look," she continued, "Rachel asked me to help them find Niels. But they don't want its purpose to be publicly known. I imagine they are afraid of the reaction."

"Rightly so," said David Armitage. "You might not have seen the news for a while, but it's getting pretty hairy out there." He wafted his hand vaguely towards the rest of the world outside of the tent. "The Great Unwashed might be extremely dim, but one thing they don't like is uncertainty."

"So why *do* the...people from the future want my machine?" asked Torben, looking at David Armitage with pleading eyes. To Hannah he looked like such a small entity in that moment. Someone who had spent a lifetime trying not to be noticed, and yet carrying a burning ache inside to help people, to make a difference in the world. She saw in him a kindred spirit in that moment, as if unlocking her own desires and ambition for herself. On the surface the two of them were so different, and yet they had so much in common. The years standing outside the school gates, being at least a decade younger than the other mothers, just wanting to fit in, waiting for one of them to come and talk to her, and instead being ignored and left to watch them exchange gossip about people she would never get the chance to know. She had never imagined that the life of a young physics graduate could share some of the agonies of a teenage mother. And yet both represented a certain path to a certain destination.

"I think it best, Torben," said David Armitage, "that the reason why the humans from the future have returned to this particular time and require this particular machine should remain a secret for just a day or two longer. The ramifications of it becoming public knowledge would, to say the least be..." He twirled the fingers of one hand as he searched for the word. "Far-reaching. Do you not agree, Hannah?"

Hannah paused before replying. His smirk was really starting to get up her nostrils. She knew that he was right, of course, which only enhanced her irritation towards him. It was the reason she had not told Gareth; why she had kept the truth from Torben. The stakes were as high as it was possible for stakes to be, and she had no experience that might guide her as to what she should do. If word got out that the aliens had come to take a select few people away because all life on the planet would end in eighty years' time, the impact would be unthinkable. Quite aside from the fact that the spaceship would be completely overrun with people trying to escape, the remaining inhabitants of the world, not known for their ability to cooperate in a crisis, would descend into an unimaginable hell.

It had also occurred to her that this news was not exactly

new, that scientists had been providing the same predictions for decades now. Despite this, the population of the planet had, by and large, continued to insist on their freedom to live their lives as they wished, and to deny the fact that it was going to end in the destruction of their species. Now that incontrovertible proof had arrived in the form of humans from the future, the reaction would either be total panic or global apathy. Either way, making the news public would serve no purpose. The future was written, and it was not bright.

The future had already happened, at least for Rachel. The ultimate destiny. It could not be changed, which meant that Hannah had no part to play. As she had always tried to instil into Gareth, only worry about the things that you can control. In which case, there was very little point in thinking or worrying about the end of humanity.

There was something in that sentence that just didn't feel right. How could you just sit on your hands and do nothing if there *might* be something you could do?

Hannah looked at the man in the impossibly perfect clothes and the professionally enigmatic smile of a movie star. He carried himself in a way that made it clear that it would be his decision who went on that ship. And she had no doubt whatsoever that, as far as he was concerned, she and Gareth were *not* going to be among the chosen few. Yet Rachel had promised. She hated this man with all her might, with his smug nature and dominance over their future. Right now she especially hated the fact that he was right: she needed to keep this secret, irrespective of the promise to Rachel. She had no choice, and the fact that it was this smug little man telling her only served to double the irritation she felt.

"Who are you?" she said to him. "I mean, obviously you are someone important. Someone who was able to summon the most famous and exclusive people in the world. I assume that *was* your doing?" He bowed his head, yet even that came across as smug. "You tracked Torben down, had us all followed, and Ted was scared of you. And you are now the person who has come in to interrogate us – no, not interrogate, to smarm all over us. That again suggests you have considerable power and influence.

So I don't think you are just someone from the Secret Service, someone employed by the government. I think you *employ* governments." Still he just sat there staring back at her, his eyes filled with a malevolent twinkle. They reminded her of a cat's eyes, highly attentive and yet uninterested. "You are 'The Man', aren't you? I have a feeling I should be extremely afraid of you."

David Armitage threw his arms out wide as if to show he had nothing to hide. "I am an entirely benevolent force, I can assure you, Hannah."

"Then tell me your name."

David Armitage laughed. "You *are* a tricky one," he said, the laugh descending into the smile that Hannah was fast wanting to smash in.

"Will you *please* just tell me what these people want," shouted Torben. "What do they want with my box machine? Sir, you have to tell me."

"Torben," said Hannah, not taking her eyes off David Armitage, "I believe that you are a lot safer not knowing." Torben yelped in exasperation as Hannah continued. "I also suspect that we are not as free to leave as this man may have wanted us to think."

"Let us just say that, until we know how we are going to deal with the situation in which we find ourselves, you may indeed be safer under our watchful eye."

"And our phones? I want to call my son."

A chuckle came where no chuckle was required. It sat in the room for a moment like an unexplained smell. David Armitage shook his head sadly. "Well, we wouldn't want you accidentally informing the world of what you know, would we? You will both stay here as our guests for the time being. Your son has been informed that you are involved in some important governmental work and that he is unlikely to hear from you for a week or so." Hannah jumped to her feet even as David Armitage turned to address Torben. "We have not informed anyone of your...stay with us. It would not be unusual for you to be out of contact with your parents for a month or so, and you have no one else who we felt would miss you."

"What the fuck did you say?" said Hannah.

David Armitage looked affronted. "I am merely being pragmatic," he said with a shrug. "Torben has no friends."

"And he *is* right," said Torben, staring at the table.

"Not that. What you said about Gareth. He *is* on his way." Her voice became staccato, bristling with anger. "They. Have. Flights. Booked."

"All flights from Europe to the UK have been postponed. We need the airspace."

Hannah's voice was barely able to contain her anger as she leaned heavily on the table in the direction of Armitage. "That spaceship will not leave without me. I have an agreement with Rachel. And *I* do not leave without my son. And his family."

For just the merest of moments, David Armitage recoiled.

"That spaceship returns to the future with the white box," he said, composure regained. "That is their mission. That they succeed is evidenced by the fact that they are here, right now. I will deliver the box to them – rest assured, Torben. However, Hannah, the history of the future gives us no indication as to whether you – or, for that matter, your son – are also on the spaceship. As I have already offered, I will arrange for a private plane to take you to your son. Perhaps in two days' time. After we have left." Hannah felt like climbing over the table and pummelling his smug, tanned healthy face, but she had a strong feeling that, if she did so, a number of large men – probably dressed in black – would emerge from somewhere to stop her. And probably much worse. Even so, she still considered it for a moment.

"In the meantime," he continued, "the two of you will stay as our guests. We cater for the most important people in the world – a categorisation which, I am sure you would agree, now includes the two of you. The food and wine are therefore of the very highest quality." He waved an arm in Hannah's direction even as she drew herself up to launch another round of vitriol at him. "I am sure you will find our catering services to be to your taste, so please, do make the most of your stay with us. When you leave the mess tent you will find someone waiting to help you find your way to where you need to be." He turned and walked out of the room, Hannah's glare burning into his back as he went.

Chapter 28

The History of the Future

David Armitage left Hannah and Torben and walked across the field to the briefing tent, checking his watch as he did so. A few minutes to nine am on Friday morning. Two hours before he planned to address the world in a broadcast that would surely go down in history. A history which, it seemed, only had eighty more years to run, at least on this planet. The occasion would be pivotal not only for the world, but also for himself. The moment when he stepped from the shadows into the limelight.

First, however, came the chore of briefing the world leaders. He smiled at the irony of that expression. The world leaders weren't doing a great deal of leading right now. He was.

Inside the tent, the elite of the world had once again gathered as instructed. At the other end of the television cameras were many hundreds of politicians and business leaders. It was a TV channel available only to those who had, whether through choice or duress, pledged their loyalty to David Armitage.

The premiers of Great Britain, Russia and the USA took the three vacant seats in the front row. Immediately the Archbishop of Colchester stood from his seat in the back row, walked around the side of the seats and stopped in front of the British Prime Minister. He started barking a barrage of questions, his finger pointing and jabbing in the general direction of the seated man's chest. The British Prime Minister looked up at him with disdain.

David Armitage entered without fanfare and took his position at the lectern at the front of the room. The Archbishop of Colchester, realising the room had fallen silent, reluctantly returned to his seat. David Armitage waited until the archbishop had regained his seat, then raised his eyebrows in his direction as if to say 'If you're *quite* finished…'

"Ladies and gentlemen," he began. He allowed himself a momentary bask in the moment, the feeling of history forming into solid lumps out of the very air around him, out of the very air he exhaled. The anticipation was so great that even the most powerful people in the world had stopped in mid-sentence when he had entered the room. Would his words be repeated down through the centuries, perhaps inscribed around the base of his statue in the Parliament Squares of the future? He had never bothered to waste time on thoughts of his lasting impact on the world; he had been so busy building the present. He was not a man to be distracted by concerns of time stretching out in front of him – he had seen the results of such rampant egos, all legacy and legend. The outcomes of which they dreamed, masquerading under the myth of 'destiny', rarely came to pass.

David Armitage did not believe that the future was written. Fate is a concept that losers deny and winners credit. He had met many a person who thought that their success had been entirely of their own making, ignoring the lucky encounters and friendly gestures that were so key to their seemingly meteoric rise.

From a young age, David Armitage had believed in making his own pathway, and in taking every bit of help that fate would give him. In the early days he had quickly realised that the more drinks evenings he attended, the more likely he was to have a chance encounter. It was just a question of numbers, and attending the right events. As his 'little black book' of contacts had grown and his sphere of influence had widened, so the idea of his having a 'place in history' had become a genuine possibility. He would then redouble his determination to ignore its charms; to continue rolling the dice. Now, however, he was being given the chance to cash in on that hard work. Maybe it was time to accept. Like Croesus, he knew that the assessment of one's time stalking this Earth can only be made after you leave it. Time is a magician, distracting with one hand while holding the real truth in the other, only to be revealed once the illusion of happiness is complete. Was history forming within this assembly of the privileged arrayed in front of him, or was it to *himself* that the future was swarming?

"I have news," he announced. "The leaders of the United Kingdom, Russia and United States of America and I have met with the aliens and can advise you of the real reason they are here on planet Earth." He looked around the room at the pathetically eager faces. Control just came so easily. He allowed the pause to take effect before continuing.

"They are tourists," he said.

After a few incredulous moments, an animated murmur broke out around the room. Ignoring a conspiratorial wink from the President of the United States, David Armitage raised his hand to restore the silence before continuing.

"The aliens have been searching the galaxy, seeking life on other planets. We are the first that they have found, and they decided to engage with us. As well as wanting to find new life with which they may communicate, they are also seeking to share knowledge and understanding. As such, they are on an entirely peaceful mission.

"As you all know, we have, for some years now, given our space agencies the task of finding a planet that would be capable of sustaining human life, with a view to the long-term colonisation of that planet." He ignored the exclamation of outrage that came from the Archbishop of Colchester. "This was one of the first issues we raised with the aliens, and I am delighted to confirm to you all that such a planet does, indeed, exist. After much negotiation, I have managed to secure agreement with the aliens for them to assist us in beginning the colonisation of this new home for the human race."

He paused for a moment to allow the excited cries and yelps to subside. Now he caught a knowing nod from the Russian President.

"There are two additional spaceships which are ready to arrive. Between them, these craft are able to transport some two thousand people, along with building materials. The aliens have therefore agreed to take an initial group of specialists and experts to this new planet in order to prepare the way for a larger expedition in the future.

"This initial group of people – these pilgrims – will be away from Earth for some ten years before returning. We have already drawn up a list of the best people in their respective fields. The decades of training that astronauts usually undertake are no longer required, owing to the advanced nature of the alien spaceships – the journey will take only a few months and will be in the greatest of comfort. The aliens will be leaving in three days' time, and my people are already contacting the chosen few. I will be announcing this momentous news to the world. You are therefore to return to your respective countries and tell your people that their lives will continue as normal, while the reach of humanity expands beyond our wildest dreams."

Before the final words had been given the chance to swim in the silent air, the Archbishop of Colchester put up his hand to speak. With a sigh, David Armitage wafted a hand in his direction.

"Leaving aside the extremely concerning news of the deception of the Church regarding the real reason for the untold wastage of money on space exploration, who has made this decision that populating a new planet is a good idea? We need time to consider this in detail. We cannot just—"

"With the greatest respect," David Armitage interrupted. He had raised his palm like a traffic policeman to stop the archbishop talking, and now leaned his arms across the lectern in front of him as he continued to speak. "Actually, no, fuck it, without any respect whatsoever: would you please shut the fuck up. I would imagine that you would have enough on your plate, trying to work out how your belief in a one true God sits alongside the discovery of alien life, to worry about decisions that those of us who are actually in charge are busy making." He glared to underline his point, following the eyes of the archbishop as he slowly retook his seat. That felt good. "We will be populating this new planet because at some point we are going to run out of room on the one we have. This is an inevitability that some of us have been concerning ourselves with while others of you have been making rulings on subjects about which nobody actually gives a shit." He glared from the Archbishop of Colchester to the Pope and back again. "Now, I think you'll find I wasn't actually seeking questions. I have told you what will happen. You must now go and tell your flock." He wafted his hand airily in the direction of 'away from him'. He looked around the room. "That goes for the rest of you too. I will be making an announcement to the world later this morning. The Brigadier will coordinate your press releases to ensure that you are consistent. Nothing goes out without his approval."

David Armitage leaned forward across the lectern. Apply the Stern Face. Adopt the Voice Of Gravitas. "Now, listen to me, everyone. The world is on the edge. You will be aware of the riots and unrest currently taking place on all continents. People do not like uncertainty. What we are about to give them is the greatest dose of hope that humanity has ever received." He pointed his finger at the Archbishop of Colchester, who had been about to protest, before waving it across the congregation. "You must deliver this message exactly as I have set it out. A new planet has been found. People do not need to change their habits in order to prevent climate change. Their freedom to continue to consume has been protected. This is the message they want to hear, and you, my friends, are going to be the ones to deliver it to them. I have given you the tools with which to calm your people. Now go and apply them."

He stood up straight and stared at them, indicating not only that he was done, but that they were now to leave. Everyone stood up, chatter immediately filling the room. The British, American and Russian leaders also stood, but they continued to look to the front. David Armitage indicated with the briefest of nods that they should follow him, and he turned and walked back through the door from which they had come.

In the anteroom, the British Prime Minister spoke first. "Oh, David, I must say, that really was very good," he blurted. Armitage ignored the compliment.

"I am going back to speak with Rachel to sort out the details," he told them. "I need you three to follow my instructions, the same as everyone else. In the meantime, and with the utmost secrecy, prepare your plans. You are each able to bring with you five people—"

"Five!" said the American President. "But that barely covers my…needs!"

"He has six mistresses in America alone," laughed the Russian President.

"You could use two of my spaces if you like," said the British Prime Minister. "Most of the people I know I can't wait to get away from."

"Five plus yourselves. Anyone you like. I will have the skills needed for the new planet covered in the other people who will be coming with us – you leave that to me. Along with the animals, building materials, and so on. What I need from *you* is to keep the world from panicking. We need to depart this dying planet with those idiots thinking they are safe. If word gets out about the real reason for the arrival of these spaceships, the panic it would create across the world would mean we would probably never get away alive."

He watched the three of them walk away, jabbering and elbowing each other like newly elected prefects walking back to their classes. Just intelligent enough to do what they were told and to know a good thing when they saw it. They would make excellent princes in the new world.

Thirty minutes later, David Armitage sat at the cocktail bar inside the spaceship from the future with an ease that possibly only he, out of the entire population of the planet Earth, would have been able to achieve. His was the languorous sway of a batsman in cricket avoiding a ball travelling towards his head at ninety-five miles an hour; the elegant shifting of balance of a downhill skier taking a corner at a speed greater than the limit on a British motorway; the calm decision-making of the scrum half as he kicks cross-field to an isolated winger. He seemed to have so much more time than other people. For many, such a talent would be used for the accumulation of medals and awards. David Armitage had chosen to put his flair for grace under pressure towards the quiet accumulation of power.

He sipped at a Virgin Mary, nodding his appreciation to the unfeasibly tall member of crew behind the bar.

Perched on the edge of a bar stool next to him, Rachel was reading a piece of paper. Every few moments she placed it on the bar and, using a pen that David Armitage had placed in front of her, scribbled a few notes.

After a few more minutes of reading and scribbling, she handed the paper back to David Armitage.

"That seems fine. I don't agree with your gender ratio, and I have added a few specific skills that I think you will need. At the end of the day, however, it doesn't really matter because—"

"Because you are sat here. Yes, I know," said David Armitage, "but you are not the one going to settle on a new planet. You will drop us off and return to your own time, having set the wheels in motion. You know it works out in the end. However, you have already told us that you do *not* know exactly what happened at the beginning. *That* is *my* problem."

Rachel shifted weight on the bar stool. She was on her third Sex On The Beach and Dan, the cocktail waiter, was already mixing the antihol version. "What are you going to tell the people you select?" she asked. "I am just curious. I assume you will not tell them the truth. You cannot trust two thousand people to keep this a secret, and if the population of the world finds out, there will be widespread panic. We are here to collect the pilgrims, but we do not wish to leave behind chaos."

"Only the four people who you told will know the reason for your coming back in time."

"Four?" Rachel looked confused.

"Yes. Four. Myself and the three men who you told the last time I was aboard the ship."

"And the lady, Hannah, of course. She also knows. But I believe we can trust her. I rather like her."

"Oh yes, and Hannah. Of course. She is working with us."

Rachel eyed him carefully. "Will she be on the ship? I think I would enjoy her company for a little longer."

"Oh, of course. She has been essential in helping us to find Niels. She was one of the first on the list."

"And her family to come with us as well. I made her a promise."

"They are being flown here as we very speak." The smile flashed.

"And you definitely have the white box, the time machine?"

"Oh yes, indeed we do."

Rachel regarded him in the same way that a gopher regards a rattlesnake. She very slowly lifted her glass to her lips and took a drink, not for one moment averting her stare. She then held her glass in front of her for a moment, before slowly placing it back on the bar. David Armitage shifted his legs to move his weight from one buttock to the other. Rachel waited a few more underlining moments before she spoke again in a considerably lighter tone.

"There is *one* person who I would be very interested to meet before we leave. The inventor of the machine. It is not essential to the mission. But it would be quite fun to say that I met the person who saved humanity. Would you be able to bring him up to meet me? I assume that you have brought him here to be one of the pilgrims?"

"Of course you can meet him," David Armitage replied in a voice of camomile and honey. "He is in the camp at this very moment. Although I would ask that you descend from the ship to meet him. It would make things...easier as we prepare for departure."

Rachel studied the man for a moment, struggling to hide her disdain as she finally concluded with certainty that she could not trust a single word that he uttered. Then the smile of the preordained spread once again across her face. "Of course," she said. "As you wish."

"There is one last requirement I would like to request," said David Armitage.

"Can one actually request something that is required?" she stated matter-of-factly. "Surely a requirement is not something that leaves the option of being denied. Otherwise it tends to come across more like a demand than a request." The smile had not withered so much as a fraction.

David Armitage paused. It was an elegant pause, accompanied as it was by an almost imperceptible nod of the head. It was not too short and not too long. It was the pause of a man at ease with greatness, and when he spoke, it was with the timing of a comedian. "You are, of course, entirely correct. I expressed myself poorly." He took a sip from his drink, holding eye contact as if assessing the next move against a formidable opponent.

He sat up straight like a chess grandmaster about to make the defining move of the game. "We have an interesting relationship, you and I. We both know that whatever we do doesn't matter in terms of continuing the human race, because that has already been achieved in the future. Your bargaining position is therefore a weak one. You cannot force me to do anything, because you know that me agreeing or disagreeing will make no difference to the success of your mission. Likewise, I cannot demand anything of you, for the same reason." He paused, theatrically lifting the glass to his lips, then equally slowly returning it to the counter even though no liquid had passed his lips. "I do, however, hold one significant card that you do not. I don't care. I have no dependants. I am unconcerned about the future. You therefore have no power over me. Do I really want to be one of the pilgrims? I do believe that, right at the moment, I am ambivalent on the subject. I live in ultimate luxury on Earth, whereas if I travel with you to a new planet I will be going at best into the unknown, at worst into severe hardship. Why would I want to do that?"

"Because you will not go down in history if you stay here," Rachel replied. "If there is no future, there can be no history. Who do you think will remember you? If you come with us, you will be the founding father of a new civilisation. I am assuming, by the way you have adopted the role of spokesman and organiser, that you plan to be the leader of the new world. You intend to secure your place in the history of the future. A future which, if I may remind you, I come from, and whose history I do, of course, know."

The two of them looked at each other for a moment, sharing the mutual respect of two people at the very top of their game when one of them had just made a winning play. David Armitage finished his cocktail and slid from his stool. "Thank you, Rachel," he said, brushing down his suit. "I now understand my role."

"So what is your request?"

"I do, indeed, wish to be declared president of the new world. I therefore require that you make this decree to the pilgrims before you leave us on the new planet and return to the future."

Rachel shrugged. "Fine with me."

David Armitage walked to the door which led back into the main reception room, then turned in thought. "There are many practicalities to sort. Although I chose them myself, it is fair to say the three world leaders you met earlier were selected from a limited pool. I do not trust them to keep this secret for long. I don't actually trust them to be able to run their own countries, which is why I do it for them. I therefore need to move swiftly. Do you think it would be possible to leave after two days?"

"That is up to you to assemble the people and equipment that you want to go. My mission is successful. How comfortable the colonisation is for you, however, is entirely up to you."

Chapter 29

Sympathy for the Mouse

Hannah was perched on the edge of her cot. Torben sat at the table. The outline of the soldier could be seen outside the entrance to the tent. She had given the two of them a cheesy grin and a double thumbs-up as they returned from the mess tent.

The news that none of them would be on that ship to the future – and that Gareth was not, in fact, on his way to join her – had hit hard. She felt as though time was being sucked away from her. The extinction of humanity would be in eighty years' time. She would be long dead, and even Atticus might not be alive then. But what sort of life would he have? When would the reality bite? The descent of mankind was going to be far more brutal than the ascent. Humans had not been subject to a natural predator for many centuries. With nothing to fight, we had instead turned to fighting ourselves. The prospect of this narrative coming to its unnatural conclusion made Hannah shudder with fear.

She realised that the opportunity to gather her family close to her again had been driving her actions. She had even been mentally prepping for a change in her relationship with Monique. She had imagined greeting her with a kiss on both cheeks. She would avoid any critical comments, allow her daughter-in-law to help in the kitchen if she wanted to, or let her *not* help if that was what she wanted. The prospect of having her family around her had brought to the surface the reality of her loneliness. She wanted them near again, and she was willing to do anything to make that happen.

Hannah wondered if she and Torben should try to escape; but to do what? She couldn't tell the world what was happening, because the man was right: there would be panic. These were not stakes that Hannah had ever dealt in before. Saving humanity, finding new planets to populate, a stolen time machine. How was one supposed to know what to do when faced with issues of this magnitude? She had spent her life feeling marginalised; now the world had, quite literally, come knocking on her door. She wasn't equipped for this.

The morning sun baked through the white canvas of the marquee. She looked at Torben, some twenty years younger than her. The man responsible for saving humanity was staring glumly at his feet. He had created a machine from theories he only half-understood, and that made him a true explorer. He was intense in a way that she could never hope to achieve. Hannah liked beginnings and endings, an ordered world with rules that needed to be followed. That was how she approached life. As a preordained path. The task of getting through was to climb over the blockages to that path. Walk around, blast to smithereens, tread on, shove to the side; anything but expect the path to offer options. There had been times over the last few years when she had felt that she was just doing whatever was required to get through each day until reaching the destination. Head down, get on with life. Right now, however, she felt like a person who had been desperately trying to avoid stepping in puddles, only to finally look up and realise that the road was disappearing into a lake.

Torben was different. He didn't worry about where the road was going. He had stopped and revelled in the joy of simply splashing around in a puddle.

"Torben."

He looked over to her.

"Chin up." His expression did not change. She smiled, but knew it did not carry the conviction that was required of it, and it consequently drew no reaction. Then she remembered that English was not his first language. "Things could be worse, you know," she said.

He looked back at the ground. "What is there to be happy about, Hannah? They have taken from me the only thing I have ever been proud of. I was nothing, and I am again nothing. In between I think I might have been something. Who knows? I could even have made a difference in the world, but no one will ever know, not even me."

Hannah stood from her cot and went over to the table. She sat down next to Torben and leaned forwards, resting an elbow on the table and her cheek on the hand. She reached over and held his hand, looking at him imploringly. He looked up and returned her gaze, all the sadness in the world held in his eyes. She had the overwhelming feeling for a moment that Torben had not experienced much in the way of happiness in his life. Loneliness is more than just the removal of social contact. Hannah had the feeling that Torben had never even known that contact in the first place, that he was suffering from the absence of something that was, to him, mythical. Love. Companionship. Faith. Like a plant that cannot grow without light, she wondered how he had managed to create something so extraordinary in the absence of the faith of others.

"*I* know, Torben," she said. "You *are* a genius. That is something that you can always hold with you."

Torben scoffed. "I am not a genius. I'm just curious. I got lucky. I just put lots of theories together. I am the infinite monkey. That's what my professor called me."

"Oh, tosh," said Hannah, letting go of his hand and sitting back. "You have to study very hard to get that lucky. You invented a time machine!"

"Well, I had a lot of time on my own as a child."

"Were you the only child?"

Torben looked up at her. He looked as if he was struggling with himself for a moment, his forehead creased with the effort of the ignored. Hannah sensed that he was about to tell her something that he may have never said out loud before.

"I was adopted," he said. "My mother lost a baby in childbirth and was unable to conceive again. So my parents decided to adopt. They got me, six months old." Torben was breathing hard, the words coming slowly, like lava turning into newly-formed rock.

"After two years, my mother got pregnant after all. She had two children of her own, and spent all of her attention on them. She realised she had made a mistake in adopting me. It was, however, too late, and I grew up in a house with my family but separate from them. My mother could not bear the sight of me. I went to a different school, had a television in my room, and ate my meals in my bedroom while they ate together in the kitchen as a family. I think my father felt guilty, but he could not cross my mother. He would bring me books to read, and, with evenings spent in my room on my own, I devoured everything I could find. When I read Stephen Hawking's *A Brief History of Time*, it was like everything shifted, as if someone had taken the jigsaw puzzle of my understanding and moved all the pieces to form a different picture."

"Torben, that is awful. How could your mother treat you so callously?"

Torben shrugged. "It was not awful. It made me who I am today. How can I call that awful? It would be to wish that I were someone else. I do not. My mother set me on a path. My wish to help, to make a difference, came from being ignored, from not having a family. It led to this time machine. It was my past. I accept it."

"Did no one show you any care?"

"Yes. My father's brother came to visit me when my mother was out of the house. He would bring his guitar up to my room. He tried to teach me how to play, though I had no talent for it. I remember once, during one of the first lessons, I said that my fingers hurt. '*Du godeste*', he said to me. 'Imagine being someone unwilling to bear a little pain in order to make beautiful music.' I understood in that moment what he meant and what my life needed to be.

"I dedicated myself to the study of science, physics. I was not concerned that I did not have friends or that I was laughed at by others. I had my books, I had Niels Bohr and Stephen Hawking to guide me forwards. I realised that there *is* a god, a divine spirit guiding us, but it is the god of chaos, of infinite possibilities and random events. The ultimate destiny of everything is to become food for something else. There are only a certain number of atoms on Earth, and they have been constantly rearranged over billions of years. Sometimes they form themselves into dinosaurs, sometimes into giant redwood trees. Just at the moment, they have formed into me, and I believe that is for a reason. I just do not know what that reason is yet." He turned away finally, with a frustrated shake of his head. "I do not understand why everyone wants Niels so badly."

Hannah looked at the earnest young man sat opposite her. He was driven by a desire to do something; he just didn't know what it was. She envied his passion. She seemed to remember a time when things had mattered, when she had wanted to be in control, to make a difference. A time before she had felt that all her choices had been bad ones and somebody was punishing her for them.

The two of them looked at their chosen spot in the room for a moment, lost in their thoughts. Hannah spoke first.

"Torben, what are we going to do? I feel so helpless sitting here, and yet I'm not even sure if we *should* intervene. They are going to take your machine away on their spaceship, and that's wrong, but...well, what will change if we stop them?"

"Hannah, I am very simple. I only know that there is a right and a wrong thing to do, and taking Niels from me is a wrong thing. I want to get him back."

It was a decision. It was something to do, which must surely be better than not having anything to do. Hannah stood, emboldened by having a cause. "Right. Let's do *something*. I'd rather be making a decision or two of my own than sitting here waiting for whatever that man decides is going to happen to me." She waggled a limp hand in the direction of the mess tent as if David Armitage might still be there.

She walked to the exit of the tent and went outside into the sunshine. The guard raised her eyebrows and smiled warmly.

"Just, uh, getting some air," said Hannah.

"No problem," said the guard. Then she saw Torben behind, and smiled at him too. "Hi!" she said to Torben, and nodded again at Hannah.

"Hey, say, something has just occurred to me," said Hannah. "I think I left something over there." She pointed vaguely in the direction of the mess tent. "Well, to be more precise, we both did. We're just going to go over and get it, okay?"

"Oh," smiled the guard, "No, I'm afraid not. Nah, I can't allow that, I'm afraid. Sorr-ee. I've got my rules to follow like everyone else." She rolled her eyes. "Got to keep you here," she continued, gesticulating with her gun back into the tent. "Got new instructions to, you know, shoot you if you try and leave. Don't want to have to do *that* now, do I? Ha, Lord, no!" Hannah and the guard both gave a short false laugh to each other as Hannah stepped back into the tent. The guard tilted her head and gave an extra nice 'sorry' smile as Hannah's shoulders slumped. She stepped back inside the tent, closing the flap behind her.

"You see?" whispered Torben urgently. "I told you! This is serious! We are prisoners, and that must surely mean that they wish to use my machine for bad reasons. We have to stop them, Hannah!"

"Yes, but it would be pretty dumb to die in the attempt, right? That wouldn't help anyone."

Torben shrugged. "I am not concerned."

"Yes you are, you just don't know it yet. If we run out of there and she starts firing her gun at us, I'm pretty sure you'll suddenly start caring, right? Am I right?"

Torben paused for a moment, then nodded his agreement, with only a little reluctance.

"Look," she said, putting a hand on each of Torben's shoulders as she spoke to him, "what they are planning, it is...big, yes. But I don't think it is something we have to stop."

"You *do* know, don't you? You know what this is really all about."

Hannah allowed her arms to fall slowly back to her sides. They had known each other a ridiculously short time, and yet he was looking at her as if she held all the answers to his future. The last person to look at her like that had been her son when he was a boy, and she had ensured that he grew out of *that* particular habit soon enough. There was something of the child about Torben; he was determined and decisive in some matters, but desperate to be told what to do in others.

She so badly wanted to tell Torben about the future of humanity; the enormity of it was almost too much for her to bear alone.

Besides the danger of the news becoming public, she had no idea how Torben would bear up under the weight of such knowledge. If she told him, and he tried to act, then both their lives would be in danger, and nothing could be achieved. The future was written. Rachel had come back from a future that took place on another planet. That meant inevitability for those left on planet Earth. The future was decided because, in this very rare instance, it was known. She felt angry, frustrated. The man had given her no options but to wait while the future was prepared without her.

She looked again at Torben, standing like an impatient puppy waiting to be fed. How much should she tell him about what he had set in motion with his invention? How was he going to be able to cope with the news of his role in the history of humankind? Was he the saviour of humanity, or the person who had doomed the inhabitants of Earth?

Chapter 30

The Ever-Moving Shadow

On a typical Friday mid-morning in late summer, Tanning's Farm, at the heart of the Mendip Hills, would usually be surrounded by empty cars. Parked on either side of the road which runs next to the farm, the owners of the cars would at that very moment be cycling across the footpaths of Black Down. On this Friday, however, a slew of black Range Rovers with even blacker windows lined the road. Two identical vehicles were stopping any traffic from coming down the road and past the farm entrance.

As he sat at the table in the middle of a large kitchen, David Armitage wondered why it was that farmers always lived in such huge houses. As the old joke went: how do you know that someone is a farmer? They tell you. How do you know how hard it is to be a farmer? They tell you. And how do you know what time in the morning farmers have to get up? They tell you.

And yet, despite such protestations of poverty and misery, farmhouses were almost always sprawling piles of main house and outbuildings. In the early days of the Armitage Foundation, when favours had been won by providing access to the inaccessible, farmhouses had been among the most sought-after properties for conversion by many of his customers.

If the rustic décor of the living rooms had not been to David Armitage's taste, the kitchen suited him perfectly. It had all that he required. Broadband, a decent signal for his phone, and two lockable doors. Throughout the previous night and now into Friday morning, he had been coordinating the selection, contact, movement and, ultimately, removal of two thousand people from the planet. He was arranging for the selection and collection of animals and plants that would be sufficient to feed the pilgrims. As well as domesticated animals, there were decisions to be made about which wild animals would best survive the inevitable period of captivity. The installation of giant aquariums to house selected species of fish. On more than one occasion he had mused as to how Noah had coped without the availability of international communications.

Delegation was an art form that Armitage had perfected many years ago, the objective being to extend one's influence across as many levels as possible. He had once arranged the removal from office of a troublesome (i.e. incorruptible) president of a medium-sized African country while walking up the fairway of the third hole at Wentworth, simply by placing a call to the CEO of an international aid organisation. Eight further calls had resulted from the original made by Armitage, with only the original CEO being aware of the originator of the action.

With the various world and business leaders busy getting themselves ready to leave the planet, David Armitage had been clear to assume the responsibility for updating the world on events relating to the spaceship. One call to his communications manager had meant that, within twenty minutes, all the news agencies and social media outlets around the world were informing an eager public that wonderful news regarding the aliens would be announced at midday. A makeshift studio had been assembled in front of the farmhouse. Make-up had been applied. Now, with ten minutes to go before the live broadcast, David Armitage was reading once again through his speech and preparing for his grand unveiling.

Like the falling tree in the forest that has no one to hear it crash, what use was power if nobody knew that it was you wielding it? He had always drawn his satisfaction from holding the largest amount of control of any one person in all of history, and yet was entirely anonymous. He was unarrestable in any country in the world. He waltzed through airports and borders, and yet no border official or policeman knew who he was. They would simply run a check on his ID and receive the response that the person should be waved on their way immediately, with the highest possible authority. He could walk into any bank in any country, present his ID, and within twenty minutes would be given access to as much money as he required. And yet his picture – let alone his name – had never appeared in a single newspaper article. His was a level of anonymity not available even to the most wealthy.

For decades this had been enough; ideal, even. But now a new temptation had been placed in front of him. The chance to lead as well as control. To have a taste of real power, visible power; to be acknowledged. For many years he had anonymously controlled individuals and the fate of nations. Now he had the chance to go down in history as the man who changed the destiny of humanity itself.

He had seen the effect of power on a person many times over. The changes to their character as they begin to discover that they have control over the thoughts and actions of others; as they start to feel more inspired by themselves than by others; as they begin to wonder whether they weren't somehow built differently to other people; as others start to treat *them* differently. Finally the hunger for power itself obscures the sight of the goal and, in a final confirmation of the rampant ego, they begin to refer to themselves in the third person. That was when the person most revealed themselves.

He had trained himself in spotting such signs. David Armitage had become increasingly adept at taking control over the powerful. He followed his one simple rule: control the thing a person wants the most.

Was this now happening to him? Was he finally succumbing to the honey trap of power? Did he feel different to everyone else? Yes. But then, he *was* different to other people. And he had been controlling the thoughts and actions of others for a very long time now. He knew the traps and would be able to spot them. No, this elevation was inevitable. He hesitated for a moment, and thought: yes, I *will* use the word. He looked at himself in the mirror that the make-up artist had left on the table for him, and said under his breath, "David Armitage, this is your destiny."

There was a knock at the door.

"We are ready for you, Mr Armitage."

He stood, turned, and walked out of the door and into his future.

*

David Armitage was half-sitting, half-leaning, elegantly against a table. In the background were two rustic bookcases that had been carried out from the front room of the farmhouse.

The woman standing next to the camera began to count down from ten, the last five with only her fingers, and the red light on the camera flicked on. An estimated five billion people were now staring at him, live.

"Ladies and gentlemen of the world. My name is David Armitage. You do not know me, and yet I feel I know each and every one of you." Sincere smile, micro-hand gesture towards the camera. "I have been asked to speak to you on behalf of the aliens currently hovering in their ship in the United Kingdom.

"I would like to take a few moments of your time to tell you about this alien spaceship. I will tell you why they are here, and what is going to happen next. And don't worry – it's great news!" Knowing smile, double hand-spread.

"As you will have seen from the videos posted by Hannah Siggers, these aliens are friendly. Indeed, they are here to help us. We know that climate change is altering this planet that we inhabit. We *could* use less electricity. We *could* have smaller families, stop throwing rubbish on the floor, stop watching videos of kittens on our phones and use bicycles rather than sit in our cars, but who wants that, right?" His quick laugh was genuine, as he imagined the confused and awkward chuckles of a race being told what it doesn't want to hear.

"The time has come for us, the human race, to find somewhere else to live, in order to continue our expansion. Governments have, for many years now, directed the space agencies to search for a suitable planet, one that exhibits the atmospheric conditions necessary to support human life. And I am delighted to be able to tell you that one such planet has been discovered." Pause for effect.

"This joyful news does come with a 'but' attached, however. This planet was identified several years ago – however, it is beyond the reach of man. It would take three hundred and twelve years to travel to this planet. We do not have sufficiently powerful space vehicles to take people to this new planet and begin colonisation.

"This is where the aliens enter our story. Their ships are much more advanced than our own. For the last decade we have been sending messages into space, in the hope of finding life on another planet. These messages have proven to be successful beyond our wildest dreams! These aliens – these friendly aliens – have come to help us to colonise this new home for humankind.

"Two additional spaceships will shortly be arriving at Washington and Moscow. Together, these three spaceships will be taking an initial seeding party of two thousand settlers to our new planet.

"We have carefully selected the people who will form the first party to travel to the new planet. They will face great danger. These brave pilgrims will require a wide skillset, as we do not know the challenges to be faced. I am sure we carry your goodwill with us.

"I will be leading the party and, at the request of the aliens, will assume presidency of the new planet in order to coordinate the colonisation. Once we have built the infrastructure to support civilisation on this new planet, we will return for those who wish to join us.

"By establishing this new population, we create an overflow for planet Earth, and a solution to the climate change crisis. Much like explorers of a different age, we humble few take these giant steps for the betterment of all.

"Your future is secured. You are now safe. May your god be with you."

Phase 3

The Future Arrives

Chapter 31

The Calendar and the Clock

The sound of voices in disagreement reached Hannah and Torben through the canvas. Initially indistinct, they had been getting louder, then seemed to stop just beyond the point at which they would be heard clearly. The words were being spoken in staccato, as if the person wanted to raise their voice in anger yet needed to keep the volume down in order not to be heard. It created an effect a little below a commotion but certainly more than a conversation. They looked at each other quizzically. A sense of urgency seemed to invade Torben. It was more than just his face; his whole body seemed to suddenly become impatient. The anxiety in the tone of the voices outside the marquee travelled in to Torben, and now continued its journey to Hannah. Maybe they would be separated, maybe...well, maybe anything.

"Hannah," he said to her quickly. "You know what is happening, don't you? I can see it in your eyes. My time machine is what enabled them to get back here. I am guessing they need to take it with them in order to build another box to communicate with Niels. Okay, that makes sense." He paused, looking through her as he processed what he had just said, thinking through talking. He leaned forwards and towards her, the bench squeaking as he did so. He clasped his hands together in a double fist and turned his head slightly upwards to look at her. When he eventually spoke, it was with the inquisitive voice that had been his default during almost the entire short time that Hannah had known him. "But why would they want to do that?" he asked. "There must be a reason. And how do they get it back to before their time in the future, to be able to build their machine? What is the reason behind all that is happening? I want to understand everything."

She leaned forward herself, reached across and took both his hands in hers. "That is the one thing I can't tell you, Torben. I promised Rachel. You have to trust me. I just cannot see any other option than to sit here and wait. I am sure that, when they leave, we will be released."

"And my machine will be gone. No. That is not good enough." He stood abruptly, turning away from the table, flushing in the face. Hannah now stood too and placed her hand gently on his shoulder.

"Torben, please. I know it is hard to see your machine go, but sometimes the best thing to do is nothing."

He shrugged her hand off his shoulder, then whirled around to face her.

"No! This is not good enough!" He took a step back and stood very still. Turning his head to the side so as not to look at her, he took three deep and deliberate breaths. He paused for a few extra moments, listening. The voices continued outside, no nearer nor any clearer. Then he turned back to Hannah and spoke urgently, as if aware that they were about to be interrupted. "Do you know why I became interested in time, Hannah? Why I studied this subject so much, why I even started to build a machine from the theories of time? It is because I wanted to change things. To change how we talk about time, how we are so obsessed with getting things done, with being efficient. We got set deadlines at university to hand in our work. Why? Learning should not have a time limit. We hold exams at the same time each year. Why? What relevance to how much I have learned does how far the Earth has rotated about the Sun have? My entire life has been dictated by the clock, by stakes in time placed there by others. Imagine if we broke free, Hannah. Imagine if we could move around in time. Imagine if we lived our lives by the calendar and not the clock."

He thrust out his arms towards her. "Look at my wrists, Hannah. What do you see?" She looked, but shook her head slowly. "No watch. I have never worn a watch in my life. It is the demand of others that drives the obsession with time, not *my* needs. If my mother had not been concerned with time, she would

not have adopted me, and then she could have been happy. I..."
Torben choked back his words for a moment, before continuing.
"All I ever wanted, Hannah, was a life with a purpose. And
purpose does not have a deadline. That box has given me purpose.
I don't know why it is so important, but I am not going to simply
let them take it before I find out."

A slow handclap came from the tent entrance, which Torben
had obscured from Hannah's view. Torben turned, and they saw
the source of the sarcastic clapping. David Armitage. He was
flanked by the Brigadier. The soldier who had been on guard
stood at their shoulder.

Armitage stopped clapping. "Fine words, young man," he
said to them. "A fine speech indeed. I hope someone was writing
that down." He turned to the Brigadier. "Were you writing that
down?" The Brigadier impassively shook his head in reply. David
Armitage looked around as if asking a crowd of people the same
question, even though only the three of them had entered. He
turned back to address Torben with a mocking sad face. "Well,
isn't that a shame," he said. "Nobody wrote down your speech,
Torben. It would seem that nobody will remember it. Rather
appropriate, really. You see, it is not only history that is written by
the victors. It is also the future."

Hannah regarded him through narrowed eyes. "You really
are a self-absorbed little prick, aren't you?" she said.

David Armitage spoke quietly into a walkie-talkie, and they
could hear his voice crackle just outside the entrance. A soldier
entered the tent carrying Niels, then walked to the middle and
placed the white box on a table.

"Your insults do not affect me, Hannah," he said. "I have
dedicated my life to helping others to achieve what they desire.
And I now intend to save humanity. The fact that I also gain from
the process does not change the good in what I am doing."

Hannah folded her arms and glared at him with all the
venom that a lifetime of being patronised could summon. "Oh,
I do understand all of that entirely. It doesn't, however, change
the fact that you are a prick. All you have just done is to describe
how you are a prick. It is relatively simple to justify any actions –

something I suspect you have spent a lifetime doing. Explanations, justifications, call them what you will – these things do not define how much of a prick you are. It is your actions, the facts, that speak for themselves. You are a prick because you act in your own self-interest to the detriment of others. *Why* you do that is irrelevant. *That* you do that is what makes you a prick. And, if I may add, one of the biggest pricks I've ever had the displeasure of coming into contact with."

David Armitage appeared to be momentarily stumped for words. From the effort he was making in subduing a laugh, Hannah wondered if she and the Brigadier might have enjoyed dinner together if circumstances had been markedly, enormously, different.

The Brigadier suddenly cocked his head, then stepped aside and back to hold the tent flap open. Rachel and Clarence entered. He stopped next to the Brigadier, she strode on into the room. She placed her hands on her hips and looked quickly around the room, clearly searching for something. She did not acknowledge Hannah or Torben, but her face lit up the moment she saw Niels.

"Is this the machine you require?" asked David Armitage.

She walked over to it and chuckled. "It seems so strange to see it here. But yes, the handwriting on the side is the same. This is definitely our machine."

"Rachel," David Armitage said, gesticulating to Torben. "I believe you wanted to meet the inventor of the time machine."

Rachel turned and stared at Torben. She regarded him like a child seeing a hippopotamus in the zoo for the first time. It was as if her brain were shifting gears, working things through, getting up to speed. Then, as slowly as the dawn, realisation began to spread across her face. Her hands came back up to her hips as her expression continued to go through the emotions; past realisation, into a smile, finishing with a full-blown chortle. It was the laugh of someone who has just got a joke they had been told three weeks previously. It was as if she had just realised the why of everything, and she couldn't believe it was all so obvious.

For the first time, Hannah began to find Rachel's calm and happy demeanour rather irritating.

As the guffaws and the groans finally subsided, when Rachel had herself under control again, she looked briefly at Hannah, and then at length at Torben. He held her stare, his own countenance being of someone with their own realisation. "So are you Torben?" she eventually asked him.

"It's you," he replied to her.

"You are the inventor of the time receiver?"

"I am," he said. "And you. You are the woman I saw. When the machine worked."

Rachel stared at him and gave a half-smile as she comprehended what Torben had just said. Her expression was kind, that of a person who had met someone with whom they had shared an experience that few others could ever understand. Then her brow furrowed, and she regarded him more as an animal in a zoo, full of realisation and confusion to a degree both equal and alternating. It was as if she were trying to work out the answer to a puzzle that she just could not solve.

"You are black," she said.

Hannah looked at Torben to share surprise at such a comment, but Torben did not return the look. Instead he glared at Rachel for a moment before replying.

"Yes. I know," said Torben, through tight lips. "You, I am guessing, did not."

"No. No, I didn't," said Rachel. "Although it does explain a few things."

"What are you talking about, 'it explains a few things'?" said Hannah, hands on hips and eyes darting accusingly. "Exactly *what* does the fact that Torben is black explain?"

Torben now turned to look at her. "Hannah, you are so very lovely. But you are also blind. Look around you. How many non-white people do you see? You were on the spaceship. You met the rest of the crew from the future. How many non-white people were there?" He looked at Rachel, who looked at the floor, avoiding his eye. "I am guessing there were none. Imagine the people who this man" —he gestured dismissively towards David Armitage— "will be packing onto those three spaceships. The self-titled 'great and the good', the people who run the world.

233

How many black people do you think will be included? How many non-white people will they be taking with them?"

Hannah looked at the ground, unable to hold his gaze momentarily. "It...it didn't occur to me."

"No," Torben said. "It doesn't tend to. I, however, have spent a lifetime being ignored because of the colour of my skin. I was the only black-skinned child at school. I was bullied because I was different. To defend myself I retreated into my studies, because I could not continue to accept that—"

"With the greatest respect, could you shut up now, please?" interrupted David Armitage, stepping forward. "We have a lot of work to do, Rachel. You wanted to meet the inventor of the machine, and now you have. Can we please get on?" He turned sideways, showing her the exit.

Rachel did not move, not even to turn her head and acknowledge that she had been spoken to. "Torben, I offer my apology. I only remark upon the colour of your skin because it was unexpected. I care not either way, but humans are an entirely white race of people in the future. I pass no judgement on this. Maybe the pilgrims made this a conscious choice, maybe it just worked out that way because we landed where we did. A quirk of fate, perhaps. It does, however, make for a rather lovely irony that it was a black man who invented the receiver." Rachel stepped forward and offered her hand. "May I thank you, sir, on behalf of myself, of the people of the future. On behalf of all humanity. I would like to tell my government upon my return that I shook the hand of the man who invented the time receiver."

Torben eyed her for a moment, looked at her hand then looked at Hannah. "Pilgrims?" Then he turned back to Rachel. "I think I understand. You have just told me that I do not go wherever it is that you are going. I won't be one of your 'pilgrims'. That I don't make the cut. Because I am black. And then you ask to shake my hand. Madam," he continued, the rage building in his voice, "You may go back to your government, tell them that you offered to shake my hand, and that I then told you to go fuck yourself."

Rachel stood up straight and pulled her arm back to her side. She looked sad for a moment, disappointed. The momentous moment had not turned out as she had dreamed it might. Suddenly, she brightened. "No," she said. "I think I'll still tell them that we shook hands. After all, there is nobody here to dispute it."

Chapter 32

The Future Is Ours

Torben flushed. His whole body became a ball of involuntarily tensed muscle as he stretched his arms downwards and simultaneously pushed his shoulders back and up, as if seeing how high he could make his head go. He held his arms tightly by his side, fists held horizontally, clenching then unclenching like a grabber in an end-of-the-pier claw machine. He rocked up onto tiptoes and back down again. His head shook minutely for a moment. Hannah reached out and held him gently but firmly on the arm. Torben turned his head violently in her direction, and she could see the fire and anger in his eyes. Armitage had retreated to the back of the tent and leaned insolently against one of the poles, arms crossed and one foot across the other. He coughed to get Torben's attention, then turned towards the Brigadier, as if inviting Torben to notice that his number two had drawn his pistol and now held it at his side. Torben slowly removed Hannah's hand from his arm. He stopped rocking and his shoulders relaxed a little.

"Well," said Rachel flatly. She turned as if to leave, then looked at David Armitage. She paused, then, reaching a decision, spoke to him. "Just wait one more moment," she said. "He deserves to know. It is only fair." Then, turning once again to address Torben, she said, "What you have created, Torben, is a time machine."

"I. Know." Torben replied slowly and deliberately, the adrenalin rush having passed. "I have worked out *that* much. But you mentioned 'pilgrims'. That suggests you are leaving with some people – presumably to take them back to the future? I would like to know why. Why is all this necessary?"

David Armitage righted himself and stepped forward. His matter-of-fact tone was that of the chairwoman of the local choral society deciding that the committee had deliberated quite long enough about which flowers should be presented to the conductor at the end of the upcoming performance and that it was time to move on to Any Other Business. He took one extra step in order to be in front of Rachel and spoke to Torben and Hannah with the tone of someone who was only going to say this once. "They are not taking us to the future, Torben, they will be taking us to populate another planet. There is going to be a mass extinction on Earth. The human race will be wiped out from Earth in some eighty years' time. A small group of around two thousand people – the pilgrims – will go to another planet to continue the species' existence. Your time machine is a receiver, and it must therefore go with the pilgrims so that they are able to build the transmitter in the future, enabling Rachel and her crew to return to the present, thereby saving the human race." He spread his arms out. "Okay? Hm?" He looked at Rachel with eyes raised. He then turned to the Brigadier and gave an impatient nod toward the exit.

Torben stared back at him with the blank expression of someone who had been given either wonderful or terrible news. It was as if his brain required all its power to process the information it had been given, leaving none left to power the facial muscles. His mouth sagged slightly, and a small amount of drool threatened to make its exit at the side. Hannah elbowed him sharply, and he awoke like a sleeping princess kissed by a prince. He turned his head slowly toward her. His empty stare went through her.

"Torben," she hissed. "Torben, what is the matter with you?"

Words began to form silently as he moved his lips. Eventually he managed to silently mouth the words 'save the human race'.

"Yes", said Hannah. "I couldn't tell you before. But yes. Torben, you have saved the human race."

For a moment she thought he was going to explode. Tears were leaking from his eyes and rolling down his cheeks. He turned back to Rachel. "How does it work?" he asked her.

"I don't know," said Rachel. "I leave that to the experts back home. All I know is that this is a receiver, and we had to build a transmitter." Hannah saw Torben mouth the word 'transmitter'. "It took us a long time to get around to it, but we eventually set to work on building a machine that would dial in to connect to your machine. Then we had to find the exact second that you pressed the button, which was a matter of trial and error. Then, eventually, everything clicked and, hey presto – here we are!"

Torben was now beaming like a boy with a new bike on Christmas morning. To Hannah, the transformation from the rage-filled indignant young man standing next to her a moment ago to this peaceful, beatific person was nothing short of remarkable. He turned to her and pulled the sort of face that a husband might show to his wife at an awards ceremony having just been announced as the winner. It carried a mixture of amazement, thankfulness, and gratitude that it had all been worthwhile.

"This is destiny," he said to Hannah. "There is nothing I can do to stop what has already happened." Turning back to Rachel, he said "Please. Take the machine with my love and blessing." He swept his arms towards them and bowed slightly.

David Armitage smiled at the young man, and said, "Well, actually we already have. But, yeah, you know, thanks and all that." Then he turned to Rachel. "We have an awful lot to do. If you're done with this historical moment of yours, can we please now go?"

Now it was Hannah's turn to feel her bile rising. It was as though Torben's anger had needed somewhere to go on leaving him and had found her. She glared at David Armitage as they turned to leave. He had everything. He *owned* everything, and everyone. He could have used that power for good; instead he had used it to accumulate wealth and power for himself. He, as much as anyone, was responsible for the problems of the planet, and now, rather than face them and deal with the consequences, he was simply going to leave.

"Wait!" she shouted. Rachel turned round and smiled benevolently.

David Armitage stopped but did not turn around; instead he looked upwards and sideways, and sighed. *"Really?"* he said. "Do we need *another* speech?"

"Yes, we damn well do," said Hannah. She took several steps to stand in front of Rachel. "We had a deal," she hissed, pointing her finger in the other woman's face. "You've got the machine. You now need to keep your part of the bargain. Me and my family must be on that ship when it leaves." Hannah poked her finger twice into Rachel's breastbone. "We had. A deal."

Rachel stared dumbly for a moment, then turned to address David Armitage. Hannah went back to stand next to Torben.

"She is right," Rachel said. "I did promise her that she and her family would be on the ship. Arrange it, please. We will wait until they are safely on board."

"No."

Hannah could feel the early afternoon heat soaking through the tarpaulin of the huge tent. Outside, the coos of a wood pigeon sitting on the apex of the roof of the tent could just be heard above the sounds of multiple generators. Helicopters had been arriving every ten minutes, and she could now hear another in the distance making its way down to the landing pad. Inside the tent, however, there was silence. Rachel opened her mouth to speak and then let it slowly close again.

Rachel and David Armitage stood facing each other, holding each other's stare. Armitage, legs apart to twice the width of his shoulders, head lolling insolently to one side and arms folded. Rachel in the same neutral stance as always, feet not quite together and one hand held in the other in front of her tummy. The Brigadier stood behind the shoulder of David Armitage, still holding the gun. Hannah had barely noticed Clarence until now, who had moved to be standing near enough to Rachel to provide support if necessary.

It was Rachel who spoke first. "Mr Armitage, this is *my* mission. *I* am the captain of the ship that you plan to be aboard to travel to the new world. I am therefore *requesting* that you arrange for Hannah and her family to be on the ship when it is ready to leave. And I do expect my requests to be granted." This was the

239

first time Hannah had detected a measure of grit in Rachel's voice. She approved – it rather suited her. Rachel smiled her saintly smile and continued. "Besides, we know the mission succeeds. There is no need for argument or disagreement. Please – just make the arrangements."

David Armitage continued to stare at her. Hannah saw nothing in his eyes other than calculation and assessment. "We do, as you have so often pointed out, know that your mission is a success," he replied. "The fact that you are here proves that a group of pilgrims successfully colonises your planet. Your ship and crew will return to the future as heroes. There is, however, no evidence to suggest that you will be among them."

In one fluid movement, David Armitage reached down and behind him. He took the gun from the Brigadier's hand and lifted it in front of him at head height. With barely a pause to register the look of protest on her face, he pulled the trigger and fired a bullet through Rachel's forehead.

The violent intrusion into the tent of the noise of the gun was truly shocking. As Rachel's brains left the back of her head, both Hannah and Torben physically recoiled and took a step backwards. As Rachel fell to her knees, Clarence let out a scream and clutched his palm over his mouth. As she folded forwards and landed face first into the grass, David Armitage handed the gun back to the Brigadier by holding it up to his shoulder. As the Brigadier reached forward to take it from his grasp, David Armitage turned to Clarence.

"I am in charge of your mission now. I will be captain of your ship, and you will take orders from me and no one else. Do you understand?" Clarence was still staring down at the inert body of his former commander. David Armitage raised his voice. "Do you understand?"

Clarence looked up at him and slowly nodded.

"Good. Now, get back to your ship, please. We proceed as I have instructed." Without so much as a glance at Hannah and Torben, he turned and walked out of the tent. The Brigadier also turned away without looking at them, but his gait was of someone desperate to avoid their accusing stares.

Clarence again stared at the body of Rachel, crumpled at his feet. His hand now slipped so that it was held to his face only by the fingers hooked into the bottom lip. One soldier took his arm and gently led him from the tent, his stare ripping from the inert body on the floor only when the flap of the entrance folded back into place.

The guard from outside the tent now came inside, stepping over Rachel's body to Hannah and Torben. She gestured that they should also leave the tent in front of her. They dumbly followed the instruction and walked back to the mess tent.

Hannah briefly considered trying to overpower the soldier, but she felt as lifeless as the body they had left on the floor behind them. Nothing mattered any more. The future was finite after all. She felt overwhelmed by the enormity of what she found herself in the middle of. The fact that she would not have Gareth and family with her, let alone that none of them were to be on the spaceship. The fact that Atticus would not have children who would survive; that the future contained a full stop. There would be no more history, because there would be no one on the planet to talk about the past. That one life could stop so abruptly, that all life would be going the same way. The fact that a man could do what he had just done, and with so little concern. She sat heavily at one of the tables, sitting sideways in order that she could continue to stare at the grass in front of her. Torben sat on the bench across the table.

"Hannah," he said to her gently. She stared back, barely acknowledging that he seemed to be coping with the shock of what they had just witnessed better than she was. "Hannah," he said again. "We are okay. We must focus on the good things. You are okay. Your family will be all right."

She looked up at him and saw the kindness in his eyes. The love he had to give that had nowhere to go. The need to love and to be loved.

Then, to her surprise, he smiled. Now, after what they had just seen, he chose this moment to smile? He held both her hands in his. She swivelled sidewards to face him, their hands now clasped together across the table.

"Hannah," whispered Torben. "That was shocking. I know.

I too am shocked. But I have realised something very important and I need you to listen to me. It is okay to let them go. I can see everything so clearly. The future is ours now."

She continued to stare blankly at him, the words hitting her with a delay. What was he talking about? The humans from the future had come back to save just a tiny number of people. The rest were being left to become extinct. Gareth was stuck in Switzerland, his new home. She was in the middle of making a history that had a finite shelf life. What sort of sick joke was fate playing on her now? She felt like the nameless character in an episode of a long-running TV show, destined to be killed off long before the end.

Torben seemed to still be talking. She zoned back in.

"Do you not see?" he was saying. "My invention will save the human race. I made a better future. I now have everything I have ever wanted. Now it is *your* turn."

"My turn? Torben, I don't understand. What can I do? That man…he…he has won. He gets to go. We have to stay. We all die. There is no choice here. How can that future be changed?"

"I will show you how. You will be able to make choices. You actually have so many choices right now. There *is* a path. I have seen it. Can *you* find it?" He was grinning at her now, as if wanting her to answer a riddle that he had already cracked. Torben's intensity somehow gave her the smallest sliver of hope where she thought there would never be hope again. He didn't speak, but his expression seemed to be urging her to work something out.

All she felt was resignation. Was this really it? Had the final scene actually been played? Was the future now set, and all that was required was for them to play out the inevitable? If there was truly only one path stretching ahead of her, surely the only action remaining was to take that first step, back into her life, return to the river of her destiny to float through to the inevitable conclusion. The destiny that Rachel had foretold; that which had already happened and therefore had to happen.

And yet.

She looked at Torben without seeing.

There was indeed something that nagged and niggled at her.

Something ill-fitting, out of place. Destiny was supposed to be immutably logical. Fate was supposed to fit perfectly as the reality of the future combined with the circumstances that led to it. That is how history works. Things just *mesh*. And yet now there was something out of kilter that she just could not shake. The shock at what she had seen ten minutes previously, mingled with the anger that those who had done so much to cause the extinction of humanity were going to be the ones to escape to a new life. But there was something deeper in the logic of the time machine that was troubling her. What had she heard that had managed to lodge itself somewhere within her, like the proverbial grit in the oyster?

"What am I missing, Torben?"

He didn't answer. He wanted her to solve the mystery herself. But she did not even know what the mystery was. The future was not only written, it was also known. Rachel had told them. The grim reality depressed her, and yet, even though such thoughts were useless to her, they still infiltrated her thoughts.

She realised that she was still looking at Torben. In a few days' time, they would be the only two people on the planet who would know the future of the civilisation of Earth. What was she supposed to do now? Just get on with her life? How was that even possible, knowing what she knew about how the future was going to end?

Endings. Was that what was nagging at her? There is no such thing as an ending. Once a goal has been reached, life continues on. There are things that happen *after* endings. So, if this is not an ending, what is it? Beginnings and endings are an artifice around which to weave a journey, a narrative. Something to hang time on. So was this the convenient end of this particular story, or just a pause in the narrative arc?

"Endings?" she said. Torben nodded, eyes wide now, encouraging her to go on.

She did not want it to end. Who decides the point at which to end this story? There is no author to make such calls. It is time for the players to take over the control of their own tale. It might have already been told; Rachel had made that clear. Hannah's future was Rachel's past, yet who the hell was Rachel to determine Hannah's future?

"You said I will have choices, Torben. Choices. Options."
He smiled like a parent watching a baby taking their first steps.
"If the ending has been written, then there cannot be choices. So
maybe the ending has not been written. But how can that be so?
Someone has come back from the future and told us. We have
eighty years."

And now something else approached her. The logic of time.
Now that Hannah allowed the possibility that she might shape
her own destiny, she approached what she knew from a different
direction. And suddenly the pathway became clear. Torben let go
of her hands and she sat up straight.

Eighty years. That's all the time in the world.

Hannah felt something change within her, like the final piece
of a jigsaw puzzle clicking into place. There was a chance that she
might have a destiny after all, one that she could influence.

Torben sat back, revelling in the dawning realisation that had
been creeping across Hannah's face. He clapped his hands together
once, held them together under his chin, and looked at Hannah
expectantly.

It was the realisation of someone who had awoken to find
themselves not where they expected to be. Of someone who has
realised that they are not stuck in traffic, but that they *are* traffic. Of
someone who has been complaining about litter, then realises that
they could always just pick up the litter. Of someone who had only
started working behind a bar while they waited for a better job,
but now described themselves to people at parties as a bartender.
Of someone who did things not because they made a conscious
decision to, but because they just happened, and as a consequence
was never actually happy because they always wondered what else
might have happened. It was the dawning awareness of someone
who liked a glass of wine to relax after work, thought it was cute to
say you couldn't leave a bottle unfinished, then realised they were
an alcoholic. Of someone eating sushi for the first time aged fifty-
three. Of someone nearing the end of their final school holidays
after leaving school, only to realise that they weren't actually on
holiday at all but had entered adult life. Of someone becoming
irritated at waiting for the receptionist at a small hotel, only to

realise they hadn't read the sign that politely asked them to ding the bell for service. Of someone changing their definition from 'woman' to 'mother' then forgetting to change it back again. Of someone realising that they are not only the problem, but also the solution.

Hannah was about to answer Torben's hopeful gaze when the tent flap was again peeled back. The Brigadier entered with six soldiers, each wielding an automatic weapon.

The Brigadier addressed Hannah. "We have come to take you home," he said.

Chapter 33

Here Be Dragons

At one in the afternoon that same Friday, Clarence returned to his ship to tell the crew the terrible news about their captain. At three, David Armitage gave the crew their instructions for the loading of the three ships, which had now landed at their designated points in America and Russia. Over the next few days, activity around each of the spaceships increased dramatically as they were prepared for departure.

The perimeter of the compound that spread out from beneath the spaceship had been moved back by a mile on all sides, which meant it now passed just the other side of Hannah's cottage. A giant and impenetrable fence had been erected around the whole compound in the sort of short timeframe that only becomes feasible when the lives of the politicians who approve the budget are at stake. Two huge gates represented the only way in and back out, and were repeatedly opening to allow traffic to the spaceship, closing immediately the vehicle had passed through.

Around the gate, but kept at a distance of a hundred metres or so, was the media village. Groups of reporters lounged in the weekend sunshine on collapsible chairs, unaware of the gravity of the real reason for the dramatic increase in activity. Although there had been nothing new for them to report on for some time, they remained ready to jump up and pester anyone who walked past their camp. The reporters themselves held their microphones on their laps; the camera operatives sat with their equipment on the grass beside them.

Army trucks thundered across the Mendip countryside to the spaceship throughout Friday and Saturday. The ground was churned into mud as the lorries trundled across the fields from the road and on through the gates, leaving a trail of squashed wildlife in their wake. There were five fields to be crossed even before they reached the perimeter. The five-bar gates at each side of the fields had been removed but that still left an insufficient gap for the trucks to pass through, so they had simply driven through the hedge. The first had tipped over the nest of a lesser whitethroat, the eggs being crushed under the wheels of a second truck that followed shortly after.

The area underneath and immediately surrounding the spaceship was covered in activity. The moles, voles, badgers and birds that had previously occupied the fields had now fled completely. A large door had appeared at the rear of the ship, serviced by a second and much larger lift, this time with a floor. The trucks drove around the ship in a wide arc, eventually delivering a seemingly endless succession of crates for loading into the ship. Most of the crates were sealed, some marked 'Fragile'. In one area was a long line of cages containing various animals. Most of the animals were destined either to be eaten or to be bred to provide the food of the future. A few of the cages contained animals that would form an intended zoo. The line that curved away from the rear of the spaceship mimicked animals waiting to board Noah's Ark, only with metal bars.

One particularly intrepid family of rats made it onto the ship by eating their way through the corner of a crate filled with bags of seed. Queues of large crates sat two by two on the grass waiting to be loaded. A man driving a fork-lift finished the chocolate bar that constituted his elevenses, threw the wrapper out of the cab and onto the rapidly diminishing grass, put the vehicle into gear and recommenced unloading the crates from the Army truck in front of him to the end of the queue.

All weekend, Hannah and Torben listened to this activity from inside Hannah's cottage.

At mid-morning on Sunday, the first helicopters began to bring the first pilgrims. Throughout the day they continued to buzz constantly back and forth from the airport. They flew over the media village like enormous attention-seeking bugs, sending newspapers, plastic coffee cups and water bottles spinning into the hedges, from where no one attempted to retrieve them.

The helicopters landed some one hundred metres or so from the spaceship, their passengers disgorging then running in a crouching position as if they were actors in a movie about the Vietnam War. They were waved onwards to the base of the ship by a succession of soldiers wearing elbow-length white gloves. From there, in groups of four, they giggled and shrieked their way into the air and up to the door via the invisible lift.

A few of the more prescient travellers stopped at the doorway and looked back, taking one last look at a world that they had been told they were unlikely to ever see again.

As they stepped into the ship, each person shared a very similar expression. Still amazed by the feeling of flying that the invisible lift gave them, they would then step gingerly into the first big room, looking around expectantly. They were then met by one of a series of attractive young men and women, hosts and hostesses, who would usher them through a door which led to the rest of the ship.

At around three o'clock on Sunday afternoon, the fifty-two-year-old British CEO of a large European petrochemical company, his twenty-eight-year-old Danish mistress, a sixty-one-year-old middle-ranking but extremely loyal politician from Italy and his twenty-nine-year-old supermodel wife of six months all made the auspicious journey into the air to the threshold of the spaceship. As they took their first gawping stare from the entrance door, there was so much to take in that they did not notice the now former British Prime Minister standing in the doorway to the cocktail lounge watching their embarkation. He sipped at a large gin and tonic. He delicately spat a juniper berry back into the glass.

He turned, wandered back into the cocktail lounge and joined the only other person in the room: David Armitage, who was seated at the cocktail bar. David Armitage proffered his glass; the two of them clinked a 'cheers' and drank.

"Tell you what, David, old chap," said Douglas, the former British Prime Minister, smacking his lips. "Any chance we can take this cocktail waiter with us? He does knock up a fabulous G&T."

"He will be going back to the future, I'm afraid, Douglas. However, rest assured I have included enough quantities of the finest wines and spirits to last a lifetime, as well as the winner of the World Bartender of the Year 2017, who also happens to be a dab hand at carpentry. He makes model churches out of matchsticks in his spare time."

"Well, Armitage," said the former British Prime Minister. "You certainly have this all under control. It's like you've been waiting for this moment all your life."

David Armitage gave the singular mirthless laugh of someone untroubled by modesty. "In many ways I have, Douglas," he replied. "For many years I have been collecting people the way Davis collects businesses and Sergei collects political opponents. I have taken particular notice of people with multiple areas of expertise. I had no particular reason for doing so – it just seemed a sensible thing to do. And now here we are. Heh! I guess you could call it serendipity. Or perhaps fate."

"When will you tell them the truth?" asked the former British Prime Minister.

"Not until we are well away from Earth," David Armitage replied. "They have already been told to have little expectation of seeing their loved ones in person again, but nevertheless we do not want to take the chance of a revolt before we have left."

"*Ciao bello!*" came a voice from the other side of the room. The others turned to see the now former Italian Prime Minister occupying the doorway. A beautiful young woman stood just behind him. "Hey there, my clever friends," he shouted at them. "Are we ready to reboot history?" He cackled, then, noticing their stares, stepped forward, bringing the woman into the room by the elbow. He gestured towards her. "This is Martina." She nodded to them, they kissed on the lips, then she turned and left the room. The former Italian Prime Minister walked over to join the two men at the bar, his face beaming as broadly as a child who has just been given a certificate in assembly for Best Attendance.

The British Prime Minister spoke first. "Crikey, Marco, what happened to your wife? I mean, Maria. Where is Maria?"

The former Italian Prime Minister winked at him in response.

The former British Prime Minister winced slightly. The former Italian Prime Minister did not notice. "Hey," he replied, with a shrug. "We are settling a new planet and continuing the human race. We want the future to be beautiful, do we not?"

"Well, of course," said the former British Prime Minister. "This is very true, but it does beg an obvious question: why, then, are *you* coming?" He and David Armitage leaned towards each other and cackled loudly. The former Italian Prime Minister wobbled his head as if to say: 'You guys!'

The former British Prime Minister slowly stopped laughing, then put his glass on the bar. "Mind you," he said, almost to himself. "I *liked* Maria. I had hoped she would be my bridge partner."

"So," said the former Italian Prime Minister to David Armitage, "I assume Sergei and Davis are on target for their own spaceships to be ready. How did they take to the idea of you being top dog of the new planet?"

David Armitage drained his glass, emerging with the grin of a victor. "Let's just say I don't think it came as a surprise. However" —he paused to look earnestly from one to the other and back— "I will be counting on your complete support just in case any ideas...develop. I don't wish to have any discussions about the fact I will be the leader of the new world." He looked at the former Italian Prime Minister, who threw his arms to the side and took a step backwards in complete submission. Satisfied, he then turned to look at the former Prime Minister of Great Britain.

"You're welcome to it, old pip," said the former British Prime Minister with a scoff. He turned to address the former Italian Prime Minister. "I didn't even want to be leader of my own party. Only did it because Armitage here had some pho...had given me little other choice. I'm glad to be out of it."

After a brief silence, the former Prime Minister of Italy seemed to decide that a clearer display of his loyalty might be appropriate at this juncture, and chose to elaborate on his response. "David," he began, with a weary sigh, as he oozed his backside onto a bar stool. "I have been in politics all of my career. It has brought me great power and wealth. Has it brought me happiness?" He shrugged extravagantly. "I am not sure I even know what the word means. I have been forced to do things the memories of which I keep locked in a box in my mind, for if I allowed myself to dwell upon them I would certainly..." He tailed off for a moment, then sat up straighter in his chair. "No, I have reached the top, and I found it barren. My desire in our new society is to have a place at the top table. I have had a degree of power for so long that I would not know how to live without it. However, ultimate power wearies me. I always assumed the end of my addiction would come with a bullet in the back of the head or a jury trial. Instead I have the chance for a new start, and I intend to take it. I am more than happy to serve."

Without even the merest movement of his head, David Armitage looked at them both in turn. He stared directly into the eyes of one former leader, slowly closed his eyelids, then, when he reopened them, he was staring at the other. He went from one to the other and back again.

Eventually, with the silence and tension drawn from decades of unspoken threats filling the room to near elephantine proportions, David Armitage spoke to them. It was not so much a monologue as an address. They both had the distinct feeling that the former President of the USA and the former Prime Minister of Russia would have received the same speech.

"Gentlemen," he began, "do you know what Roman map writers used to write on the areas of the maps that they could not chart, that were beyond their knowledge? They would simply write, in large letters across the virgin territory, 'Here be dragons'. No one had ever seen a dragon – how could they, given that dragons do not and have never existed? They had no knowledge about what might have been in those territories. There might have been dragons, theoretically, but they did not actually know one way or the other. Man being an animal that cannot admit to ignorance, however, they had to pretend that they *did* know. And so they wrote 'Here be dragons'.

"We, gentlemen, are heading into uncharted territories. We do not know what awaits us. This" —he gestured around the cocktail bar—" is a luxury that we must savour, for it will not be available to us for very long. Life on the new planet will be harsh to begin with. We are loading the spaceships with everything we need to erect shelters quickly then build houses and homes. We do not, however, know what beasts there might be on this new planet. This is not the time to be writing 'Here be dragons'. It is the time for admitting that we are heading into the unknown, and preparing accordingly.

"This is what David Armitage has been doing. While you have been choosing partners, I have been organising. Preparing. The leadership skills needed in the new world will not be the same as the ones that have propelled you gentlemen to the top of your respective greasy poles. David Armitage will be the leader in the new world, and you gentlemen shall be my generals. Our first task will be to set up the legislature for the new community that we will be starting. All that is required to ensure this new system works is that you, along with several other chosen ones, remain utterly loyal to me. Divided, we will fall. Unite in support of David Armitage, and none of you will have anything to fear from the dragons."

He reached forward and held his hand palm down in the middle of the three men. The others looked at each other. Douglas, future Chancellor of the Exchequer, put his hand atop that of David Armitage. Marco, future Secretary for Home Affairs, followed suit. The hands of Sergei, the former Russian Prime Minister and the future Minister for Justice, and Davis, the former President of the USA and future Secretary of Commerce, were with them in spirit.

"To new beginnings – to the future!" said David Armitage. He pushed his hand upwards, and all three men lifted their arms into the air in declaration of their alliance. They settled back onto their chairs and drank as if to seal the alliance.

David Armitage stood up on the foot rail of his stool and leaned over the bar. He reached down, searching, before bringing back a bottle of vodka. He unscrewed the lid and poured three measures into three glasses. They chinked, and he and the former Italian Prime Minister and future Secretary for Home Affairs downed theirs in one gulp. The former British Prime Minister and future Chancellor of the Exchequer, however, had paused with his glass held in mid-air.

"David," he said slowly. "Can I ask you a question?" He paused, though he was not waiting for an answer. "Are there any trees on this new planet?"

"Trees?" replied David Armitage. "Well...I don't know. Why?"

"You mentioned that you are bringing a carpenter. I just wondered if there will be any trees. You know. For wood."

The three men looked at each other in silence.

Chapter 34

The Vanishing Point

The newly expanded perimeter fence meant that Hannah's cottage was now fully inside the compound. She and Torben had been marched across the fields back to the cottage in a daze that Friday afternoon. They had been partly in shock from witnessing the callous murder of Rachel, but also reeling with thoughts about what they had realised, and what they might do about it.

In the cottage they had found enough food and wine on the kitchen table to last for several weeks. The reporters were no longer camped outside her door; however, soldiers had taken their place. David Armitage was clearly taking no chances of Hannah somehow preventing the departure of the three ships. The Brigadier had lent her a phone in order that she could call Gareth. She had eased her son's fears, promising to call him again in two days' time. The Brigadier had then left them, taking the phone with him.

All Friday afternoon, the two of them had sat at the kitchen table, talking. Often one would be sitting while the other paced around the room. The only two people on the planet who knew the reality of the noisy activity outside the cottage throughout the day and night were making plans.

Hannah had initially expressed her understanding of the situation to Torben hesitantly, feeling her way as she attempted to articulate a concept that she had only just grasped herself. It had been as if making the idea real through words contained a power that she was reluctant to release.

"Rachel is the one that has delivered to us the knowledge that the human race is to die out," she had slowly begun, hoping the pieces would come together by the time she finished speaking. "That knowledge will be taken with the pilgrims who will colonise the new planet. They pass that information through their descendants, where it will eventually reach…Rachel. Who brings it back from the future as a fact." He had beamed at her now. "It's a loop, Torben. Which means it is not real. The future, our future, is still uncertain. Nothing has been decided. And nothing has changed."

He had clasped her hands in excitement. "Oh, but it has, Hannah, it has. Because we have had a spaceship land. Everything has changed. And we will be the only persons left on the planet who were in contact with the supposed aliens. You brought the message of the arrival to the world, and the people of the world will listen to you again. You can tell them the truth about what the future will be if we do not change. They will listen to *you*." He had underlined the point by poking her in the arm.

The enormity of what he seemed to be proposing had taken a few moments to permeate. She, Hannah Siggers, a no one, an everyone, delivering a message of that magnitude? She had shaken her head involuntarily, in denial. Finally, she had found her voice.

"Torben, for all our lives, for generations, the future has offered possibility and excitement. Computers and jetpacks, economic growth, endlessly increasing house prices, the internet with its access to cheap shopping and free porn. Even Mad Max had a cool vehicle. The future was a place we wanted to be, and we couldn't wait to get there. And now I'm going to come along and tell everyone that the future is a disaster. That we're in danger of being Wile E. Coyote, sprinting over the cliff edge, our legs pumping away as we look down and realise it's too late.

"People don't like to have their dream taken away from them. You can't sell reality. People have tried to tell this message before, and we just laughed at them, idiots in the street with their placards. 'The end of the world is nigh.' It's a standard joke. Why are people going to listen to me?"

"Because we've never had people from the future come back on a spaceship and tell us that we're all doomed before."

And so they had begun their planning, a simple campaign which could – which must – affect the course of life on Earth.

Late in the afternoon, Hannah's eyes had alighted on the cigar box that remained where she had placed it three days ago. Had it really been only three days since she had resigned from her job? She had thought of the little girl whose picture was inside the box, who had presumably buried the time capsule. She would be fifty-something now, if she was still alive. Had that life been all that the child dreamed of when she placed the time capsule in the ground? Of course not. Nobody gets everything they expect, good or bad. Life is not about riding the pre-written script, of allowing your destiny to happen to you. It is about reacting to what happens in the best way you can. That is what Hannah needed to do, she had realised. She and Torben knew something that nobody else on the planet – or at least who was going to remain on the planet – knew. That the future was not written. That it could be changed.

She had opened the lid and looked again at the contents – the photographs of the girl's family, the lock of hair from the beloved family pet rabbit. Three days earlier, she had been pondering whether to add something of her own to the box before returning it to the ground. Now she wasn't completely sure if there would be anyone on the planet to open it again. She had thought of all the time capsules around the world, buried with the expectation of being dug up one day, instead just destined to rot in the ground. Messages sent but never received, like the last telephone ever to ring.

She had felt the urge to bury the box again. She had wanted to honour the intention of that little girl, but there had been something more. She also hadn't wanted to admit that humanity was doomed. She had wanted to make her own statement that there *would* be someone to dig up that box in the future. What might she add to the box, what gift to the future could she bestow? Something personal? It had felt an uncomfortable notion. Acts driven by ego were not what was needed right now. The future needed someone in the present to act in something other than their own self-interests. This box did not belong to her. She had closed the lid, locking the family together inside once again. As she stared at the cigar box, she had realised that she had a duty to that little girl; to accept the fact that she had been placed in this position of knowledge. To take action.

And so, when the Brigadier had come by for one final time on Saturday, Hannah had asked if she might be allowed to speak with Clarence before they departed.

By Sunday morning the rolling news dominating the output of radio stations provided constant updates on the exciting and selfless adventure that the brave pilgrims were about to undertake. There were profiles of the brave souls who had volunteered, tributes paid to the business leaders and politicians who were selflessly heading out into the unknown. The mysterious David Armitage had gained particular attention but, try as they might, journalists could find nothing about him, other than press releases from the Armitage Foundation. Consequently, Armitage was portrayed as a saintlike figure, a combination of Christopher Columbus, Mother Teresa and Nicolas Cage.

The radio delivering this white noise of news into the cottage was turned to a high volume in order to counter the sounds of lorries delivering supplies, and helicopters delivering people, to the spaceship. Only Hannah and Torben knew that the people were elopers, not crusaders; that the supplies were to build a new world that no one else on Earth would ever see. The deceit and betrayal being handed to the entire population of the planet would have been almost too much to bear, had Hannah and Torben not been too busy making their own plans.

Now, just as Armitage and the others were congratulating each other, Hannah sat at the kitchen table nursing a mug of coffee. Torben had not yet surfaced from the spare room. She lifted Agnes onto her lap. Agnes did not attempt to resist arrest, instead wriggling into the flat-on-your-back-legs-in-the-air-like-you-just-don't-care position to afford the greatest tickling opportunities. Hannah was now absentmindedly stroking the dog's tummy.

Clarence sat on the opposite side of the table. Hannah had placed a mug of coffee in front of him, but it was as yet untouched.

He sat scrunched up like a nervous schoolboy in front of the headmistress, hands in his lap, feet flat on the floor, staring at the table.

Clarence clearly believed that he was abandoning the population of Earth to their extinction, given that he was now sitting in front of her looking as penitent as the Pope. When Hannah had answered the knock at the door ten minutes earlier, he had requested to talk to her with the air of a husband asking to be allowed back home after his infidelities had been discovered.

"I'm surprised you aren't needed on the ship," she said to him, breaking the silence. He looked up at her with eyes that were even more baleful than usual.

"I have nothing to do," he said with a shrug. "That man has taken over. He gives orders to the crew. At first they looked to me for confirmation that they should do as he told them, but after a while I stopped answering. Instead I spend my time thinking... preparing for our return."

"What will you tell Rachel's family?"

Clarence stiffened a little. "That she was a hero. Which is true. This expedition will be seen as a success. We have the box, and we will deliver the pilgrims. Her name can now go down in history as a great explorer. I will make sure of it."

Seemingly cheered a little, Clarence reached forward, picked up the mug and sipped the coffee. "Oh boy," he said, "clearly Mr Armitage forgot to pack some decent coffee. We don't get this in the future."

"Why not take some with you?"

"You know it does not work like that, Hannah. If they had taken some with them, we would have coffee in the future. I can't try and change that. If I give them coffee to take then something must happen that will result in its destruction."

"No, not *them*. *You*. Here." Hannah stood and entered the larder in the corner of the kitchen, reappearing seconds later with an unopened box of coffee. "Give that to your scientists in the future and see if they can reproduce it." She put it on the kitchen table and sat back down.

Clarence stared at the packet for a moment. "Our instructions for this mission have been very clear: that we must not do anything that might change the course of history. This is why we have been so very careful, why we have barely left the ship. The choices made by the people in this time must be their own choices. However, I am not sure that anyone considered the possibility that the future *we* return to could be improved by something that I brought with me back from the past." He picked up the box. "Thank you."

There was something innocent about this man that Hannah found herself drawn to. He was like a puppy, something you wanted to protect. Pathetic, yet endearing.

"What is your world like?" asked Hannah, folding her arms and legs and leaning back in her chair. "On your planet in the future."

Clarence shook his head sadly but firmly. "Hannah, you know I cannot answer that question. My job here is—"

"Yes, yes, I know. Do as little as possible and do not interfere. But you'll all be gone later today, and I cannot leave this building or contact anyone. So what does it matter if you tell me? Come on, loosen up a little."

"How do I know you are telling me the truth? What if you post another video, and someone who is about to get on the ship sees it? I cannot take that chance." Clarence shook his head sadly.

"They gave us back our phones, but they have been disconnected until you leave," Hannah replied. "It seems there is nothing that man cannot arrange. But that doesn't even matter, because you are from the future, and nothing you do can change things. So you could tell me everything, and it wouldn't make any difference to people getting on the ship."

Clarence laughed dryly. "Yes, it would. They wouldn't come with us at all!"

Hannah sat up. "What? Why?"

Clarence looked awkward. "No reason. Nothing." He mimed zipping up his mouth.

Hannah looked at him slyly. "They don't all survive, do they? Rachel told me that your history records don't go back that far. She was lying, wasn't she?" Clarence looked away, pretending he hadn't heard the question. "This is a brand-new planet you are taking them to. I watched them on the news, loading up. I saw the sort of people they are taking with them. There seemed to be a lot of very attractive young people. I recognised quite a few of them. The rich and famous all lined up. Politicians, the jet set. Models and pop stars. The celebrity fund managers and executives. I remember thinking that these are not the sort of people to build a new world. How many actually survive, Clarence? How many people are you actually descended from?"

Clarence looked sheepish for a moment, then slowly raised his hands. Seven fingers were raised.

"Seven?" Hannah bounced with excitement. "Seven! And is Armitage one of them?" Nothing. "Do you even know?"

"We have very advanced genetic research. It is true that we do not have records of the very first decade or two. We have concluded that the early years were too traumatic for the keeping of records. We do know, however, that all of the people in our population are descended from seven people."

Hannah was now sitting right on the edge of her chair, leaning across the table. "Yes, yes, but is that wanker Armitage one of them? Come on, boy, spill!"

Clarence looked around him for a few moments, as if checking there was anyone in the room listening to them, then shook his head almost imperceptibly.

Hannah rocked backwards and clapped her hands twice. She burst out laughing. "Yes!" she shouted. "Result!"

Clarence put his finger to his lips. "Shh! I have told you nothing," he said. "Okay? Nothing."

"Oh, don't you worry," said Hannah, "do you think I want those people to remain on Earth? No, thank you! Good riddance, them! You are doing us a favour. With them gone we might actually have a chance of surviving."

Clarence looked sad again. Hannah understood. He had travelled back in time to meet the founding fathers of the people of his planet, only to discover them to be a bunch of egotistical power-seekers. It must have been like growing up to realise that you don't like your parents.

"I am glad you asked to see me," he said. "I wanted to apologise to you."

"Apologise? What for?"

"I imagine you wish that Rachel and I had never knocked on your door."

Hannah gawped at him. "Are you kidding me? I should be *thanking* you. You brought me into the middle of the most exciting thing to happen to the world! The only complaint I could possibly have is that I now have too *much* purpose in my life!"

Clarence seemed to blush for a moment. Hannah wondered what sort of people the pilgrims would become over the next few hundred years. David Armitage and his cronies were an unpleasant bunch, but they were also taking a few labourers, workers. Settling a new planet clearly was not going to be a simple thing to do, and if only seven of them survived, maybe it was those with humility, who were able to work together, who made it through.

"I do have one more request of you, Clarence," Hannah said. "I need to record one last video. With you. I'd like you to come and sit next to me."

"What do you wish me to say?" asked Clarence, rising from his chair pensively. "You know I am not allowed to interfere."

"Are you kidding me?" laughed Hannah. "You just landed three dirty great big spaceships and took away two thousand people, including all our major politicians and business leaders! You can't come back from the future and pretend you haven't affected things! And besides, your past is the future of the people on those ships, not the ones you are leaving on Earth."

"Yes, I do see your point. So what is it that you want me to say?"

Hannah took out her phone. "I want you to say goodbye. In style."

The spaceships left in the same inconspicuous way that they had arrived. There was no giant explosion of fire and fuel. There was no slow graceful ascent or jettisoning of fuel pods. There was no gazing into the distance trying to see the spaceships for as long as possible until they could be seen no more. No sense of a goodbye. It was simply a case that there was an absence of space in the air where the spaceships were, followed moments later by clean, fresh air where they were no longer.

It could have been described as something of an anticlimax, had anyone but Hannah and Torben understood the true importance of what the spaceships had taken with them.

Chapter 35

The Year Two Thousand and Ninety-Seven AD

Atticus Siggers sat back in his chair, satisfied but utterly drained. He had been on his feet, addressing the United World Council, for some twenty minutes. Despite being as fit and healthy an eighty-three-year-old man as any other on the planet Earth, the emotion that had been building to this day – to this speech – suddenly hit him, now that it was complete.

He allowed himself to absorb the standing ovation currently being adorned upon him, their leader, by the representatives of the four hundred and sixty-seven independent nations of the world. Today was D-Day. Desolation Day. The day that the humans from the future had predicted when the last human would die, as told to his grandmother. Atticus was the only person alive who knew that they had not, in fact, mentioned a particular day; however, his grandmother and Torben Christiansen, the Danish scientist, had assessed – correctly – that people would be more likely to believe the prediction if it were specific.

Of course, he had been just a baby when the political and business leaders had been removed from the Earth, and his grandmother's crusade had begun with a simple video. Eventually the whole story had been revealed, including the delicious irony of the search by the humans from the future for the now mythical machine called Niels Mark. They had believed that they were searching for a person capable of spreading a message, but instead they had unwittingly created that person themselves. Hannah had been 'chosen' because the spaceship had landed closest to her house. Being the person who had posted the first videos of the aliens who turned out to be humans from the future had meant that Hannah could command the attention of the world.

And so when she had posted the third video, featuring the alien called Clarence who was revealed to be a human from the future, the message had been spread immediately across the planet; onto every phone and computer, into every home.

There had been limited response from the remaining political and business leaders, for the simple reason that the most powerful were no longer on the planet. Just by taking the twenty-five richest people in the world away from it, fifty per cent of the entire wealth on the planet had become available for redistribution. In fact, one hundred and thirty of the wealthiest people had boarded the spaceships. Without the time or inclination to deal with their affairs before they went, their assets were frozen. Soon, faced with the inevitable destruction of humanity unless massive changes were made, their estates were dismantled. Other wealthy people began to follow suit. Over the following decade, Mammon was decapitated.

Politically, a vacuum had been created overnight in all the major nations of the world. The rich and the powerful were no longer in charge, and those who were aspiring to be rich and powerful were busy making their moves to be the ones to take their place. As they were doing so, however, a new political class had emerged from the ranks of the youth. They were impatient and energised. They had just seen the removal of the blockage to a better future, and were not going to allow the opportunity for salvation to be taken away once again.

And then had come Hannah and Torben's stroke of genius. Atticus's grandmother had not spoken to those who would be king. She had instead addressed the people, via social media. She had talked of a new era, of a new type of leadership. She had spoken of the opportunity to start again, a fresh hope. She had spoken of changing the future, of wresting the power from those who sought to have it, and giving it instead to those who saw the future of the human race and the planet on which it resided as being of greater importance than their own careers.

She had urged the interested and connected, the benevolent and the benign, the insightful and the energetic, to engage with politics now that the leaders were no longer there to hold them back. Take this chance, she had told them, before the gap gets closed. Step into the fray and change it from being a fray. Vote for candidates who promise to do the best for everyone, not those who will look after only those who voted for them. Vote for those who will look after the whole planet, not just the bit they happen to be standing on. She had called to the people of the world to make the future a place that our grandchildren would want to live in – that would be *there* for them to live in.

And they had. The people had responded. Cautiously at first, as if blinking into the light after having been asleep for a hundred years. Slowly, even those 'old guard' still clinging to their posts had begun to realise that nothing would ever be the same again. Some had changed their attitude because they saw the light, others because of expediency. Some had never changed, and had continued to insist that the old ways were the best ways.

Slowly but surely, however, the religious, political and business classes had all started to make the changes that for so long had been called for, in order to prevent what had previously seemed inevitable.

In time, when the call for a unifying President of Earth could no longer be ignored, Hannah had been pressured by the public to stand. She had done so reluctantly, then had won the vote by getting twenty-three times more votes than her next opponent. At the end of her first term, a successful campaign to ditch the requirement for a regular vote, and instead make Hannah the President for as long as she wanted it, had been started by a fifteen-year-old girl from New Zealand.

Gareth had given up his job in Switzerland, and the family had returned home to help his mother with her activism. Monique and Hannah had found that they had far more in common than they thought, now that her true purpose had been revealed. Atticus Siggers had therefore grown up in both a household and a world run by the same benevolent dictatorship.

Over the decades, even the number of people on the planet had begun to fall, not through any government-enforced measure, but because people had realised that there was no other option.

Humanity had blossomed in conjunction with everything else on the planet, and not at its expense. By the time of Desolation Day, no species had become extinct for forty-one years.

Eventually Hannah had stepped down, and her grandson had been voted in to take her place in a landslide victory only marginally smaller than his grandmother's. Hannah Siggers had eventually died, surrounded by her family. The world had mourned as one.

The ovation slowly died down; the members of the United World Council retook their seats. The man that Atticus had proposed to be his successor was now delivering his own speech. It was a short speech, in praise of the vision of Hannah Siggers. The words were by way of an introduction to the video that not a single person in the Council would not have seen a hundred times or more. Yet they had decided to show it again on this day, D-Day, to remind themselves what could be achieved by humility, vision, and a cheeky grin.

Atticus smiled as he saw his grandmother, younger than his earliest memory of her, appear on multiple screens around the auditorium. She was smiling. If there was one memory he had of his grandmother, it was of her smiling.

Atticus sat back in his seat and listened for the thousandth time to the video clip that had changed the course of history.

The screen shows Hannah in her kitchen. She is holding the phone and smiling. There is no one else in the shot.

"Hi world, it's me again, Hannah Siggers." She gives a little wave. "I'm joined by one of the aliens."

She turns the phone to show Clarence, who gives an awkward circular wave: "Hi!"

Hannah stretches her arm out and directs the phone so that they both appear in the frame. "So, listen, the spaceships are literally about to depart for their new planet. Clarence here needs to join them – you wouldn't want to get left behind." Clarence laughs awkwardly. "But before he goes, I want to let you in on a secret." Clarence looks at her, eyes narrowed.

"Now," Hannah continues, "people of the world, brace yourselves. Because I've got some pretty big news. First up, my buddy

Clarence here isn't actually an alien at all." Clarence continues to stare at her from the side, his mouth slowly dropping. "He is actually a human from the future." Clarence looks around him in mild panic. "Perhaps the man himself should explain."

Hannah directs the camera towards Clarence, remaining in shot at the edge.

Clarence looks into the camera, his mouth opening and shutting a few times. "Go on," says Hannah, now looking at Clarence from the side. "Tell them why you are here. They won't get to see this until you are gone, so it doesn't affect your mission."

Clarence is clearly uncomfortable. "Um, well, yeah. This is a bit awkward, people of Earth. The fact is that…well, you have eighty years left. As a race, I mean. That's why we've come to take some of you to populate a new planet, to keep the human race going." Then, out of the side of his mouth to Hannah, "I can't believe you are making me say this to the population of Earth!"

Hannah becomes centre-screen again. "What Clarence is trying to say, people, is that all life on this planet is due to end in eighty years' time. Right, Clarence?" She looks at him again.

Clarence, who looks as if he wishes he could be anywhere else but in that room, replies. "The simple truth is that this planet cannot cope with what you have been doing to it, what with your ever-increasing population and pollution and everything. The planet is going to stop being able to support you quite soon, which means that the human race will become extinct. In eighty years time. Um. Sorry."

Hannah now takes up the dialogue again. "So that is why that David Armitage fellow has taken all his mates with him in the spaceships. They've left us here to die. But chin up, everyone. Because there is a stinger to this story. A twist in the tail." Clarence looks quizzically at Hannah, clearly wondering what she is going to say next. "You see, the future is *not* written. How does Clarence here *know* that humanity is going to become extinct? Because their ancestors told him. And how did his ancestors – those bozos on the spaceships waiting to abandon us – how did *they* know? Because Clarence told *them* a few days ago!" Clarence's eyes dart left and right, then realisation dawns across his features. Hannah's eyes were shining brightly. "Do you get it? It's a circle! Clarence tells the people in the past, who then tell the people in the future! It's doesn't actually *have* to happen!"

"So," continues Hannah. "All is *not* lost. We *can* change the future. What has been stopping us from making changes in the past? Why, our leaders, of course. But now they are gone, and *you* can take charge of your destiny." She points at the camera, and grins. "This is a new start! We can make our own future!"

Clarence is now staring at Hannah with admiration and the dawning realisation of someone who has been rather brilliantly duped. Hannah is beaming broadly. Clarence looks at the camera for a moment, then turns back to Hannah, and opens his mouth again to speak to her.

Video clip ends.

Appendix

Chapter Headings

Some of the chapter headings are taken from other sources. These are:

Chapter 7: A Pollinating Zeal

                                         From Twitter, @Robin1969

Chapter 12: The Butterfly Collector

                                           A song by The Jam

Chapter 16: Blinking Lights and Other Revelations

                                           An album by Eels

Chapter 17: Moving Clocks Tick More Slowly

                  A line used by scientist Brian Cox in his show

Chapter 23: The Geography of Hope

                              Wallace Stegner, *Wilderness Letter*

Chapter 24: The Prospect of Immortality

                                  A book by Robert Ettinger

Chapter 26: Our Nature Lies in Movement

                                  Blaise Pascal, *Pensées*

Chapter 30: The Ever Moving Shadow

                          Part of a quote from Frank Lloyd Wright